Buford, Candace, author.
Good as gold

2023
33305257354674
ca   06/09/23

CANDACE BUFORD

HYPERION

Los Angeles   New York

First Edition, June 2023
10 9 8 7 6 5 4 3 2 1
FAC-004510-23111

Printed in the United States of America

This book is set in Albertina MT Pro, Avenir Next LT Pro,
Baskerville MT Pro, Courier New, Grotesque MT Std/Monotype; Caslon Antique Pro,
Hand Stamp Slab, Jelena Handwriting, Minion Pro/Fontspring.
Designed by Tyler Nevins

Library of Congress Control Number: 2022951495
ISBN 978-1-368-09025-4

Reinforced binding

Visit www.HyperionTeens.com

SUSTAINABLE FORESTRY INITIATIVE
Certified Sourcing
www.sfiprogram.org
SFI-01681
Logo Applies to Text Stock Only

PROLOGUE

The beam of his flashlight scanned the tree line, casting spindly shadows against the dark woods. I held my arms close to my chest, trying to make myself as small as possible as I hid behind a large spruce. My chest rose and fell in short spurts, my breathing harried. The sound of water thundering through the dam dominated the air, but I covered my mouth with my hand so that he couldn't hear me.

I crouched there for a while, waiting for the searchlight to shift focus to the other side of the woods. Then I sprang up and took off in the direction of my car. The old coins clinked in my full pockets, making me sound like a rattled piggy bank. I pressed my hands against my sides to silence them.

"Get back here, Casey!" he howled.

His footsteps came quickly behind mine as I ran through the patch of trees, his flashlight in a tailspin as he matched my hurried steps. Leaves and twigs snapped and snarled beneath his swift footsteps. The light grew brighter. He was faster than me, and he was getting close. Too close.

I shoved my hand in my pocket and grabbed a fistful of coins, then tossed them over my shoulder, praying that it would slow him down—that he would drop to his knees and search the forest floor for my treasure.

But he didn't stop. He didn't want the coins. He wanted to know what else we'd found buried in the depths of Langston. He wanted to know *exactly* where to find it.

And then he wanted to silence us forever.

A gunshot sliced through the noise of the dam, through my ragged breathing, through my pursuer's footsteps. I fell to the ground with a thud.

For Grandma Essie, who told me our histories and encouraged me to keep them in the light

To my writing buddy, Mister. You were so loved.

ONE

Old Colonel Langston loomed large in all of our lives. Prominently placed on the pristine lawn of the roundabout in our community's hub, his marble statue was hard to miss. He towered above his pedestal atop a horse mid-canter, his chest puffed up proudly as he gripped the reins with his famed hands—hands that a hundred years ago had transformed the abandoned mining town of Toulouse into a lakeside retreat named after him. His inscrutable gaze followed you, or at least that's what people said. But that was just something for the tourists to eat up.

A family posed for a selfie in front of the statue, angling their camera so that they could capture the colonel and the gleaming country club behind them. I often wondered why visitors wanted to snap a picture with a confederate officer. It was *weird*. Sure, local lore claimed that Langston was different from the others, that he had atoned for his sins through various charitable acts. But maybe that was yet another thing for the tourists to eat up—after all, their business was the lifeblood of our Blue Ridge Mountain economy. Maybe we were just lying to ourselves.

I dodged the tourists and hurried across the street, my eyes darting to the colonel's before returning back to the Gatsbyesque facade of the club. Framed by bowers of ivy climbing up crisscrossed lattices, the marble entryway had an imposing yet enticing feel. The hallway gave way to a large foyer, paneled in mahogany with gilded frames featuring old photos of the town's construction—Colonel Langston inspecting marble stone and overseeing the building of the town; even a frame of the original deed to all of the surrounding land hung there. It was part of our history, the pride of Langston lined up in a row for all to admire. Nonmembers could access the hall to view this makeshift museum, but they weren't allowed to cross the velvet rope into the rest of the club.

I'd crossed that threshold countless times, never really seeing the splendor. And now that my family had lost its membership—along with almost everything else—I missed those lazy days lounging on the deck, watching the sunset over the veranda.

But those days were over. I wasn't here to kick up my feet. I was here to work.

Taking one last glance at the front of the club, I walked along the unevenly laid path to the back of the restaurant, where tree roots had pushed up the brick pavers in jagged directions and opportunistic weeds had sprouted up between the gaps, standing in stark contrast to the club's carefully curated facade. The glitz of old Langston was more muted in these unkempt back shadows, because members didn't venture here. I didn't even know this entrance existed before I got a job here. But Langston was two-faced like that.

I'd used every ounce left of my family's goodwill to land this job, and I was lucky to have it. Admittedly, it was weird waiting on tables at which I used to sit, but the alternative was even scarier. With graduation on the horizon and my college fund bare, I needed the money to help pay for books and moving expenses.

Sure, I could mope around the house like my dad often did, or complain like my mom always did, or completely check out like my sister had. But I was choosing to pull myself up and make my life happen—grasp on to opportunity before it passed me by.

I was a doer, after all.

Pushing through the service entrance, I wove through the crowded hallway, sidestepping serving carts and beverage crates, navigating like a pro. After living in my grandma's old house for three months, where the rooms were chock-full of my family's furniture and hers, I was getting good at cramped spaces.

The only thing Grandma Bernie left me in her will was her ruby ring, which arguably should have gone to her daughter, my mom. I didn't know her reasoning behind that, and now that she was gone, I'd never know. But I wore it almost every day, even when I was in my server's uniform. She'd always told me that Black women had to dress and act beyond reproach—a Black woman had to be *flawless*. This bezel-set ruby, with its halo of diamond baguettes, her crowning glory, certainly was flawless.

Hopping over a misplaced mop bucket, I walked through the steamy dishwashing station and into the side galley, where I grabbed an apron off the door hook and hastily tied it around my waist. I pulled my coils into a high bun, just as the manager, Ms. Harold, liked it, adjusting my pearl-studded hair comb so that it wouldn't get tangled. Before I could get my hair into the hair-tie, a broad shoulder slammed into me.

"Watch it." B glared at me, her thick eyeliner barely visible through her bushy bangs. Her thinly veiled disdain for me rippled off her shoulders as she carried two entrées balanced on her forearm to a table in her section.

Ms. Harold glided quickly across the dining room, nodding her head with a polite smile at each table she passed. A man held up his hand, wiggling his fingers to catch her attention. She leaned over his table, and nodded at something he said, then her head snapped up, her sharp gaze fixed on me.

"A moment please?" She waved for me to join her, pursing her lips as she watched me weave through the half-full dining room. I fidgeted with my fingers, already running through a dozen excuses for why I was two minutes late, but Ms. Harold ticked her head toward the wineglass in front of the man seated next to us. "This gentleman has been trying to get your attention for a while now. To order another glass of pinot."

"Uh." I tilted my head to the side. "I'm sorry, but I just started my shift."

"Oh." The man squinted as he peered up at me. Slowly, he nodded his head and drawled, "Now that I think on it, I believe it was the other Black one. Sorry, hon."

I nearly choked on my tongue as I tried to swallow the string of curse words fighting to break free. I opened my mouth to push back, but Ms. Harold cleared her throat.

"We'll get your server ASAP. And that glass of wine is of course on the house." She raised her eyebrows at me. "Send Barbara to me, will you?"

"Okay." I nodded, barely concealing an eye roll as I turned on my heel. My feet faltered as I darted to the back of house. I felt like such a chickenshit—I should have said something. Better yet, Ms. Harold should have stuck up for me. But that wasn't the world we lived in.

I was in a huff by the time I made my way to the time stamp station. I leaned against the wall separating the tearoom from the kitchen and clocked in. A throat cleared behind me.

"I spy somebody late." A familiar voice came from the private dining room, closed to patrons unless specially reserved. I poked my head through the doorway to find Tanner standing over the glass-ware steamer, his gloved hands holding a wineglass over the vapor.

"Yeah, because of the asshole at table fourteen," I grumbled under my breath. I slicked a loose curl into my bun and checked the schedule scrawled onto the wall calendar near the time stamp machine. I was also scheduled for dish duty with Tanner, likely for the large private dinner party later in the evening.

My elbow grazed his arm as I rummaged through the linen cabinet for a spare pair of gloves, and my heart rate ticked up. I yanked my arm away and shut the cupboard, intent on ignoring my body's reaction just as I did every time he brushed past me in the kitchen or waved at me in the dining room. The fire wall between us remained intact at school, but he was unavoidable at the club.

I'd never spent much time with him before I joined the staff at the club—he was always just another server in the dining room, a vaguely recognizable face at Langston Academy, our private school where he was on scholarship for the swim team. But he was from downstream, near the side of the lake where noise from the dam dominated the air, where all the bumpkins lived. I should know—I currently lived there in my grandma's old house, but I wasn't *from* there and neither were my friends. That was a key distinction.

He didn't mix with my crew, and I didn't mix with his.

Sure, he was funny, even charming sometimes. But guys like him would end up right where they started—right here, serving tables for the rest of his life, smoking joints outside the service entrance without an ounce of ambition. Definitely nothing much to entice me.

There was of course that one time I went to a swim meet, because my friend Fatima was crushing hard on Ian Jemmings. And, well, let's just say Tanner looked great in a Speedo.

He nudged my shoulder, and I nearly screamed. If he could hear my thoughts right now, omg.

"Do you think I got all those pesky fingerprints off the glass?" He held the wineglass up between us, and I could see his playful grin in the reflection of the glass. The corners of his gray eyes crinkled as his smile widened. "Because you know the *charmies* want only the very best."

Charmies—that's what they called us. The charmed ones, born with silver spoons in our mouths. I used to think the name was harmless, but now I wasn't sure how I felt about it. The downstreamers had a way of adding an edge to it.

His gloved hand reached for a water goblet in front of me. He was so close, I could feel his breath brush across my face. My cheeks started to heat. Good grief, I wished he didn't have that effect on me. I flinched and slid farther away from him.

"You're jumpy today." He hovered the glass over the steam, looking at me in the corner of his eye. "What's got you all riled up?"

"Wouldn't you like to know," I deflected, batting my eyelashes suggestively. I'd rather him think I was late because I was off doing something interesting—not at home, playing referee between my parents and their never-ending feud over the state of our dwindling finances.

"Now I *am* curious."

I rolled my eyes and took a step farther down the countertop, maintaining a safe distance.

Squid skidded to a stop in front of the expediting station, wiping his hands against his white uniform before sneaking a fry out of the fryer basket. He was always on the hunt for food, maybe because he had such a high metabolism, or maybe it was because of his rigorous job as the towel boy—or client services specialist, as he preferred to call it. His wiry arms and gangly legs were always in motion as he carted piles of towels to and from the laundry room.

"Hey," he said to Tanner through a mouthful of fries. He held a plate just beneath his chin to catch any scraps escaping his lips. "You working at the shop tomorrow?"

"Yeah, why?" Tanner sighed and set his goblet into the row of clean glasses.

"Because I was thinking we could get another poker game going."

"Not a chance." Tanner ran his gloved fingers through his messy brown curls, shaking his head. "I lost too big last time. And you know I'm saving up."

"Don't miss out on a chance to double your money." Squid raised his eyebrows, his hopeful eyes widening.

"Ron hates when we crowd the store. Why can't you get a game together at your place?"

"Because my grandmother is sick, bro, and she hates gambling." He bobbed his head from side to side, looking to the ceiling as he thought more about it. "And loud noises."

"Yeah, well if she hates loud noises, she should maybe check right under her roof—"

"Shut up about that, dude." Squid's brows furrowed, and his eyes flitted to me, like he was worried I'd overhear their conversation. But he wasn't exactly being stealthy, and it's nothing I didn't know already. I knew what they all did on the mountain near the old mine. Shooting bottle rockets and getting high. I could hear it from my house.

Like I said—that's what downstreamers did.

B strolled in. Her fingers tapped quickly across the touchscreen as she put in a long order from memory. She never seemed to write down any of her orders. Maybe that's how she'd forgotten that guy's glass of wine.

I said, "Ms. Harold wants to speak to you ASAP." I held my chin up, bracing myself for B's ire, but she only gave me a fleeting glance before returning her attention to the screen without a word of acknowledgment.

I'd count that as one of my more successful interactions with her.

"Hey, chica." Chef Alessandra leaned her elbow against the steel expediting rack, waving a fork in our general direction. Her eyes honed in on B, ticking her head toward a plate of short ribs resting on the counter. "I need your taste buds for a sec."

The scowl slid from B's face, leaving a sly grin in its wake. She stepped away from the register, her hand raised toward Chef's fork, but Squid sidestepped in front of her. His greedy eyes were fixed on the short ribs.

"Not you." Chef Alessandra waved her hand, shooing him away.

"Sorry, Chef." Squid bowed his head, properly chastised.

B elbowed his side and pushed past him, then dipped the fork in the beef. It sliced through easily.

"Mmm. That's dope." She closed her eyes, sighing with satisfaction. "What is that?"

"You tell me." Chef raised an expectant eyebrow.

"Brown sugar and red wine reduction. White onions." B speared another forkful and brought it to her mouth. She shook her head. "No, those are shallots. And butter, obviously."

"Lots of it." Chef pursed her lips, nodding at B's assessment. It appeared that her informal training had served her eager student well. She looked over B's shoulder at Squid, who was still eyeing her new dish. "Fine, you can have some. But get from behind the line."

Squid wiggled into the tight space behind the counter and

reached for the fork, but B snatched it away. She took another bite, ignoring his grumbles over her shoulder.

"And...citrus. Maybe orange?" B said, passing the fork to Squid's impatient fingers.

"Very nice." Chef snapped her fingers and threw her head back with a laugh. She beamed at me and Tanner. "This is my future sous chef here."

"Yeah, right." B shook her head dismissively. "Like I can afford culinary school."

"You'll find a way like the rest of us did." Chef ticked her head down the line at the cooks working beside her. With a hopeful smile. "And then maybe one day I'll be working at your joint."

"I think that red wine is getting to your head." And then B flashed one of those rare smiles, one that reached her eyes, mirroring the hopefulness in Chef's. And I couldn't help but be curious about the side of B that allowed herself to dream. I'd like to know that B. But she wouldn't even talk to me.

"So, poker?" Squid turned his attention back to Tanner, his hopeful eyebrows upturned.

"I'll play you." B looked over her shoulder, her mercurial gaze locked on Squid. "Heads-up style, Vegas rules?"

"Wow." I snorted under my breath, wondering what they were teaching over at the public school. B had one hell of a poker face. I'd never seen Squid in action, and I wasn't exactly sure how to play the game. But she would surely smoke Squid.

As if Tanner could hear my thoughts, he leaned toward me and whispered, "He's toast." Then his head popped up, and he rejoined the conversation. "Remember, I've gotta split early to babysit the twins."

"You got it. I'll cover for you." B nodded then dug in the cutlery bin to get more rolls of napkins. "Still trying to teach Gemma how to be a linebacker?"

"You laugh now." Tanner chuckled. "But she's going to be in the NFL, I swear."

"How many jobs do you have?" I asked, mentally juggling all of his odd jobs—babysitting, working the dining room, working at his parents' pawnshop.

"Three," Squid said through another mouthful of fries.

"Four if you count swim team." Tanner nudged me again, and this time I couldn't hide my grin. He was so playful, unlike any of the other guys I knew.

"Hey, who changed the schedule for Saturday after next?" B's nostrils flared as she looked at the calendar hanging above the cash register.

"I asked Ms. Harold if I could switch." My chest tightened as B's glare bore into me, but I held my chin up. I needed that day off. "Come on, it's prom."

"Great." She clenched her teeth, her jawbone twitching. "And I guess you're taking off for the centennial, too?"

"I'm sorry...." I blinked away from her, feeling the hair on my neck prick up.

Admittedly, I'd also asked for that day off months ago. The Centennial Founder's Day celebration was even more important than our school dance. As one of the cochairs of prom committee,

I was determined to at least make it a good time, but anything I had planned was no match for the city council's budget for fireworks and sprawling tents and live music on the green. The centennial promised to be the biggest event our town had seen in ... well, a hundred years.

Of course I would be there—that was definitely my kind of party.

"B, it's okay. You can make great tips working the event," Tanner cut in with a soft, reassuring pat on her shoulder. "Plus, the other party doesn't get started until late anyway. You can just catch up with us later."

"You guys having a party?" I looked up at Tanner, wondering why he would want to go to a downstream party on the same night as the centennial. It was hard to imagine anything topping the town's shindig.

"Our thing isn't for charmies." B snapped her bubble gum between her teeth, her smug grin faltering as she looked through the French doors over my shoulder. "Shit, Harold alert."

We all returned to work, B busying herself with rolling more napkins while Tanner and I doubled our efforts. Squid stowed his plate underneath a pile of menus, gulping down the last of his fries as Ms. Harold walked into the galley.

"Mr. Sciuducci, how many times have I told you to stay out of the kitchen?" She folded her arms and cocked her head to the side.

"I was just, uh—" He dove for a bottle underneath the wash station. "Grabbing some bleach for the towels. We ran out. It's shaping up to be quite a messy season."

"Oh, well, just bring it back." Her shoulders relaxed, and she turned her attention to the expediting counter, shifting order tickets down the production line.

"Oh, Ms. Harold." B tapped her on the shoulder, her voice sounding sweet. "Is it okay if I take my break?"

"First, make things right with the gentleman at table fourteen, and then you can go." Her eyebrow arched as she looked down at her watch. "But, Barbara?"

"Yes?" B pivoted on her heels, her nostrils flickering at the sound of her full name. No one got away with calling B anything but B. Except Ms. Harold.

"Make it a five-minute break. You know we're shorthanded today. And please do get rid of your gum." Her eyes tightened at B, who immediately stopped smacking on her gum. "Casey, can you handle Barbara's tables while she's out?"

"Sure thing." I took off my white gloves and squeezed past the manager, brushing against B.

"Enjoy table three." She smirked, leaning closer so that only I could hear her. "Those bitches look *thirsty.*"

With a carafe of water in hand, I made my way to B's section, my stomach tightening as I saw the splash of wavy blond hair draped over a dainty shoulder that could only belong to Dylan. Across from her lounged Fatima, who twiddled her fingers at me when she spotted me. Dylan turned in her seat, her lips pulling into a smirk. She flipped her hair to her other shoulder, her pearl-encrusted clip on full display in her hair. Fatima had one, too. It was our thing—our pearl charm.

We were charmies.

"Oh my gawd!" Dylan jutted her bottom lip out in her signature pout. "I was hoping we'd run into you here."

"It's almost like you know my exact schedule." I smiled widely, hoping to be convincingly lighthearted. She lifted the corner of my apron, and I swatted her hand away.

"Look at you in your little outfit. Aww. Smile." She held her phone up, and before I had time to duck out of the shot, the camera flashed. Sinking back into the tufted leather chair, she mumbled, "I wonder if there's a TikTok thread for working-class hotties."

My smile faltered. Behind the compliments and cute pouts, I got the sense that Dylan wasn't actually being friendly. It had become increasingly clear over the past few weeks that she was one of my best friends in name only. She was there to document my fall from grace and loving every minute of it.

If I had any regrets this year, it was confiding in Dylan about my dad's business going under. I ran to her house and told her about the foreclosure notice on our front door, about the impending bankruptcy proceedings, about my parents fighting. Dylan had said it wouldn't change anything between us, that we'd always be best friends forever, that she wouldn't tell a soul. But Dylan was a liar.

So much for best friends forever.

"What can I get you guys?" I tapped my pen against my notepad.

"Where's that other waitress—the one with the face?" Fatima scrunched up her face into a scowl, imitating B.

"Yeah, she spilled water on my sandals." Dylan dabbed the side of the leather straps—this season's Chanel. For once, B's bad attitude had worked in my favor. But I turned my toes inward, suddenly self-conscious about my worn-down loafers.

"Your order?"

"Let's see." She crossed her legs, a small devious smile tugging at her lips. She was clearly enjoying herself; making me wait on her was something she'd draw out. "What's in the raspberry vinaigrette?"

"*Omigod* you know exactly what's in the vinaigrette. You order it all the time." Fatima snatched the menu out of her fingers and rolled her eyes. "We'll both have the spring salad with avocado, as usual."

"Thank you, Fatima." I snatched the menus out of her hand and set the carafe on the table. I turned to leave, but Dylan tugged on my apron again.

"Just sit with us for a second. Come on, no one will care."

She patted the chair beside her, but I shook my head; instead I lowered to sit against Fatima's armrest.

"Skyler Dawkins just asked her to prom," Fatima blurted out before Dylan had a chance to tell me the news. "So much for the pact to go with each other."

"But I'm not going with him." She waved her hands in front of her. "I'm still down to party with you ladies—I'm booking the sickest limo for us. Hos before bros. Right, Fatti?"

"Don't call her that." I closed my eyes and sighed.

"Um, thank you." Fatima rested her head against my arm. "I need your earth sign energy."

"Oh, hi, girls."

I looked up to find Mayor Hornsby beaming down at us beneath a broad-brimmed hat that almost completely shaded her eyes from view.

"Good grief, it's hot out there." She fanned her face with her hand, then plopped into the chair next to Dylan with a huff. "I heard from the principal at the academy that you've nearly transformed the school with prom decorations using the new 3D printer—the one that *I* raised money for last year. Anyway, I hear they look fabulous."

"Wow, thank you." I gripped my chest, feeling proud that my designs had reached all the way to the mayor's ears.

"I was hoping to maybe steal some of what you have for Founder's Day. Upcycling is what we like to call it at the office. It's good optics not to appear wasteful, you know." She leaned forward. "Maybe even get you gals to join the planning committee. We need some fresh blood."

"Would that mean sitting at the table with *you*?" Dylan covered her mouth with her hands. "Omg, or on the stage!"

"Not the stage, honey." The mayor arched her brow. "But I'll make sure you're at the front."

"We'd love to ma'am, but we're already on the prom committee," I said.

"What's prom compared to the glitz and glamor of Founder's Day?" Mayor Hornsby held her hands up with a shrug. "Come on. It'll be fabulous."

"Yes, we're in." Dylan nodded vigorously. Even Fatima seemed on board with this idea. But I was wary about taking on yet another responsibility. Between work and school and prom committee, applying for scholarships and trying to keep my family together, I barely had enough time to sleep.

"I don't think I can swing it."

"Poor thing. I know you are busy with...so much. Just keep your chin up." She tutted, her eyebrows upturning like she was genuinely sad. Her lip jutted out like Dylan's did when she donned her fake pout, then she handed me her menu. "Oh, and get me a turkey club while you're at it. No mayo though. Thanks, you're a doll."

I blushed as I got up from Fatima's armrest and grabbed the laminated menus. I was clearly being dismissed. There were limits to my charmie status. I could feel it shrinking by the day. I was one of them, but now that I lived downstream, I also wasn't one of them. I existed in the space in-between—a place that made both downstreamers and charmies confused.

As I walked away I heard over my shoulder, "He hasn't left the house in days, bless his heart. But you didn't hear it from me."

And I knew who they were talking about—my dad.

My face burned with embarrassment as I typed their order into the system. The room was spinning. I saw B walking in from her break, and took that opportunity to run outside and let the wind cool down my face.

TWO

Poor thing—that's what people thought of me, and I hated that. I wanted to be strong, but my tough exterior was chipped, and I felt my weak, tender bits showing. Feeling sorry for myself, I collapsed into the armpit of where the dock met the end of the boardwalk, and watched a group of amateur divers huddled around one of the instructors, who looked like he was teaching them how to use a breathing regulator. He held the round mouthpiece up to his lips and blew into it, his cheeks inflating as he simulated how his students should clear the water from their pipes underwater.

Squid ran up with a bundle of mesh bags, which he handed to each diver.

"Just in case you find some treasure. Here's where you can put it."

My shoulders rumbled as I snorted a laugh—the things we told tourists just to hold their interest. People flocked to Langston Lake not just for the quaint shops and homemade custard or for Langston Academy, its top-notch private school, but also to see the ruins of Toulouse, the abandoned mining town that lay scattered at the bottom of the reservoir, eighty feet below. Forcibly submerged by the dam a hundred years ago, the town's remnants served as kind of a marketing gimmick to attract tourists. The charter companies tried to make it interesting with ghost stories about the Lady of the Lake and tales of pirate gold. In truth, there wasn't much down there except for piles of old brick, schools of sunfish, and an easy, albeit sort of boring, dive for beginners.

Personally, I thought the lake was kinda gross—like a murky brown color with floating bits of moss and bark. In a wet year, the water would have been higher, reaching well above my calves, but a prolonged drought had lessened the lake levels to unprecedented lows. The last time I could remember seeing the shoreline this shrunken was over ten years ago, when my sister and I splashed and played in the shallows in front of our house, digging our toes into the mineral-rich soil that hadn't kissed the air for over a decade. That summer we were covered in mud from head to toe. Even my mom got a little dirty.

I wanted to go back to the way things were. We were happier then. But there was no going back, was there?

I heaved myself off the wooden planks of the dock and brushed my apron off, mentally stuffing my grief into the corners of my mind. Regrets and pining after a life long gone did me no favors.

A passing Jet Ski caught my eyes. It zoomed around the ring of buoys in the center of the lake known as the Drop Point—the space reserved for the scuba diving excursions tourists could book through the club or cheaper charters on the other side of town. A larger boat eased into view, flanked on one side by another Jet Ski. Instead of stopping at the edge of the Drop Point with the growing flotilla, it veered off to the right—headed straight toward me.

The Jet Ski whirred closer and I recognized the paint—the ice blue streak and the cursive *Wavebreaker* scrawled across its side. It belonged to one of the last people I wanted to see right now—the mayor's son. I staggered backward, my soles catching on the uneven boards of the dock as I prepared to duck back inside. But he'd already spotted me and was waving.

Awkwardly, I waved back as Devin slid to a stop, sloshing water against the shoreline.

"Casey! I thought that was you." He ran fingers through his wavy hair, which looked like he hadn't cut it since the last time I'd seen him. With the back of his hand, he washed the sweat off the top of his lips—lips that only last summer had been locked with mine. We'd sloppily made out in front of everybody at his senior prom and later hooked up in his boathouse as a last hurrah before he left for Dartmouth.

"I've been meaning to say hi, but it's been so busy!" I waved my hands in the air, displaying more excitement than I actually felt. It wasn't exactly the truth. I'd worked three shifts since Dev returned to the club. If I'd wanted to see him, I could have. But last year was a lifetime ago, and if I was being honest, I was kinda hoping our hookup would have been the *last time* I'd see him. A last-minute fling held the promise of no strings attached, and that was all I was willing to give Dev. That was all I was willing to give anyone these days. I'd walled myself off. I was an island unto myself, and I wanted to keep it that way. I dropped my hands to my sides, an awkward smile tugging at my lips.

"I heard you're working at the Dive this summer. I thought you hated diving."

"Yeah, well, my dad didn't really give me much of a choice."

We both let that revelation hang heavily in the air. Because gossip traveled at the speed of sound in Langston, I had of course heard the rumors about how Dev spent most of his first year of college partying and almost failed out of Dartmouth. He was probably on thin ice with his father and working as penance at one of the family businesses.

His Jet Ski drifted closer, and I could see the bags underneath his eyes, a dent from a sheet mark on his face, and his puffy eyelids—the signs of an interrupted sleep even though it was already afternoon. I recognized that look. Dev was hungover, a common occurrence for him.

Squinting my eyes, I could just see the wet suits jumping off the stern of one of the boats and into the Drop Point. There must have been eight of them sloshing around in the circle of buoys—an unusually large crowd for such low water levels. One diver stood on the steps of the stern, gripping the railing with one hand while gesturing to the waters below.

"Which story do you think he's telling them?" I nodded toward the divers, where the tourists were probably being fed one of Langston's tall tales. "The one about the coffin cove? Or the one about the railroad tycoon's lost fortune? Man, I wish you'd come up with better material."

"You and me both. If I have to hear another story about Langston's gold, I'm going to drop dead." He shook his head, making his hair swoop across his forehead.

He guided the Jet Ski closer to the dock, then turned off the motor. Hiking his leg over the seat, he hopped expertly onto shore, his sea legs wobbling as he shook off the excess water. He snapped his fingers at Squid, who was on his way to the guest services booth with a stack of freshly folded towels.

"Hey." He waved his hand expectantly, privilege and entitlement oozing from every gesture. "Hand me one of those, will you?"

Squid's eyes tightened, but he didn't say something snarky. The Hornsbys were important people. You didn't mouth off to them. He clamped his mouth shut and walked over to us. Steadying the stack of linens underneath his chin, he pulled out the bottom one and placed it into Dev's expectant hand.

"Thanks, bro." He wiped down his face then moved onto his legs.

"Charmed," Squid said through tight lips. There was that word again—this time with more bite than I'd ever heard.

I tried to catch Squid's eyes as he walked away. I wanted to apologize on behalf of Dev. But he just looked impassively by me.

"Hey, dude, catch!" Dev yelled as he tossed his towel at Squid's retreating figure. It hit his back with a soft thud, leaving a water splotch on the back of his shirt. "My, bad, bro."

"Seriously, sorry, Squid." I called after him, my cheeks burning with embarrassment. I whipped around, frowning at Dev. "You can't walk ten steps to throw your own towel in the bin?"

"What? The dude is the towel guy. That's literally his job." He squinted and shook his head. "I'm creating jobs."

"He's a client services specialist." I smile, remembering Squid's preferred job title.

"Who cares? He is here to serve us."

"*Us?* Not me. Not anymore." I stepped backward, feeling my charmie status receding even further than it had in the dining room. "I'm here to serve, too. So, I guess I should get back to doing just that."

"That's not what I meant." He grabbed my hand, his thumb stroking the inside of my wrist. "You're still *you*. Even if you ..."

His voice trailed off, and he lowered his head, suddenly more interested in the zipper on his life vest than looking me in the eyes. But the rest of his sentence hung heavily in the air.

Even though you live downstream. On the other side of the lake—the poor side.

Everyone in town knew about my dad's bankruptcy, about how all our belongings were catalogued and sold to the highest bidder, no matter how hard my family tried to keep it quiet. Nothing in Langston could stay a secret for long.

"Look, I'll apologize to him later. I promise."

"I should get going." I pried my hand from his grasp. My five-minute break had gone *way* over my allotted time. That meant that B was covering for me. I'd owe her a favor if she hadn't already set all of my tables on fire.

"Right. Work," Dev said, sounding disappointed. He cocked his head to the side. "Only a week until prom. Then graduation and freedom."

"Barnard, here I come." I smiled widely. I couldn't help it. College was the biggest bright spot on my horizon, even if I didn't quite know how I'd cover the cost.

"Well, we should hang out sometime," he said with a shrug, his cheeks reddening. "Or you know, we could even go to prom together."

"You can't ask me to prom. You're not even a student here anymore."

"I know, it's just that we had so much fun last year and ..." His eyes flitted to mine and then back to the zipper on his life vest. "Anyway, I'm here if you need a warm body."

And then I looked at him, this guy that could be the answer to all my problems. I'd have a prom date who'd probably even offer to pay for the limo I obviously couldn't afford. Maybe if I played my cards right, he'd ask me to be his girlfriend and shower me with gifts.

God, I sounded like my mom.

Last year's sloppy hookup was a one-time thing, and right now I had bigger worries than who I was taking to prom—like maintaining my dignity. I didn't want to lead Dev on, and I certainly didn't want to use him for his money. I wanted *my* money back—or at least a small piece of it—for college and to help my parents out.

The diving instructor from the end of the dock walked up to Dev, his eyes narrowing as he looked at his clipboard. "Can I talk to you for a sec?"

"Kinda in the middle of something."

"The inventory doesn't add up." He nervously clicked the end of his pen over and over again. "Did you put away all the equipment yesterday? Your dad is asking."

"Yeah. Everything. I think. Hey, we'll talk later?"

"I should go anyway," I said.

I waved at Squid on my way back inside. He gave a small smile then turned away from me. I wrapped my arms around myself, feeling the chill of his cold shoulder.

THREE

When I opened the back door, it predictably banged against my mom's large credenza—a relic from the entryway of our former house. It obviously didn't fit on the back wall—or anywhere else in this tiny house. In fact most of our furniture, made for much larger, grander rooms, was crammed too tightly together, jutting out into the walkways and creating an obstacle course from one end of the house to the other. We'd been in this house for three months, and still hadn't truly moved in.

I squeezed through the door, sidestepping the legs of a claw-foot lamp, shimmying past a stack of picture frames that had yet to be hung, and tiptoed quickly down our narrow hallway. Our new house was small, and sound traveled quickly—and I seriously didn't want to get roped into a discussion with one of my parents. Thankfully, someone was using the shower, so the running water masked my footsteps. Careful to skip over the floorboard that creaked, I rounded the corner to my room without being seen or heard.

Once safely inside my room, I sank to my bed and kicked off my shoes, leaning to rub my sore arches before sinking into my mattress. I lifted my phone and scrolled through emails, searching for my financial aid decision, even though the office was closed on the weekend. But I couldn't help it—I was impatient to have my college tuition taken care of. I closed my eyes, letting sleep overtake me. I didn't care about eating dinner. I was just so tired.

A loud shriek came from the bathroom across the hall, and I heard the faucets abruptly shut off. I looked back at my phone. I'd only shut my eyes for six minutes.

Six effing minutes.

My mother ripped open the door, her terry cloth robe haphazardly tied around her waist.

"I swear to God. No hot water *again*," she fumed, adjusting the towel on her head, then stalked down the hall in the direction of the water heater.

I rushed down the hallway after her, hoping to prevent another argument between my parents. When I got to the kitchen, Mom was already tearing up.

"I said I'll fix it." My dad rolled up the sleeves of his cardigan. He took a step closer, placing a soft hand on her shoulder, but she jerked her arm away.

"Don't," she snapped, turning her back on him to open the fridge. She brought out a carton of milk, and said softly, "So help me, Richard, if it's not fixed by the time I finish dinner, I am going to Margaret's for the week."

Staying with my aunt in Atlanta was a common threat Mom pulled out from time to time. I sidled up next to my dad, nudging him in the direction of the garage and the utility closet.

"The plumbing book is on the workbench." I smiled encouragingly at him. "Godspeed."

He shuffled out of the room with his shoulders slumped over, looking defeated before he even tried. He looked like that a lot these days. Mom ignored him, choosing not to offer any words of encouragement. Instead, she set a box of cornflakes, the milk, and two bowls on the kitchen table, then slumped wordlessly into a folding chair.

That was dinner, I guessed.

We sat across from each other at the tiny kitchen table, chewing our cereal quietly in this house that didn't quite feel like home. The pipes behind the pantry groaned, and my mom whipped her head in the direction of the noise. The towel wrapped around her hair wobbled and started to unravel. A trail of shampoo escaped down the side of her forehead.

"I swear to God," she mumbled under her breath. She wiped the soap away with the back of her hand before it got into her eye.

I tucked my lips between my teeth, trying to hide my smile. Mom looked so disheveled, so unlike the perfectly buffed and manicured queen I was used to seeing. Truly, our new life was bizarre. I couldn't help but nervously laugh. Mom's eyes narrowed, her lethal glare fixed on me.

"You think this is *funny*, Casey?" Her voice hitched up an octave.

"Mom." I sighed, covering my face with my hands. "It's either really funny or super depressing. I choose funny."

"This is the second time the water heater's conked out this week. It's depressing." She stabbed her spoon into her bowl and brought up a mouthful of cornflakes. She looked over her shoulder at the moaning wall, glaring. The eating nook was *just* big enough to fit our family, but it hardly seemed big enough to house my mother's frustration. Before she finished chewing, she said, "This is all your father's fault."

I took a deep breath and focused on finishing my dinner quickly. I didn't want to hear all the wrongs my dad had inflicted upon our family, the laundry list of grievances my mom still harbored against him. It didn't help the situation at all. It only made everyone feel miserable.

"This is worse than a dormitory. And the dorms are really just glorified jail cells. Just you wait." She sniffled into her bowl, no doubt thinking about my college acceptance gift—the swanky New York condo they'd been forced to sell during the bankruptcy proceedings. I thought about it too sometimes.

I shook my head, pushing the image out of my mind.

"Plenty of people stay in the dorms and like it." I shoved away from the table and walked my bowl to the sink. I honestly couldn't wait to be at Barnard, even if it meant sharing a dorm room with a weirdo.

It could *not* be worse than my current living situation.

"Lucile lives with two roommates, and she seems to like it," I said, leaning against the counter.

"Your sister has always been a trooper. Built like your grandma. But you and I aren't made for roughing it."

"Don't go to Atlanta," I said in a low voice. Part of me feared that beneath my mom's empty threats of packing up and leaving Langston, there was a kernel of truth and that one day I'd wake up and she'd truly be gone. I lifted my chin, an idea brewing in my mind. "Maybe you could call Lucile and ask her to come up for the weekend. We could have an at-home spa day or something."

"I will not call your sister away from school while she's studying for the GRE. She's far too busy to come here."

Lucile had a life in Atlanta, and she was almost finished with her junior year at Spelman. And if she could nail down a good test score, she was going to start law school soon. She had been virtually untouched by our family's financial crisis. She'd gotten past high school relatively unscathed, even if she was a dork she didn't have college debt, she didn't have to carry the shame that I did every day. And she didn't have to watch our parents' marriage slowly fall apart every day. I'd lost count how many times I'd begged my sister to come back to Langston. I missed her tough love, her assertive tongue, her resilience. I wasn't sure what I expected her to do once she got here. Maybe she could whip my mom into shape. Maybe I was just dreaming.

"She'll come if you ask her to."

"I said *no*." My mom's voice quivered. "And don't you go asking her either."

I raised my eyebrow and fished in my skirt pocket. I had no intention of following this order. Lucile had stayed away for far too long. And part of me didn't blame her. I needed her to come home and help me hold this family together. It was too much to do on my own. I shot her a quick text.

Come home. Please? Emergency.

The pipes behind the wall groaned, and the kitchen faucet sputtered to life, coughing up gouts of water before continuing with a normal stream.

"What about now?" my dad called from the garage, where he was no doubt on his knees, praying for a win.

I held my hand under the faucet, feeling the cold water rush between my fingers. My mom flinched when she heard me sigh. Before she had a chance to threaten packing up and heading to Atlanta again, I pushed off the counter and walked to the garage door. I knocked softly on the door. I was always afraid of disturbing him here. The garage was his sanctuary.

I knocked harder, and a muffled grunt made its way to the door. I pushed it open to find my dad crumbled on the floor in front of the water heater, a wrench held loosely in his limp hand. The garage door was open, and any passerby could see the defeated man on the floor, sitting on a pallet of old couch pillows he'd taken from the love seat in the garage.

The *Plumbing for Dummies* book lay on the workbench through a minefield of old chip bags and candy wrappers and discarded puzzle pieces strewn about the concrete floor.

This was what he did all day—paced, listened to podcasts about money markets he wasn't in charge of anymore, and did jigsaw puzzles. Dad was the shell of the man he once was. Six months ago, he would have been immaculately dressed in a suit. But now, he was in his sweatpants—the *same* sweatpants—for at least the third day in a row. He claimed to be following leads for a new job, but he wasn't following anything, not even the directions to fix the water heater.

I was tempted to shut the garage door so that no one would see him. But clearly by the way the mayor was talking, the word was out. My dad was a broken man for all to see. I picked up the trail of trash on my way to snag the book, then return to my defeated father. Tripping over trash and puzzle pieces.

I bent down to pick up stray trash on my way over to him. I held the book out in the space between us, the wad of wrappers crinkling in my tight grasp. When he grabbed it, his arm plummeted to the ground under the weight of the book, as if he was so diminished, he could barely hold it up.

"I think—I think it's the thermocouple. And that takes a real professional." The wrench fell from his hand with a clank. "I can't do this."

"Sure you can." I tapped the book with my toes. He'd fixed the water heater last time, and he needed to fix it again. We couldn't afford to get it repaired or replaced. I lifted my hand with the trash in it. "I'll put this in the can, and then we'll work on it together. Find the thermos-whatsit chapter."

My bare feet padded against the smooth concrete of the garage to the rough asphalt of the driveway on my way to the metal trash can by the mailbox. We were the only house on the block that had our bin on the street. And that's because I forgot to bring it in yesterday.

Seriously, was I the only one working in this family?

I dragged the can across the yard, grumbling under my breath as I put it against the side of the house. I was scooping mail out of the overflowing mailbox when a loud crackle ripped through the air, throwing me off balance. Instinctively, I flinched and crouched to the ground.

But after my heart rate skipped a beat, I quickly recovered. Squaring my shoulders, I stood straight, then turned with a scowl, looking up the tall hillside to where the burnouts and flunkies shot bottle rockets and guns from the old mine—a constant source of irritation, more fodder for my mother's endless complaints about our new situation.

I couldn't believe that's where Tanner, Squid, and B hung out. Especially Tanner. But then again, he was a downstreamer, and downstreamers got mixed up in all the trouble.

When I got back to my dad, I dropped the stack of mail on the ground, then plopped down next to it. He sat hunched over the book. I sidled up next to him to look at the diagram on the page.

"Have you tried unscrewing that panel?" I pointed to the bottom of the water heater near the pilot light.

He grunted in response and slid to the ground, lying on his side to see underneath the heater. I sat with him to keep him company and to offer him any advice I had. Although, to be honest, I didn't know how much value I could add to this situation.

A yawn swept through my chest as I flipped through the stack of mail—mostly junk and flimsy coupon pages. I carefully folded a page with coupons for meat and cheese and slid it into my back pocket for safekeeping. I stopped at a small envelope with a red banner wrapped around the front that said FINAL NOTICE.

I rapped the letter against my dad's leg. "Dad, what is this?"

"What?" He propped himself up on his elbows and squinted at the envelope. "Oh, just set it aside. I'll take a look at it in a second."

Casting the letter aside, I sorted through the rest of the stack. I tilted my head to the side as I plucked another red envelope from the stack. This one said: URGENT. THIS MATTER REQUIRES IMMEDI-ATE ATTENTION.

This time I didn't even bother to ask my dad what this letter was about. I ripped it open and pulled out the page, my fingers trembling as I read through.

> As of April 27, we have not received back taxes for 1732 Mead Lane. Taxes must be received within sixty days, or property will be levied against you, proceedings to commence sixty days after receipt of this notice.

I read it over and over again as if I could change the wording somehow. The blood drained from my face, and I got woozy whip-lash thinking about the last time this happened. My dad had stopped tinkering and was eyeing me from underneath the water tank.

"Did you know about this?" I shook the page at him.

"I told you I would take care of it. These things can always be deferred until next year. I'll file a protest."

"It says final notice," I said louder, my angry voice echoing off the walls. "That doesn't sound like you've taken care of it."

The back door swung open and we both whipped our heads around to find my mom on the threshold, clasping the collar of her robe tight against her chest as she looked from me to my dad's flushed face.

There was no hiding this from her—not after she'd heard us arguing, and maybe that was a good thing. My family had been ruined by secrecy and betrayal, by my dad covering up his failing financial advising business. She slid the page from between my fingers and read, her eyes widening as she scanned toward the end of the letter.

"No." Her breath hitched, and she shook her head. "This can't be happening. Not again."

"I thought we had more time," Dad said under his breath. He scooted off the floor and reached for my mom's shoulder. "But I will talk to the assessor first thing tomorrow."

"Really, Richard? Thirty-one *thousand* dollars?" She brandished the page in front of his face.

"Can we take this in the other room?" For a moment he had the command of his former self, his hand rested assuredly on the small of my mom's back, angling her away from me.

She shook free from his guiding hand.

"Whatever you need to say, you can say it here." She jabbed her finger downward, pointing to the floor beneath her feet. "No more secrets in this house—not like last time when your business was so deep in the red by the time I found out. And we lost everything—*everything*. So tell me now. What did you do?"

"I didn't do anything. It's your mother! She didn't pay her taxes."

"Why didn't you tell me?" Her voice quivered, the hurt in it evident.

"You saw her estate. There was nothing. *Nothing* when she died. And she was suing the city. And buying antique furniture and shopping on HGTV. That's where she got the money for all of that crap—by deferring her taxes." My dad sighed, his shoulders hunching over. "And now it's catching up to us."

"What are we going to do? Where are we going to live?"

"I'll take care of it."

"Like hell you will."

"I don't see you doing anything about it."

"Guys, stop." I held my hands up, trying to pry them apart, but they continued barking in each other's faces.

I yanked the garage door chain and pulled the metal door all the way to the ground, hoping to shield our feud from the neighbors, hoping to hide our unraveling family. I crouched to the floor and snapped a photo of one of the FINAL NOTICE bills and texted it to Lucile.

Ok. NOW it's an emergency.

FOUR

Fifty-three days until we lose the house

My teeth gnashed against each other as I clenched my jaw so tightly I thought it might crack under the pressure. I stared out of the classroom window, my mind on anything but school. I'd been in a mood all day, trapped in swirl of ruminating thoughts about my family's argument the night before.

We had less than two months to pay the back taxes on my grandmother's house, or else the county would seize it. And I wasn't confident I could depend on my dad to fix this mess or that I could rely on my mom to stick around to find out. So that just left me and Lucile, and we definitely didn't have thirty grand lying around.

My nervous fingers rapped against the desk, my grandma's ring glinting every time it caught the afternoon sunlight. I wondered why Grandma Bernie had squandered all her money suing the city. Maybe it had been over taxes. I just didn't get it.

The bell rang, ripping me from my thoughts. I looked at the time. The school day was over. Somehow, I had drifted through an entire day of class barely present. How did that happen? I slowly packed up my belongings and stood from my desk. When I got to the door, the teacher cleared his throat.

"Ms. Whitecroft, a word?" Mr. Brown held his hand out, gesturing to a seat at the front of the classroom.

My shoes scuffed against the Persian rug as I shuffled to the desk. I sat in front of the sepia globe that Mr. Brown used when he taught his class, which had a different vibe than any of my other ones. He'd decorated so eclectically. Colorful rugs lined the floors, a sitar rested in a corner, and his walls were crammed full of pictures. He believed in visual learning and filled his classroom with figurines and textures from around the world—*living and breathing in culture and history*, as he liked to say. I was actually disappointed to have missed the bulk of today's lesson. I really liked him.

"Is something the matter?" I asked in my best nonchalant voice. But really, I knew exactly why I was here.

"Interesting report last week." He rubbed the peach fuzz of his nearly bald head. "Forgive me if I slightly misquote, but I think you said something like Helen of Troy got what was coming to her and should stop whining."

"Sure, it was a little editorial." I shrugged.

"You're barely *here*." He pointed to one of the desks. With his other hand, he pointed to his forehead. He meant I was just coasting, treading water until graduation. He wasn't wrong. School was basically over.

And I had much bigger things on my mind.

"You can talk to me if you need to. Or the guidance counselor is a great resource."

"I'm okay," I lied, avoiding eye contact. I was getting better at lying to people—maybe even to myself, like my father did. He seemed unhinged from the very real reality of losing another home.

I fidgeted in the small desk, tapping my fingers against the shiny surface.

"Did you hear back from that scholarship?" He folded his arms, resting against the edge of his desk. "I must say I wrote one heck of a recommendation. And I meant every word of it. Notwithstanding the Helen of Troy tirade."

"Yeah." I sighed, and then I shook my head. "They said it was a hard selection process this year. But I'm sure they say that every year."

"And the FAFSA appeal?"

"You know the drill. They take household income into account. And until three months ago, my parents' income was sky-high. So my application is still under review," I said, rattling off the details quickly. I only checked the application status every day, but he didn't need to know that. "Hey, maybe it'll come through just in time for me to miss my first semester of college."

I knew he meant well—he'd been a champion of mine during the admissions process. And he did write one heck of a recommendation letter to Barnard. He might be one of the reasons I got in. I just hoped I could pay for it. I didn't know how to pay for anything these days. Money was short, and the bills were mounting up.

"I know of a professor at Barnard offering a great work-study program. Let me talk to her about you." He clasped the edge of his desk. "And there are plenty of other loan options that you can explore. Just say the word, and I can help you with it. Really, there's no shame in carrying a little debt."

I tried not to roll my eyes. I was no stranger to debt. Right now, my family was saddled with more debt than Mr. Brown could possibly know. And what was my dad doing about it? Nothing. He was probably sitting in the garage ordering more credit cards and doing more puzzles.

Seriously, fuck the patriarchy.

I stacked one hand over the other, tamping down my fidgeting fingers. My grandma's ring dug into my palm. And an idea started brewing in my head. It was the most sentimental thing I owned, but also the most valuable. This ring had to be worth a lot of money. Like *thousands* of dollars.

The choice was clear. I needed to sell it.

"Uh, I have to go." I scrambled out of my desk, searching for an excuse that I could give. "Thanks for the pep talk. I'll be sure to let you know when my life stops being a dumpster fire, but prom duty calls." I gave him an awkward finger gun gesture then scooped down to pick up my bag.

"Oh, is that today?" he asked. His mouth kept moving but I wasn't listening. I looked at my grandmother's ring on my finger. He snapped his fingers in front of my face then waved his hand from one eye to the other, as if he was reviving me from being unconscious. "Hello? See, this is what I'm talking about. It's like you completely vacated your body or something. I'm...concerned."

"Don't be. I'm fine. Really, I'm fine. I have a good plan. But thank you."

"I'm supervising y'all, so can you leave the door—"

I bolted out of the room before he had a chance to finish his sentence. I rushed to my locker and stuffed my books in before turning around, resting against the cool metal to catch my breath. I looked at my phone, relieved to see that it was still early.

Swim practice hadn't let out yet, which meant I could still catch Tanner and talk to him about selling my ring. My breathing slowed, and I slipped my calm mask back on.

Everything will be fine.

Fatima was already at her locker, engrossed in a heinous development on her face. I looked over her shoulder, and her almond-shaped eyes widened as she surveyed her cheek in her locker mirror. She shifted the metal door closer to her face, and a small whimper escaped her lips.

"It's because Mercury is in retrograde." She prodded her cheek with the tip of her finger, tracing the faint pink outline of a pimple that was about to break the surface of her otherwise flawless skin. "I just knew something like this would happen."

"Really?" I asked deadpan, raising a skeptical eyebrow. "Was a giant zit really written in the stars?"

"*Giant?*" Her jaw fell open, and she shot me a shocked look before shoving her face closer to the mirror. "Do you think it'll be gone in time for prom?"

"Don't pick at it." I swatted her hand away from her face before she irritated it too much. "And yes. Prom is two weeks away. A lot can happen in two weeks." Like saving my family from losing our house—I left that part out. "Besides, nobody cares about prom this year anyway, right? Not with the centennial celebration coming up."

"You only say that because you're a Leo. I can't with you right now." She huffed, giving her cheek one last glance before diving into her makeup bag on the bottom shelf. She pulled out a tube of Dior concealer and squirted a glob of tan liquid into her palm. "Dylan thinks I should get Botox, and then I would have fewer stress lines, which means less nooks and crannies for pimples to form in."

"That literally makes no sense." I closed my eyes and tilted my head to the side. I brought a hand to my forehead and rubbed my temples. "Fatima, please do not get Botox."

"It works wonders for my mom." Dylan smirked over Fatima's shoulder, taunting her as she tried to blend the concealer over the bump. She jutted out her lip in a pout and looked over her shoulder at me. "If she doesn't stay on top of this, Fatti's gonna get another fatty."

Fatima flinched and shut the locker.

"I *hate* when you call me that." Fatima's cheeks flushed. She tried not to scold Dylan too hard, because in her opinion, she didn't have the strength to go to war with the Aries dragon that dwelled within Dylan's soul.

I didn't really believe in astrology, but I thought Fatima's assessment of Dylan was spot-on—aggressive and combative with a dash of DGAF and heaps and heaps of fuck-you money. She was untouchable.

And she was technically one of my best friends. Although that was more out of tradition and not by actual camaraderie or friendship.

"Here." Dylan shoved a box of art supplies into Fatima's unsuspecting hands. She gave a half smile and sauntered down the hallway toward the main staircase.

"Um, thanks?" Fatima called after her.

The door to a classroom at the end of the hall opened, and another group of students flooded into the hallway. I eyed them intently, searching for Tanner, even though I knew he was at swim practice, which was on the opposite side of the school.

"Okay, what is up with you?" Fatima asked, shifting the box of art supplies in her arms so that she could look directly at me. "You've been shifty-eyed and weird *all* day. Spill."

"Nothing. I just have to talk to Tanner about something. The swim team didn't let out early, right?" I asked, scanning the rest of the students in the hall. The only people left behind were volunteers for the student council's prom committee.

"I'm sorry, *what?*" Fatima's eyes widened, and she hastily unloaded the box onto the craft table. "Is there something I don't know about you and Tanner?"

"Fatima, don't make this a thing. I just had to ask him about the . . . schedule for work. The work schedule at the club. Unless you know it?" I cocked my head to the side, my poker face boring into hers. I hoped she wouldn't force me to continue the bluff, because I would fold. Selling to a pawnshop wasn't exactly an image I wanted floating around school.

"Okay, definitely not in my lane." Fatima retreated into her phone, probably already moving on to something else more interesting.

While she busied herself with Instagram, I ducked into the nearby maintenance closet to grab a ladder. I was thankful for the moment to recover from lying to one of my closest friends. I hated keeping secrets from Fatima, but if I told her *anything*, she'd tell Dylan. And right now, Dylan could not be trusted. I took a deep breath, then carted the silver ladder to the end of the hallway, right below the last strut for the banner.

"Hold it steady," I told Fatima, then climbed the rungs to well above my normal height. I looked down at the black tile maybe ten feet below, feeling slightly woozy. I steadied myself by focusing on the banner hook overhead. I stretched up a little, latched the first corner of the banner, then fumbled my way back to the ground. Fatima and I scooted the ladder across the hall, and I made my way back to the top.

It was really hot up here, maybe because it was early summer and the Georgia sun was relentless today. The old, stone walls of our school held on to the heat—all of the sticky air accumulated in the rafters.

But I wasn't a quitter.

Carefully, I raised to my tiptoes for an extra couple inches, then pulled the banner taut, stretching it almost to the point of ripping. The ladder swayed and tipped ever so slightly to the right, making my spotter below catch her breath.

"Holy crap on a stick." Fatima's petite frame shuddered, her knuckles going white as she gripped the sides of the ladder tighter. "You'll be super bummed if you die before prom. Just sayin'."

I gritted my teeth, bracing myself before hopping up to the

hook. The metal loop slid into place, and I released the banner. I dropped to a squat, gripping the top step of the ladder with shaky fingers.

"Yay!" Fatima released her hold on the ladder and rapidly clapped her hands together. She tilted her head to the side. "Definitely doesn't match the others, but at least we're done."

"Ya think?" I scoffed, stepping down from the ladder. I craned my neck upward to appraise our handiwork—four wide banners lined the main hallway of our school, all painted with metallic gold words.

Glitz. Gold. Gilded. Glamour.

Only one had a two-inch glitter encrusted border, and that was the one Dylan made. She knew the design scheme—I'd told her myself. But she was determined to undermine me at every corner. This was her time to shine.

A tinkering laugh reverberated off the stone walls, snapping my head toward the main staircase where Dylan was holding court with some of the football players. She threw her head back with another laugh, running her fingers through her blond hair as she ogled the quarterback at the craft table. I rolled my eyes.

Sweet baby Jesus.

All she needed was the whole damn team, shirtless, fanning her with palm leaves and feeding her grapes, and her fantasy of being queen of the castle would be complete. She sank to the bottom stair, resting her head against the stone archway, settling in for a break after doing zero work.

She had it so easy. While I was contemplating selling my last family heirloom and doing most of the work on prom committee, she was being fawned over.

I nearly lost my shit.

"Um, hi. Are we the only ones working?" I yelled down the hall, pointing at Fatima and then myself.

"I *am* working." She shrugged with a small smile, pointing at the 3D printer across from her. I peered at the glass case, my eyes following the robot arm as it slowly deposited polymer on the base of another chalice. It would take at least another two hours for it to finish, by which time we'd all be gone.

Dylan wasn't interested in working. She clearly didn't care about this committee. All she cared about was raising her profile so that she could be prom queen.

"*Ohhhmigod*, look at what Pierce did. Gimme, gimme." She snapped her fingers and wiggled them in his direction, then snatched the chalice from his hands and held it up so that I could see. Clasping her hand to her chest, she jutted her bottom lip out in a pout. "Look, Case. He painted it pink. It's charm, right?"

The heels of my boots clapped down the hall as I made a bee-line to their table. My nostrils flared when I saw the decoration up close. Hastily spray painted in pink, and not even sanded down to a smooth surface, the 3D-printed chalice was a disaster.

"The theme is *Gilded Age*, not *My Little Pony's Pimp Cup*." I forced a smile at Dylan then looked up into the quarterback's face. I reserved a genuine, soft smile for him. "Can you repaint this in gold when it dries?"

"Sure thing, boss." He smiled, his eyes glazing over as the full force of my charm hit him. I had that effect on people—except for Dylan. Her eyes tightened at the sound of *boss*.

But no matter how much she clawed at my crown, I was still student body president.

Pierce turned back to the student council craft table, which was set up against the wall near the 3D printer, and I caught him whispering instructions to the guys that pink was out and metallics were in.

To avoid any further confusion, I walked to the table myself and picked out all the colors that didn't match the color scheme—the pinks and purples and anything that didn't scream gilded glamour—and dumped them back into the art supplies crate. I kicked the box underneath the table, stowing it safely out of sight.

"To each her own." Dylan pursed her lips and slid off the edge of the table, giving Pierce an encouraging pat on the shoulder.

"This is so sweet." Pierce leaned against the glass box that housed the 3D printer, his eyes tightening as he watched the polymer clump and form.

Mr. Brown, our absentee after-school monitor, poked his head out of the classroom and cleared his throat.

"Keep off the glass, please." He waved a stack of papers at Pierce, shooing him away from the academy's prized 3D printer, then started down the hall in the direction of the teacher's lounge.

When Pierce was confident that Mr. Brown was far enough away, he returned to the glass, leaning closer than he had before. He scrunched his nose up.

"I wonder if we could like print fake money on it and like use it in stores, you know?"

"You do understand money is printed on *paper*. It's 2D, not three." Dylan squinted, her hands curling into claws. She was clearly past frustration with Pierce's lack of know-how. "So unless you think it should be printed on a brick, you're out of luck here."

"Maybe we could like print him a brain." Fatima snorted.

"He just improves with time." I patted Dylan on the shoulder a little harder than I intended. "I think he'll be able to offer you a lifetime of stimulating conversation."

"Honestly the dumbest question." She rolled her eyes with a huff.

"Now, now. No need for such ableist language, Ms. Preswyck." Mr. Brown shuffled back down the hall, folding his arms with a sigh. His eyes narrowed at Pierce, and he ticked his head to the side, wordlessly warning him to remove himself from the glass like he'd previously requested, or else he'd surely give out a detention. There were still two weeks left of school, and Mr. Brown was still in charge. He pointed his severe brow at Dylan.

"There are no dumb questions here. Actually, we could all learn something from this." His face softened as he cocked his hips to the side. "Money is actually not printed on paper. It's printed on a mixture of cotton and linen fabrics. So, you're not exactly on target there, Preswyck."

"Whatever," Dylan mumbled under her breath, low enough so that only Fatima and I could hear her.

"So next time you accidentally leave a dollar in your pocket and put it through the washing machine, you'll have the Secret Service to thank when it doesn't disintegrate."

"Like the men in black?" Pierce scratched his head, clearly confused. There were more than a few confused stares, including from me.

"Well, long before the service was used as the president's professional security detail, the original purpose of the Secret Service was to safeguard the country's first national currency and to ferret out counterfeit bills." Mr. Brown's smile widened at the murmur of wonder coming from the footballers seated on the stairs. He nodded with a hearty laugh. "I'll teach you all a thing or two yet."

"Okay, can we not?" Dylan drawled, looking at her phone instead of at Mr. Brown. Her eyebrow twitched—she was clearly annoyed. "Graduation is in less than three weeks. So, high school is a wrap."

"The smartest people, in my opinion, never tire of learning." Mr. Brown bobbed his head from side to side. "Make the world your classroom."

"Don't mind her." Fatima flicked her long black hair to the side, smiling awkwardly. "It's because she's an Aries, and May is a complicated time for her."

"Sorry, Mr. Brown." I laughed at that nonsensical explanation.

"Ugh it's just too tragic when people can't read the room." Dylan held her hand up, her bangles clanking as she grumbled under her breath about how no one wanted to be lectured to. She turned her back on our huddle and then froze.

A slow clap echoed down the hall, and we all turned to find the mayor at the main entrance.

"Nonsense. I found it very illuminating."

FIVE

Her stilettos clacked against the tiled floor, the sound echoing off the lockers lining the wall. Her assistant trailed her, followed by Dev. He had his arms crossed and looked bored already.

"Madam Mayor." Mr. Brown beamed at her and then kinda bowed his head, like he was in the presence of royalty. "What a surprise."

"Don't mind us." She scrunched up her nose, looking apologetic. "Just making an inventory of some of the decorations we're going to steal for Founder's Day—after prom's all buttoned up, of course."

"Of course." Mr. Brown looked relieved that all the hours he spent watching us after school had not been in vain. He straightened his collar, holding his chin up like he was also part of the mayor's inspection.

"Oh, these look divine." She lifted one of the silver chalices off the craft table, then nodded to the box beside them. "And all of these gold coins. How wonderful to incorporate town legend."

She looked over her shoulder at her assistant, and in a clipped voice she said, "Brenna, write this down."

"Yes, ma'am." Brenna opened her padfolio and clicked her pen. She surveyed the table then scrawled onto the open page.

"Don't you need to scuff them up a bit—make them look like they've been underwater for a long time?" Dev picked up one of the coins on the table, turning it around in his fingers.

"Actually, gold doesn't corrode," Mr. Brown said. "So, remember that next time you're training folks at I Dive—you should be able to see the shimmer with the naked eye."

Mr. Brown's smile faltered, perhaps because he'd just critiqued the mayor's family business. She'd made a fortune off peddling tall tales about haunted shipwrecks and tycoon gold at the bottom of the lake. Mayor Hornsby shot Dev an annoyed look, then turned her attention back to Mr. Brown.

"Fascinating discussion on the origins of paper money." She tilted her head to the side, her lips pursed in a tight smile.

"Well, not the origins." Mr. Brown's chest deflated, like he'd been holding his breath. "The Chinese actually pioneered promissory notes thousands of years ago, but those were made of leather."

"Mmm, yes, fascinating," she said in a clipped tone, not unlike the one she used when she talked to her assistant. She widened her smile, pumping up her enthusiasm again. "I hear you're also quite a student of town history."

"I do dabble." Mr. Brown lifted his chin higher, clearly proud.

"Oh, don't get him started." Dylan rested her head against Fatima's shoulder and groaned. It earned a chuckle from Dev, whose eyes were brighter, more awake than they had been earlier.

"Oh, I hear you do more than dabble. You've done a lot of work curating the library's section on our history." She rested her manicured hand lightly on his shoulder. "I'd love a tour."

"I'd be honored." Mr. Brown's mouth fell open. "Really, any time you want to peruse, I'll be your guide."

"How about now?"

"Now?" He blinked rapidly, looking to the table of unpainted chalices and coins. "Well, technically I'm supervising."

"I'm already here. Let's go. Come on, make time for your mayor." She tapped her foot. Clearly she wasn't accustomed to taking no for an answer.

"It's okay, Mr. Brown." I stepped forward. "You should go. We've got everything covered here."

"And Brenna can supervise while she catalogues." She clasped her hands at her assistant, begging her to agree. "Won't you?"

"Yes, ma'am." She nodded dutifully.

"And Dev honey, try to be helpful," Mayor Hornsby said. Then she linked arms with Mr. Brown as they walked to the library at a brisk pace.

"Is your mom seriously *that* interested?" I looked up at Dev, whose brow was furrowed as he watched his mom's retreating figure.

"Honestly, she's taking this centennial thing too seriously. And roped me into it, too. I think it's like the launchpad for a new campaign initiative." He ran his fingers through his hair and sighed. It was clear that he didn't want to be here helping his mom, but he was on a tight leash. His frown softened as he looked at me. "But I'll save you a seat at the Founder's Table. And, well, I guess there's always prom."

And there was that look again—the one he'd given me on the dock last weekend. He wanted to go to prom with me. I didn't know why he cared so much. We were ancient history.

"I'd honestly love to go with you again, but we all made a pact to not make a big deal about it and to go with one another." I wrapped my arms around Fatima and Dylan and pulled them closer. "I owe it to these ladies to keep my word."

"Right. Totally." Dylan wiggled her shoulders, unwrapping herself from my embrace.

Just then a trickle of students with wet, glossy hair flooded down the hallway. My heart rate ticked up a bit when I spotted Tanner with a towel flung over his shoulders, walking toward his locker.

"Actually, speaking of prom." Dylan snapped her fingers at me, drawing my attention back to her instead of at Tanner. "We need to put down a deposit on the prom limo ASAP."

"And nail down reservations at the club." Fatima waved her hands in the air when she saw my nostrils flare. "Or we can go somewhere else. Honestly, not married to the club idea."

"You can use my guest pass." Dylan blinked innocently at me, but I could feel the teeth behind her words. "You know, since you're not a member anymore."

Her eyes flitted to Dev, a smug smile dancing on her lips. She clearly wanted to catch his eye, but he wasn't paying her any attention. He was still looking at me, which under any other circumstances would make me feel awkward. But I got a kick out of watching her try so hard, so I allowed it. Dylan rolled her eyes.

"Just Venmo me for the limo, and we'll figure out the rest later."

"How much was it again?" Fatima's long, dark hair fell over her face as she bent over her phone.

"It's seven hundred apiece." She sidestepped around me and walked over to the printer, suddenly more interested in looking at the chalice's progress than at my scrunched-up face.

"Wait." I blinked rapidly, trying to wrap my head around the price tag. "Seven hundo *apiece*."

"I know. I thought it was going to be less, but then the owner let us upgrade to the stretch Hummer for just a little bit more, and I couldn't pass it up." Dylan looked over the rim of the 3D printer. "What did you expect me to do?"

"I expected..." My voice trailed off as I struggled to find the words. There was no empathy in her eyes, and I realized that I didn't expect anything more from her than ratcheting up the price. Clearly, I could no longer afford the price of admission into our clique.

My eyes drifted to the far lockers near the front door, where Tanner Holmes was hurriedly loading up his backpack with books. He ran his fingers through his wet curls, then flipped the hoodie of his sweatshirt over his head. I shoved past Dylan and walked in his direction.

"What?" I heard her whisper to Fatima and Dev, her dulcet tone feigning innocence. But she knew I couldn't afford to spend that kind of money on a limo, especially since my family lost all its money. I couldn't even afford Barnard's tuition to school next year.

"Casey, I'll pay for your share." Dylan yelled after me, loud enough for every single person in the whole damn hallway to hear—completing my humiliation. That's exactly what Dylan wanted. She was no friend of mine.

"Hey," I said, leaning against the locker next to Tanner's. I smiled widely, trying to act nonchalant. "I was hoping to run into you."

"You're talking to me. At school." His eyebrows shot up. "That's weird, right?"

"Don't make it weird." But he was right—it *was* weird to be close to him here, under the watchful gaze of my friends. I was breaking the firewall we had between work and school. "I need to talk to you."

"I'm sorry, Case. I'm really in a hurry to get to work."

"Actually, that's kinda what I wanted to talk to you about. I overheard you talking about working at the shop and wondered if I could come by."

"You wanna play poker?" He shifted his backpack strap farther up his shoulder, his face incredulous.

"God, no!" I snorted a laugh, shaking my head.

A smile crept across his face, softening his features. He leaned closer, whispering conspiratorially. "Then why would one of the charmies be interested in my family's sketchy shop?"

"This is awkward." I hung my head low, suddenly feeling too vulnerable to look into his eyes. "I've never done this before, but I have some things to sell, and I figured if I went somewhere with a familiar face, it might seem less weird than going to some random place. But I don't want anyone to know, so..."

"Don't worry." He crouched down, turning his face to the side so that his green eyes could look into mine. He wasn't exactly a friend. Hell, I barely knew him. But there was genuine empathy behind his eyes, and that's more than what I'd gotten from my friends lately. He lowered his voice to little more than a whisper. "Your secret's safe with me."

And then he winked at me.

SIX

My car purred, idling outside of the Holmeses' storefront as the sun dipped below the horizon. It had the marquee signage of the small shopping center. A large green sign emblazoned with red letters read: PAWN SHOP. CHECK CASHING. A smaller sign, posted against the frosted glass entrance said: WE HAVE HEALING CRYSTALS.

I was glad I knew someone who worked here. Otherwise, I'd never go in.

I'd been able to dip into my house to retrieve my jewelry box and a couple designer scarves and a pair of Ferragamo flats—anything I could sell—without being seen. I pulled the ring off my finger then laid it on the maroon velvet lining of my jewelry box, next to the rest of my little treasures.

"Okay, Casey." I took one last deep breath then turned the car off.

I tucked the small leather jewelry box underneath my arm, grabbed my backpack, and shoved the car door open. My feet faltered across the parking lot, then stopped completely at the smoky glass door. I knew I was about to cross a line, about to sell a family heirloom—something I could never get back.

But the alternative was having my family fall apart even more than it already had. We needed all the help we could muster. No one was coming to rescue us. So, I'd do it myself.

I pushed through the door, dinging a bell hanging from the top hinge. I wiped my feet on the doormat, which was embossed with the picture of a five-petaled black flower being held up by two brown hands. I stood awkwardly, then breathed a sigh of relief when I saw B and Squid playing cards in the corner.

"Hey guys," I said with a wave. They didn't wave back—just scrunched up their faces, looking confused. I expected this from B. She'd never really warmed up to me. But I didn't think Squid would ice me out like this. Maybe he was still embarrassed about his encounter with Dev last weekend. I cringed, remembering the way he tossed the wet towel at Squid's back.

"You lost?" B eyed me through a thick veil of black bangs. I could barely see her eyes, but the way her lip curled into a sneer, I got the feeling like I wasn't welcome here.

"I'm meeting Tanner." I held my chin up. "Is he here yet?"

She didn't answer my question. Instead she shoved out of her chair and lifted a flap in the store counter. I wondered if she worked here too, because she clearly knew her way around the store. She rounded the corner of the counters, then disappeared behind a metal swinging door.

I stood awkwardly in the long room, which was divided into three distinct sections. To the right was the consignment portion of the store, with mannequins dressed in the finest dresses the south side of the lake had to offer. Crammed over in the far-left corner was the healing crystals shop—although I doubted the plastic glowing rock figurines and lava lamps possessed any healing energy. The center counter, with glass display cases at waist level and tall ones along the back wall, must have been the pawnshop.

I waved at Squid, still sitting at the card table near the front window, but he folded his arms.

"How's your friend doing?" He leaned his elbow lazily against the card table, his head propped up by his hand. "The one with the good aim."

"He shouldn't have done that." I took a step forward, hoping to take B's seat. "It was a dick move. I'm sorry."

"It's honestly not the first time something like that has happened to me." He shrugged and looked at the floor. "But it's the best gig in town, so I guess I gotta learn to live with it."

"Please, don't be mad at me." I sank to the chair, willing him to look me in the eyes.

There were some people in this world that were truly nice and inherently decent, and Squid was one of them. I'd never talked to him before working at the club, even though I'd seen him during peak seasons, folding towels and helping out on the docks. Yet he was the first to offer me friendship when I started working alongside him. Squid was good people.

"I can't stay mad at you." He waggled his finger at me, breaking out in his toothy grin. "You're one of us now—a downstreamer."

"Yeah." A laugh rumbled through my chest, but then my breath hitched. I was a downstreamer only if I could save my family's house.

"Anyway, that dude is in deep shit with his dad, so I feel like in some way the universe is on my side."

"What do you mean?" I leaned forward, interested in why Dev was in even more hot water. He'd looked stressed out after school today, but I'd just chalked that up to frustration with his mom for dragging him into the centennial preparations. "What did he do now?"

"It's too good." Squid sank to the table, and his forehead landed with a thud. He peeked up at me through his ink-black shaggy hair. "He lost a diver—like a whole human being."

Squid covered his face with his hands and howled.

"That dude isn't lost. He obviously sold the gear and is probably halfway to Mexico by now." B leaned against the glass countertop. "How much does gear like that cost?"

"Not enough to make it to Mexico." He snapped his fingers. "Plus, he left his license as collateral when he rented the equipment."

"Oh, never mind. He's not going far," B said, snapping her fingers back at him. "That dude's gonna get pulled over before he gets out of Georgia."

"Really? You're gonna fold that easily? Plenty of people drive without a license." Squid waved his hand dismissively.

"Check your privilege, bro." B rolled her eyes.

"She's right." I shrugged, looking away from Squid. Driving without a license was easy to do if you were white. My sister forgot her wallet at home once and got pulled over. She later told me that her hands were shaking the whole time. She ended up getting off with a warning, but still—driving while Black wasn't a laughing matter. So honestly, I didn't think the missing diver could get far without a license, unless he looked like Squid and not like me and B.

The door behind the pawnshop's glass cases swung open, and a man stepped out. He yawned and stretched his arms wide, before nodding to me. He lifted the rim of his baseball cap, which had the words NEIGHBORHOOD WATCH written in large white letters.

"My stepson'll be out in a sec." He tucked a tuft of red hair behind his ear then tilted his head, studying me. He gestured to the center countertop. "You can lay your stuff out here."

I took a cautious step forward, then my feet stopped working again. They stayed firmly planted to the spot. But the door swung open again and Tanner walked onto the floor with a large box in his hands. He set it on the edge of the counter, unlatching the left side of the counter, likely on his way to replenish some of the floor displays.

Then he looked up with an apologetic smile. "Sorry, I was unloading a shipment."

"It's cool." I laughed nervously. "I was just catching up with Squid."

Tanner's stepfather motioned for me to approach the counter. Tanner's smile faltered and a blush crept across his cheeks. He turned to Mr. Neighborhood Watch and flicked his head toward me. "Ron, mind if I take this one?"

"Sure. I'll just be over here." Ron shook his head and shuffled to the far side of the counter, grabbing a newspaper off a stool before settling in for a good read.

"I have some Burberry scarves in my backpack. And a pair of Ferragamo booties." Tanner went slightly cross-eyed as I described my haul, so I added, "Um, those are names of designers...."

I slid my tote bag off my shoulder and set it on the counter. Then, I dislodged the jewelry box from underneath my arm and slid it across the glass. I pressed the clasp to open it and pointed to the ring.

I chewed on the inside of my cheek, wondering if it was right to sell it. I'd always thought that I'd keep the ring, maybe even pass it along to a daughter someday—this relic of Grandmother Bernie should stay in the family forever.

But I dismissed the thought as soon as it crossed my mind. My family needed the money.

"Can you buy this, too?"

Tanner exhaled in a rush, whistling softly. "That's uh . . . that's *quite* a ring."

The newspaper in the corner rustled and dropped, and Ron leaned forward, eyeing the specimen. Even from far away, he could tell it was something special.

"Well?" I prompted again.

"Well—" Tanner began, but he was cut off by Ron.

"I'll give you five grand for it." He nodded, his lips breaking into a sly smile.

The metal door swung open and B stepped out again, her eyes wide as she looked over Tanner's shoulder. She must have heard us through some kind of security system back there.

"Did I hear Ron throw around five grand?" she mumbled under her breath, scrutinizing my grandmother's treasure. By now, Squid was standing on his chair to peer over the small crowd growing around my ring and me.

"I thought you said we could keep this a secret?" I hissed under my breath at Tanner. A burning blush blazed across my cheeks.

"I can ask them to leave. Seriously, they're just here to play a few hands of cards. Except for Ron—he's technically in charge here."

"You could sell your tiara." B reached across the counter and flicked my pearl studded hair comb, coming so close to my face I could smell her cherry lip gloss. I jerked my head away from her.

"Goddamn it, B. Get from behind the counter." Tanner flicked his hands, shooing her back around the corner and through the gap on the counter. "You *know* the rules."

I shifted my stance to my other foot, blocking Squid and B from view. When Tanner returned, I was more than a little annoyed. Ron was still hovering, but from farther away now—maybe he didn't want to spook me out of the store after B's intimidation.

"This ring is worth a lot more than five thousand dollars." I frowned, lifting the top insert of the jewelry box to find its appraisal papers. But Tanner's long fingers landed on top of mine, making me pause. He spoke calmly, and not too loudly.

"Case, this is a pawnshop. You know, where people sell things at a price cut for quick cash. You don't need the cash *that* quickly. Do you?" And then his face softened. "If I were you, I would take this to a jeweler. They'll pay more competitively than we can."

He leaned over the counter, closer to my ear, and whispered conspiratorially. "Don't let my stepdad get anywhere near that ring."

He pulled back, winking at me... *again*.

"But we'll take all of this." Tanner gestured to the pile of scarves and shoes on the counter. "I just have to look up the pricing on my computer."

"And this." The pearl comb snagged on my curls as I pulled it out. I set it against the counter and pushed it toward Tanner.

"You sure?" He hesitated to grab it, his hand hovering over it.

I nodded. As obnoxious as she was, B had a point. There was no point in hanging on to pearls when the stakes at home were so high. Tanner swept the comb into the pile of the last pieces of my charmed life and carried them to the back counter.

Ron shuffled back to my cluster of items, his eyes fixated on the ruby ring. He reached his hand out as if to pluck it from the box, but my quick fingers beat him to the chase. I grabbed the ring.

"I think I'll hold on to this," I said, sliding it onto my finger.

"Got anything else?" He hovered over the box, his lips down-turned as he mentally picked over the contents. Aside from some David Yurman bangles and a simple pair of pearl earrings, there wasn't much of value in there—just knickknacks from childhood, things I'd collected as a kid that didn't hold much value to anyone but me.

Ron pointed to a coin buried beneath the pile of bracelets. "May I?"

I nodded. It was just an old rusty coin I'd found in the lake during the drought years ago, when the water levels were low.

"You might have something here." He brought it closer to his eye, squinting at the vague stamping, mostly covered by a greenish buildup. I was amazed—this featureless coin was by far the least interesting item I'd brought to the shop, yet Ron was transfixed. Tanner drifted over, abandoning my pile of things to nudge his way into a prime viewing spot for the coin.

"Where did you find this?" Ron's eyes darted toward mine, dilated and intense.

Before I could answer, Tanner waved his hand dismissively. "Jesus, Ron. That's just a rusty old penny. You're losing your touch, just like my mom said."

Ron's cheeks flushed as scarlet as his hair. He looked around the room at all the eyes watching his apparent mistake. He dropped the coin back into my jewelry box, mumbling something about *ungrateful brats* underneath his breath. Ron shuffled off again, and I wondered if Tanner would suffer any retribution later for humiliating his stepdad.

Still, Tanner floated over to touch the coin for himself after Ron disappeared into the back area.

"Holy shit." Tanner held a fist up to his mouth, bouncing on the balls of his feet, seemingly waiting for Ron to be fully out of earshot. His other hand was holding some kind of cloth that he'd used to rub the coin. But it wasn't very dirty, just dull and corroded. Could it be this coin from the lake—the "rusty penny" he'd dismissed not a moment ago—was not so worthless after all? "Squid, get over here and tell me what you see."

"What do *you* see?" I asked, my heart racing. "You're acting like you've just found a gold mine."

"Not gold, Casey. But as good as gold. Trust me."

SEVEN

I wanted to trust him. I really did. But he *just* told his stepdad that my coin was a worthless, rusty penny—which to be honest, seemed true. It only had value to me. I'd thought about throwing it away dozens of times, but it was a keepsake from playing with my sister all those years ago—a priceless memento of my childhood.

I'd been banking on selling real valuables, stuff to get me closer to financial security. My chest tightened as I watched Tanner turn the coin over in his hand, his hungry eyes fixated on junk that would definitely not cover the cost of college books, let alone the thirty thousand dollars I needed to save my family's home. I thought of what I said to my mom this morning.

It's either really funny or super depressing.

A nervous laugh bubbled up from my chest. I tucked my hair behind my ear, trying not to dwell on how ridiculous he was. Tanner leaned closer to the coin, his eyes tightening as he waved a hand toward his crew sitting in the corner. Squid's sneakers squeaked against the concrete floor as he skidded around the L-shaped display case.

"See right there." Tanner pointed to the side of the coin he'd wiped off. "It's a rose."

"A rose? On a penny?" I arched my eyebrow. "What are you talking about?"

"No, it can't be." Squid shook his head.

"Pennies don't corrode like this, remember?" Tanner bent to retrieve a bottle of turpentine from the floor then popped the cap off of it. The cap clanked and rolled across the counter. I snatched it up before it dropped to the floor.

With the rag over the open bottle, he upturned the turpentine bottle and squeezed, dousing the rag with the solution. Then he rubbed it against the coin.

"Careful. Not too rough," Squid hissed, bringing a fist to his mouth. "You don't want to scratch it, dude."

Tanner grunted in response but slowed his scrubbing to short, gentle circles. The tarnished layer wiped off, smearing the rag with grayish-green silt. I tilted my head to the side, my eyebrows furrowing as I tried to see what they were seeing.

A gasp caught my attention and I snapped my head up to find Squid covering his mouth as he bounced on the balls of his feet. His eyes widened with every rub of the coin.

"Um, hello?" I reached across the counter and gripped Tanner's wrist. His eyes darted toward my hold, and then he blinked up at me, a blush creeping across his cheeks. I yanked my hand away, clearing my throat. "Tell me what's going on."

"See this petal outline?" He pointed to the edge of the coin. "That's the Black Rose."

"As you can see, his mom and Ron are pretty obsessed with it." Squid nodded to the tchotchkes on the shelves, to the doormat at the entrance. All of them had the black rose.

Of course I'd seen it before. You couldn't walk into the tourist shops around the lake and not see a million roses. It was an unofficial symbol of our town—nothing more than a gimmick for selling keychains with tales about how Colonel Langston turned a failing mining town back into a prosperous city by building the dam.

"Wait. You think..." I sighed, hanging my head low. "You think this is from the lost treasure?"

I was hoping they'd tell me I was mistaken. Because the town's mythical treasure was just a story we told tourists to make them spend more money in our small town. Their deep pockets were the real treasure. The lost gold wasn't real. But they all nodded their heads. Even B was uncharacteristically solemn as she nodded along.

"You can't be serious. It's not even gold. *Look* at it." I pointed to the coin, then held my face in my hands, unsure whether to laugh or shriek. The legend said that Langston's treasure was a pile of gold coins. "Gold doesn't corrode."

I'd stood with the town's historian and the mayor a few hours ago talking about this very thing. I remembered what Mr. Brown said. Gold didn't get busted up, even if it was underwater for a hundred years.

You should be able to see the shimmer with the naked eye.

"This isn't gold. It's silver." Tanner picked up the coin and held it up to the light, his nostrils flaring as he nodded vigorously. "The treasure is silver."

"No it isn't. I just overheard the mayor talking about it earlier today."

"Well, the queen of the charmies doesn't know shit about the town's history." B grabbed the coin from Squid, grinning as she studied it. "She doesn't care about this town. Not really."

"And it's not Langston's treasure. It's the Toulouse Treasure. That rose was the symbol of Toulouse, or at least that's what my grandma told me." Squid tapped the glass counter, his toothy grin widening. "This could be worth a *lot* more than a rusty penny."

"What—" I struggled to find words. From what I understood of Toulouse, it wasn't exactly known for its riches, especially after its silver mines dried up and its workers left in droves. B sidled up next to me, her shoulders trembling as she tried to stifle a laugh.

"Princess is rich again." She slapped my shoulder, rumbling my stance. "You'll be back to the charmies in no time."

She cocked her head to the side, her eyes twinkling with mischief. I normally would have shrugged her sharpness off, but for some reason I couldn't. My chin fell, and I looked at all of my things scattered across the countertop. I had let my guard down to come here, had trusted Tanner to treat me fairly. And that vulnerability was met with laughter.

"So—so this is a joke to you?" I said in a low voice, barely more than a whisper. Tears pricked at the corners of my eyes, but I blinked them away. Feeling betrayed, I looked at Tanner through my eyelashes and held my hand out. "Give it back, so I can bounce."

"Wait. Case—" Tanner started, but I banged the display case with my open hand, rattling the glass panes.

"No, it's cool. Just give it back, okay?" My voice quivered, and I blinked another surge of tears away. They could continue laughing at my expense, but I wasn't going to give them the satisfaction of seeing me cry. "This was a mistake."

Butt end of a joke or not, I wanted my keepsake back. I snatched the penny out of Tanner's grasp, then quickly gathered my other pieces of jewelry, shoving them into my jewelry box before hastily tucking it under my arm.

B was laughing in earnest now, her chest trembling as she slapped the countertop. I curled my lip at her, shaking my head, and then I swiftly turned on my heels. It took me only three long strides to get to the front of the store. I swung the door open, eager to put this whole debacle behind me. The hairs on the back of my neck pricked up at the sound of B's howling, which followed me all the way to the parking lot.

EIGHT

A slow drizzle peppered my face as I burst through the door. I hugged my jewelry box close to my chest, the contents jangling as I broke into a jog to my car. Slamming the door shut, I slumped into the driver's seat, finally surrendering to the rush of tears I'd been holding back. I thought I'd fallen as low as I possibly could go before I showed up here, but I was wrong. I'd hit rock bottom and was an object of ridicule and mockery. I banged my forehead against the steering wheel, my chest heaving as angry tears rolled down my cheeks. I'd been a fool to come here.

Knuckles rapped against my window, and I jumped in my seat. Tanner bent down, wiping away raindrops on my window so that he could see my face.

"Case, please." He clasped his hands together as if he were begging me to hear him out.

"Go away," I groaned, my voice thick with embarrassment and shame. I covered my face with my hands, desperately wishing to be invisible.

"I'll leave you alone if that's what you really want, but just know that we were not making fun of you. I promise."

I flinched at his last word—another empty promise. My fingers dashed to my door panel, and I pressed the window button down and cracked it just enough to prevent any rain from coming into the car.

"Seriously, dude?" I glared at him through the crack. "You're gonna feed me a line about the Langston Treasure?"

"Keep your voice down." He hunched his shoulders and looked behind him, checking to see that no one was eavesdropping.

"Oh, because we're sitting on valuable information? Don't want the whole town to know that we've found the secret buried treasure." I snorted. "Give me a fucking break."

"Look, can we just start over?" Tan asked, his eyes pleading.

"It's cool. Seriously, I'm good." I pursed my lips, holding my hand up to block him from view. "Let's just pretend I was never here."

"If that's how you want it, fine. But I swear that coin is special." His eyebrows tilted upward. "Trust me?"

Trust. There was that deceptively complicated word again.

"Yeah, right." I shook my head, chuckling under my breath. I thought he was different. I thought he was a good guy. I was wrong. If Tanner had proved anything tonight, it was that he could not be trusted to safeguard my secrets or to handle me with care. He was now on the growing list of people I couldn't even trust along with Dylan and my own family, particularly my dad.

I pressed the button to roll up the window. It slid upward, and Tanner snatched his fingers away just before it sealed shut. He placed his palm on the window, but I didn't look at him as I put the car in reverse. His hand squeaked along the glass as I backed up.

My tires screeched against the loose gravel on the asphalt as I accelerated—a little faster than I intended, but I wanted to put as much distance between us as possible, and fast. I careened around the corner, feeling my cheeks heat as I looked in the rearview mirror at Tanner's shocked and confused facial expression.

Great. Not only was I a joke, but I was also *crazy*—a crazy girl screeching through the streets of the south side. Tanner must have thought I was such an emotional wreck.

But I didn't care what he thought of me. Right?

The tears flowed freely as I sped through the nearly empty streets of south Langston. A mixture of embarrassment and rage burned through my thoughts. I was so distracted that I almost missed the red light at the intersection. I gasped, my foot pressing the brake pedal almost to the floor. My purse and jewelry box lurched from the passenger seat and burst open on the floor.

I leaned to the side, straining my seat belt as I pawed the floor mat. I grabbed the jewelry box off the floor and set it on the seat next to me. The lid hung limply to one side, the right clasp broken from such a hard tumble. I sniffled as I gathered the other things rolling around the floor—an errant water bottle, a fistful of jewelry. Something small slipped through my fingers, falling into the cup holder.

It was the coin. That stupid coin.

I snatched it out of the cup holder and turned it over in my fingers, squinting as I studied it under the glow of the stoplight. I still could not see anything compelling. I held it closer to my face and there, under the red stoplight, was the faintest outline of a rose.

The Black Rose.

A staccato of honking snapped my attention back to the road. I looked in my rearview mirror and saw a guy animatedly waving for me to go. The light had turned green—for how long, I didn't know. But it was time to make some moves. Home was straight through the light and a few short turns through the neighborhood. There, I could bury myself under covers and forget this night ever happened.

But before I knew it, I pushed the wheel to the left, turning toward the Langston bridge. My tires bumped against the grate of the bridge as I cursed under my breath. Tanner probably thought I was ridiculous, and he'd be right.

But what if this was my chance to actually check the spot where I'd found the coin?

Fatter raindrops fell against my windshield. The storm was picking up speed. It was the first real rainfall we'd had in months. If it continued like this all night, the lake levels would be higher in the morning, and then I'd be unable to check the spot by the dock where I'd found the coin.

If it really was part of the Langston Treasure, now was the time to confirm that. I gripped the steering wheel harder, then turned and rumbled through a speed bump on the other side of the bridge, which emptied out near the end of the boardwalk. The moonlight bounced off the lake's surface, which was pimpled with gobs of rain.

The windshield wipers squeaked against the pane as they struggled to keep up with the downpour. I put them on the highest speed and wove through the streets of Langston's elite north-side neighborhood, which I knew like the back of my hand. This had been my home for my entire life. I basically belonged here.

Still the hairs on the back of my neck prickled up, and my hands started to sweat. I straddled two worlds—one where I attended school on this side of town, and one where I lived in grandma's old house on the other side. This late at night, I shouldn't be here.

Our old house came into view on Violet Drive, the soft lamp-light casting shadows on the quiet street. Easing the car to the side of the street, I cut the engine so that I wouldn't draw attention to myself. I got out and rested the car door against the frame, afraid to latch it completely closed. I didn't want anyone to hear me. But the interior light stayed on, which looked suspicious, so I bumped the door with my hip to close it completely.

For a moment, I stood in the street, drinking in the sight of my family home, passed down through at least three generations of Whitecrofts. The periwinkle trim that was set against the white wood panels was visible even in the moonlight, its windows darkened and vacant.

It now belonged to another family, and that was hard to wrap my head around. The new owners weren't home, nor were they likely to be for another couple weeks. This was a secondary summer home for them, a lake house retreat. My stomach twisted into knots at the thought of those people walking around *my* inheritance.

My paternal grandparents would roll in their graves if they knew we'd lost the house and most of their antiques. All those precious family heirlooms gone—all those memories fading.

I took the stone stairway two at a time, darting into the shadows as quick as I could. My feet faltered as I surveyed the backyard where heavy landscaping was underway. The shrubs on the far side had been torn out and replaced with tall cypress trees. It would block out the natural light that came in in the morning. The new owners would know that if they came here more often.

But it was theirs to do with as they pleased.

I fished my phone out of my back pocket and turned on the flashlight, using it to guide my steps on this altered terrain. I inched farther to the dock, the pellets of raindrops against the lake's surface growing louder as I stepped onto the floating dock. The low waterline lapped lazily against the wooden posts. Slowly, I slid down from the platform and into the sludge beneath.

My feet sank slowly into the soupy mud—mud that would soon be buried by the lake again if the rain continued at this rate. I stopped, taking a moment to dig my toes deeper, getting the same satisfaction I had when the lake was low during the last drought. It brought back the hazy memories of sloshing around in the dirt.

The soles of my feet clapped against the clay bottom of the embankment until I came to the curve of the cove near the willow tree. It was where I'd found the coin. Or at least I *thought* it was the right spot. It had been a decade since I'd stood there. I shook my head, wiping the doubt away, and knelt down, my knees sinking into the dirt. My fingers sank into the sludge, and I drove them in deeper, sifting through the crumbles. Wet curls clung to my face as my desperate fingers scraped deeper and deeper into the silt. My nail caught on something hard and my pulse ticked up a beat. I tucked my hair behind my ear before dusting around the spot. It was no treasure. It was a rock.

A freakin' rock.

I sat back on my heels, resting my filthy hands against my thighs, breathing heavily, caught between a sob and an hysterical laugh.

"What am I doing?" I threw my head back, scanning the dark sky. I wanted to scream but I couldn't. I was a trespasser, after all. Instead, I hung my head low. I thought I'd reached rock bottom going to a pawnshop to sell my grandmother's ring. But no—this was rock bottom.

Literally.

I heaved myself off the ground, smearing more mud onto my legs, and made my way to the dock. My stomach was in knots from all the shame. Shame balled into a knot in my chest, and crept up my throat. I felt like I was choking.

I scrambled onto the dock and grabbed my phone and my shoes. Then scampered toward the backyard on my tiptoes, leaving a trail of muddy toe prints on the wooden boards. When I got to my car, I slumped behind the wheel.

Headlights flickered on a few houses down, and my heart pounded against my chest. I ducked behind the steering wheel, trying to make myself as small as possible. I didn't want one of my old neighbors to find me snooping around here. Or worse—I didn't want a cop to see me trespassing. The car crept by me, the brakes squeaking a little before turning the corner, leaving the street as still and quiet as it was before.

NINE

My half-empty water bottle crinkled as I poured its contents over my knees. I leaned against the car and rubbed the mud off with a fast-food napkin I'd found in the glove box. The water ran out before I could finish getting rid of all the evidence of the most foolish night of my life.

It was dark on our street—there was no soft lamplight like there was on Violet Drive. I walked up the driveway, but something caught my eye. A burgundy sedan was parked on the street right in front of our house. My heart hiccupped.

No one visited us over here. No friends followed my parents to the poor side. They were of course nice in public, if only to whisper behind our backs.

No, this was someone else. But who?

The last time I came home to a strange car in the driveway was *the bad day*—the day the feds came to the house with a warrant, surrounding our house with several black sedans and stone-faced investigators.

Panic surged through my veins, but I calmed myself with the knowledge that it was late, that no one would be working at this hour. But with every step I took, my back tensed up, my joints became stiff, my breathing become shallow as the residual trauma crept up my spine. Despite my better judgment, I was bracing myself for impact.

The back door banged against the ill-placed credenza as I pushed it open. I squeezed past it, weaving through the obstacle course of mismatched furniture.

"Hello?" I asked, setting my keys on the counter. My ears perked up at the sound of faint laughter coming from somewhere in the house.

"We're in here," my mom yelled from the living room.

I rounded the corner and found my mom sitting on the couch opposite my sister. Lucile flashed a wide smile at me that somewhat faltered as she scanned my disheveled appearance.

"Look who decided to surprise us!" Mom nodded her head toward Lucile. My mom's cheeks were flushed, perhaps from the sudden infusion of Lucile's energy. Or maybe it was from the glass of wine in her hands. "I still can't believe you came all this way to do laundry."

"What can I say?" She tugged at the drawstring of her black laundry bag, which was so full it bulged at the seams. "It was an *emergency.*"

She shot me a knowing look at the word *emergency*. It's what I had texted her the past few weeks—even before I found out about the back taxes. I felt a little guilty about that. I had become the girl who cried emergency.

But this time it really *was*. I was glad she was finally here to weather the storm with me.

"Is that your car out there?" I pointed my thumb over my shoulder, toward the window overlooking the front yard. "I didn't recognize it."

"It's Bryant's." She sighed, tucking her leg underneath her and sinking farther into the couch. "He let me borrow it, because my gas-guzzler makes him cringe. He calls my Tahoe an *earth eater*."

"He's not wrong." I laughed. Lucile's SUV only got a dozen miles per gallon. "But does everything Bryant owns have to be in Morehouse maroon?"

Lucile flashed a fake smile then opened her mouth to respond, but my mom interrupted with an enthusiastic squeal.

"Who cares what color it is? It's a Tesla." She scooted to the edge of the couch, her legs bobbing up and down in excitement. "It's brand new. And his father is big in commercial real estate."

"Easy, Mom." Lucile held her hand up, giving my mom the side-eye. "You can stow your dossier on my boyfriend, thank you very much."

"What? I'm just saying he's a really good catch."

"He's a lot of things." Lucile pursed her lips, as if she didn't agree with my mother's limited assessment. Knowing my sister, her new boyfriend had to have more to offer than a fat bank account. "Behind that fancy car is a fierce environmentalist and passionate community organizer."

"I'm sold on him sweetheart. Hook, line, and sinker." My mom's mouth stretched into a wide grin, which she soon covered with a very large glass of wine.

Lucile bobbed her head from side to side, pleased to have my mother's approval, even if it was only because he was rich. Because behind my sister's nonchalance about status and wealth, there was a part of her that still cared. She wanted the finest things in life without *appearing* to want them. But I knew those chunky glasses were designer, and her suede tote was Prada.

"How long are you here for?" my mom asked before taking another sip from her wineglass.

"I don't know." She bobbed her head from side to side as she considered her response. "Probably just for tonight. *Maybe* until Sunday, but don't hold me to that."

"You'll need to get started on that tonight." Mom shot a worried glance at her laundry bag. She unfolded her legs from underneath her and set her glass on the coffee table before standing. "I'll go transfer the load of towels to the dryer, so that you can use the washer."

She stepped over my sister's legs, then paused.

"Might as well take this with me." She swiped her glass off the table, guzzling it down on her way to the garage.

I sidestepped her and ran to the couch, collapsing onto Lucile's lap as I wrapped my arms around her.

"You finally came." I tightened my hug. I was so relieved to have her here, I felt a pinch in my tear ducts like I was about to cry again. It was a wonder I had any tears left after crying so much tonight.

"Yeah, you said it was an emergency." She shifted her legs beneath me, causing me to lose my balance. I plopped into the warm spot on the couch my mom had left behind. "But Mom didn't mention back taxes *at all*. So, I guess we're doing that pretend-nothing's-up thing again?"

Lucile eyed me over her horn-rimmed glasses, her eyes going cross as she studied my hair. She reached up and plucked something from my frizzy hair. She pulled back holding a hardened clump of mud.

"Okay, what the actual fuck?" She brandished the dirt in the space between us. Then her gaze fell to a streak of dirt on my ankles. "You look like you've been mucking a barn. Explain."

"It's nothing." I grabbed one of the throw pillows and put it on my lap, concealing the silt. "I was…"

My voice trailed off as I considered whether to lie or to tell the truth.

"You were what?" Lucile's eyes searched me, her lips tucked between her teeth.

"I was at the house," I whispered. "*Our* house."

"What?" She flung her hands in the air. "Why?"

"You don't want to know." I threw my face down into the nearest cushion and groaned. I couldn't lie to my sister about where I was, but I wasn't exactly going to tell her the whole truth. Digging for treasure in our old backyard would have driven Lucile to commit me to an asylum.

"Okay, this is not going to happen." She hopped out of her seat and set her hands on her hips while she paced in the cramped space between the coffee table and the TV stand. "You cannot crack up right now. Dad is literally wearing a groufit and has been holed up in the garage since I got here. Mom was drinking alone, and I'm pretty sure she's on her tenth glass of wine. And now you're rolling around in the mud behind a house we don't even own anymore for God knows why." She tilted her head toward the ceiling, her eyes tightly closed, and groaned. "It's worse than I thought."

"I told you." I tucked my knees to my chest and rested my chin on my knees. "And I wasn't rolling around in the yard. That makes me sound feral."

"Um, have you looked in the mirror?" She jutted her chin out, her eyes bulging. "I legit cannot stress this enough—and I say this out of love, because you know I love you, right? But get a grip. I can't rehab Mom and Dad *and* you."

"I've been dealing with them and this stupid house every day for the past three months," I said through clenched teeth, trying not to raise my voice. I didn't want my parents to overhear the conversation. "So, give me a break."

Her face softened at the sound of my frustration, and she collapsed to the floor with a long sigh.

"Okay, I'm sorry. I'm just super stressed with finals coming up and studying for the GRE. Plus, I'm mad at myself for not coming sooner." She gave a half-hearted grin, tight with guilt, and in that moment, I could tell just how tightly wound she was. She was under as much pressure as I was—if not more. I began to wonder if she was just as clueless as I was on how to approach life's mounting challenges, including Mom's disordered drinking and Dad's depression. She cocked her head to the side, curiosity brewing in her dark brown eyes. "Have you seen them yet? The new owners of the house?"

"No." The tightness in my chest unraveled slightly at the change of subject. "But I've heard they're New Yorkers. They'll only come for the summer months."

"Figures." She leaned back on her hands, looking around the crowded living room and the furniture overflowing into the hallway. "Well, holding on to all of this stuff isn't going to bring any of it back. It's like Marie Kondo does with that 'spark joy' shit. It really cleanses your emotional state. I think there's some truth to it. My old roommate just gutted her closet, and she's much more stable these days."

My ears perked up at the mention of her fashionable roommate. "The one who is interning at *Cosmo*?" I sat up straighter. "Sis, you have got to grab me a dress from her donate pile for the centennial."

"It's done. They're already gone." She shook her head. "But you have tons of dresses. It wouldn't hurt to wear another one again."

She pulled out a stick of lip balm from her front pocket and smeared it on her lips. The gold letters FENTY emblazoned on the side reflected off the light from the ceiling fan. If my sister was trying to emphasize temperance, she wasn't doing a good job. That tube of gloss was expensive.

"Where are you getting all of this nice stuff? I thought we were broke."

"I got that work study job at the library, and they let me work as many shifts as I want. I really just sit behind the circulation desk and study." She flared her nostrils and looked away from me, a telltale sign that she was holding back. When I cleared my throat, she rolled her eyes and met my gaze. "Okay, fine. And I moved in with Bryant, so I get to keep almost my whole paycheck. But don't tell Mom, or she'll freak out and start talking about marriage and babies, and I really can't handle that kind of pressure. You know how she is."

The mention of an *old* roommate made more sense now.

"Fine." I nodded. And I meant it. The list of people I trusted was a short one, and Lucile was at the top of it. I didn't want to jeopardize it. I would not betray her secrets, and she wouldn't divulge mine.

"Okay, so I guess this weekend I'll be cleaning out the garage. But first . . ." She leaned forward, tapping the tips of her fingers, her mouth curved upward in a diabolical smile. "Where is Mom hiding the wine?"

"She's not hiding it. There's a box on the countertop."

"A box?" She blinked rapidly, clearly stunned. "Good grief, things are bad. Do you want a glass? Come on, it can't be worse than what you and your friends drink."

"Let's watch *Halloween*. I want to see a bunch of people get murdered or something."

A scary movie would be a respite, something fun to make me scream. The fear would last for a moment and then be over. Unlike my real situation, which was getting scarier and more desperate by the day.

TEN

Dylan flounced down the hallway like she was storming the runways of Milan. Her hips swayed side to side, her chin raised as she confidently claimed the center of the corridor—sort of to the rhythm of "Move Bitch." Her white uniform shirt was almost completely unbuttoned, flashing a Lululemon crop top underneath. It wasn't strictly dress code, but Dylan lived by her own set of rules, especially so close to the end of school.

She exuded power. Even the teachers gave her a wide berth.

I, on the other hand, felt like garbage. I'd stayed up way too late last night, drinking wine and eating chocolate with my sister—well past any reasonable bedtime. By lunch time, my head was still pounding from lack of sleep, and my stomach roiled from all of the overindulgence. I blew away a stray hair that had escaped my loose, hasty bun and smacked my dehydrated lips. An acidic burp gurgled up my throat, which I hid with a cough.

A group of junior girls were standing in front of Dylan's locker when we arrived. She pursed her lips and narrowed her eyes, wordlessly ordering them to move. The girls apologized under their breath and scurried away. I slouched into the neighboring locker, barely able to hold myself upright, my eyes drooping.

"What the actual fuck?" Her fingers slowed as she dialed in her combination. Her eyes tightened.

"Huh?" My eyes fluttered open.

"He's still staring at you," she said, nodding down the hall.

"Who?" I followed her gaze down the hallway and found myself locking eyes with the last person I wanted to see—Tanner Holmes. I quickly turned away from him, pretending I didn't see a thing. "No, he isn't."

"He *is* staring at you." She looked over her shoulder again, nodding slowly in confirmation. Her eyes darted to me and she raised an incredulous eyebrow. "Weirdo did it all last period, too. You would know if you hadn't been dozing off."

"I wasn't dozing off." It wasn't a lie. I had been awake—but just barely.

"It's okay. I sleep during physics literally all the time." She flashed a sly smile as she slammed her locker shut. "I told Mr. Werner that I have to wear sunglasses because I get migraines caused by light sensitivity or some shit. But really I'm full-on napping."

"So, I'm guessing you have no chance at a career in astrophysics."

"Yeah, physics can suck a dick." Her face scrunched up like she'd tasted something bitter. She threaded her arm through the crook of my elbow and tugged me around the corner, through aqua hall, the smell of cafeteria food growing stronger as we inched closer. The dining hall was chock-full of students and buzzed with noisy chatter, the lines in front of the food stations already long.

"You hungry?"

"Nah." I shook my head, feeling my stomach gurgle again. The only thing I wanted to put in my mouth was another Tums.

"Me neither." She nodded in agreement, then steered me away from the doorway. We didn't eat in the dark and noisy cafeteria with the other students. We had our own private setup outside. "I'm on a restrictive diet until the centennial, just in case I win prom queen and get to sit on the stage with the mayor. But of course I'm rooting for you, too! Let the best bitch win. But anyway, I'm doing that cayenne pepper, celery juice cleanse. I'm only allowed this protein shake once a day."

"Dylan. That sounds *super* unhealthy."

"I know, right? But I'll look so rad in my dress." Her eyes glowed—she was clearly pleased with her plan. I frowned at her, wondering if I should say something more.

At the end of aqua hall, she bumped her hip against the handlebar of the side door leading out to the courtyard. A wall of heat and humidity collided with us as we walked to the set of empty picnic tables in the center of the patio. We'd staked our claim on this hideout sophomore year, and it'd stuck. It was unofficially reserved for us at all times—where the charmed got to eat.

"Speaking of dresses, you still coming to my house tomorrow to help me pick one out?"

"Sure." I shrugged. I didn't have anything else to do. I'd done *the most* last night. Lounging in Dylan's massive closet while she sifted through her newest dresses was way more my speed.

"Ugh, this heat." Dylan sat on the picnic table bench with her back to the table, propping herself up with her elbows. She tilted her head toward the sky, closing her eyes as she soaked up the sun. "Where the fuck is Fatti?"

"Don't call her that." I moaned into my Diet Coke. "You know she hates that."

"Right, right. People should be called what they want to be called. All that bullshit." She twirled her hand in the air as she said all the right things. But she had no intention of actually following through with any of it. "Where is she?"

"Probably in line for food."

"Ew." Her lip curled up as she looked toward the double doors that led to the cafeteria.

"Again, you need food to survive. Seriously, *eat something.*"

"No, *eww.*" She slid her Ray-Bans down the bridge of her nose and pointed behind my shoulder. "What's he doing here?"

I turned and saw Tanner's wiry frame coming through the doors and heading straight toward us.

"You lost?" Dylan raised her eyebrows. She pointed in the directions of the courtyard doors. "The cafeteria is that way."

"Stalk much?" I leaned back with Dylan, raising my eyebrow. And in that moment, I channeled every ounce of charmie I had left in my bones. I had still not forgiven him for last night.

And I wouldn't anytime soon.

He gripped the straps of his backpack tighter, his nervous eyes darting to Dylan before returning to mine.

"Can I talk to you for a sec? About last night?"

"*Last night?*" Dylan chortled so loudly, I thought she'd just drowned in her celery juice. She swayed slightly, as if she was dizzy from this new piece of scandalous information.

"Right." I blinked rapidly, searching for a plausible fib. "Oh, yeah! Duh. The research project."

"Yeah." His voice trailed off. He nodded slowly and then his eye twitched as he realized what I was doing. "The research thing."

"Watch my stuff?" I asked Dylan, then hopped off of the bench before she had a chance to respond.

I nudged Tanner toward the double doors, and he stumbled forward, his long legs tangling underneath him. He recovered and bounded through the door, turning away from the cafeteria to push through the doors to the emergency stairwell. I stalked after him like he was my prey.

"Could you be any more sketch?" My voice hitched up a few octaves. "You said *your secret is safe with me.* But you just told the queen of gossip that you were with me last night. You might as well have told her we had sex. That's what she's going to think." I groaned and brushed my fingers through my hair, messing it up even more than it already was. A nervous laugh slipped from his lips, and I shot him a deathly glare.

"I will make it up to you, I swear." He backed away from me and onto the staircase. He hesitated for a moment, his mouth open like he couldn't quite figure out what to say. Then he shook his head, turning on his heels before jogging up the stairs. He called over his shoulder, "Just follow me."

"No." I stamped my foot, and the sound echoed through the stairwell. "Where do you think you're going?"

Gripping the railing tightly, I scrambled up the stairs, taking the steps two at a time just to keep up with him. But I was no match for his long legs. He pulled ahead of me with ease. When I reached the third floor, the door was almost shut. I shoved my foot through the crack, kicking it open. The door handle banged on the wall as I burst through it—just in time to see Tanner slip into the library stacks.

The halogen lights whirred, giving the ill-lit bookshelves a dingy glow. It smelled of aging paper and musty carpet—a long forgotten and neglected corner of an otherwise pristine campus. He turned a corner at the dead end of the wing, and I hustled after him. I rounded the last shelf, winded from the pursuit. My eyes widened as I met Squid's toothy grin and B's guarded stare. Squid waved sheepishly and then looked up at Tanner.

"Thought you said you were going to smooth things over?"

My nostrils flared.

"What are y'all doing here?"

ELEVEN

Squid held his hands up and walked slowly toward me like he was afraid any sudden movements would cause me to bolt. He wasn't wrong. I was *this close* to dipping back behind the bookcases and putting this crew behind me. But something about Tanner's persistence kept my feet firmly planted to the spot.

Despite my confusion and frustration, I was curious.

"Why are you in my library?" I asked Squid.

"*Your* library?" B tsked and propped her feet on the table, a sly grin tugging at her lips. "You charmies think you own everything."

I shot her a glare that would rival her own sour mug. I was not in the mood to be laughed at again—not in my school. This wasn't the pawnshop, where they called the shots. This was my turf.

"B has something to say to you. About last night." Squid gulped, his Adam's apple bobbing up and down as he turned to face her. He nodded encouragingly. "Don't you, Barbie?"

"Don't. Call. Me. Barbie." Her hand curled into a ball on the tabletop. She scooted to the edge of her seat, and for a second, I thought she might actually leap up and punch Squid. She looked lethal.

"B." Tanner's tone was clipped, serious.

"Fine." She rolled her shoulders, shedding some of the tension, and propped her boots onto the table. She blinked at me for a while before finally speaking, "I'm sorry, okay? I was only laughing because I was . . . well, I was kinda in shock. I hate to admit it, but you found a piece of Toulouse."

I wasn't expecting that from B. I waited for her to poke fun at me like she usually did, but she sat there quietly, looking earnest.

"I'm sorry for laughing, too. We all are." Squid stepped in front of B, blocking her from view. "Seriously, we didn't mean to act like such dicks."

"Noted." I relaxed my stance a bit, the urge to flee dissipating. "But seriously, you shouldn't be here. Someone might see you."

"It's technically open to the public." Tanner pulled out a chair, gesturing for me to sit in it. I shook my head—I wasn't there yet. He plopped in the seat, biting on the corner of his lip.

"Yeah, on weekends."

"Consider this my long weekend." Squid's mouth widened into his familiar toothy grin. "I like to take Fridays off."

"Geez, princess." B smirked, leaning smugly back in her chair. "Haven't you ever played hooky before?"

"Don't call me princess, *Barbie*," I said, then shoved her feet off the table, knocking her off balance. She gripped the edge of the table before she fell backward. I batted my eyelashes at her, pleased to have finally unnerved her, and took a seat at the table.

If I was searching for a toxic relationship, I didn't need to look further than Dylan. I didn't need any more friendships where I felt I always had to look over my shoulder. So if that's all B was offering—hard pass.

To my surprise, she threw her head back with a laugh.

"Okay, deal." She nodded resolutely. "*Casey.*"

It was the first time she'd ever said my actual name.

"Guys, focus." Tanner's eyes flitted to the clock on the wall. The lunch hour was already a third over, and we'd gotten nowhere.

Squid flipped a chair around and sat straddled before pulling a pile of photocopies out of the front pocket of his backpack.

"Boom." His finger jabbed the top page. "Ironclad proof that we were telling you the truth."

I slid the paper closer to me, rolling my eyes as soon as I saw the outline of the Black Rose. I would have thought he'd drawn it himself, but then I read the small print on the bottom right-hand corner of the page. The signature was cut off but the date was still legible—1862.

"I know it's just a sketch." He stroked his chin. "But that's just because there are no photographs of the treasure itself."

"You guys are really leaning into this." My hands fell to my sides. I didn't know what else to say. They really believed in a tall tale of treasure. It was ridiculous beyond words.

"You're nailing it. Seriously, a born salesman." B slapped Squid's shoulder, shuddering his stance. "But for real. We're being honest about this. We've been looking for signs of the treasure for years."

"Look, we have more proof." Tanner shuffled through the papers and pulled out an old photo. "This was taken outside of the Bank of Toulouse."

The picture showed a couple with a baby carriage in front of them. The couple was shaking hands with a familiar face, Colonel Langston, the founder of our town. He stood next to a man with an old-fashioned handlebar mustache. The storefront signage above them read BANK OF TOULOUSE. The caption underneath the photo read:

BANK OWNERS AVA AND ERNEST ANDERSON, WITH INFANT,
SHAKE HANDS WITH COLONEL LANGSTON, EUSTICE
HORNSBY. FOREGROUND: BANK OF TOULOUSE. 1895

"Is that Dev's grandad?" I squinted, doing some quick math in my head. "No—great grandad."

"Try great great grandad." Squid tapped to a faded date on the page which read 1895. "At the turn of the century, Eustice Hornsby was Langston's right-hand man. Helped him build his town."

"Once a charmie, always a charmie." B grumbled under her breath. There was a bang under the table—likely from someone kicking the leg of her chair. "Well, maybe with one exception."

Part of me thought her kindness was just to serve her own needs—buttering me up to get information on how I found the coin. After all, I had the first clue to a puzzle she'd been trying to figure out for years. And she wanted to find the rest of it. So did I. So, our interests aligned.

"Once a charmie, now a downstreamer." She looked at me without her usual mockery—with something akin to respect. She nodded encouragingly, and I accepted her peace offering with a nod of my own.

"So, now you know the treasure is real." Tanner sighed heavily, like he was relieved to have all the information on the table. He slid his hand across the surface, grazing the tips of my fingers with his. "Casey, we need to know where you found the coin we saw last night. There's a *lot* more where it came from. There has to be."

"How much more?" The words were out of my mouth before I had a chance to think. I leaned forward, sitting on the edge of my seat.

"Like factoring in inflation and the fact that they're priceless artifacts that no one has seen in over a hundred years." He ran his fingers through his hair, exhaling slowly. "A hundred million, give or take."

My breath hitched, and the wheels in my head started turning. That was more than enough to pay the back taxes on our house— and then some. I could pay for Barnard's tuition and be debt-free, maybe get a nice apartment near campus that I could have all to myself instead of sharing a dorm with a roommate. I could fix the water heater at home—shoot, I could buy my parents a new house, and my parents would be happier.

"If I were to believe you that I, in fact, found buried treasure— which is completely—"

"True," Tanner, Squid, and B said in unison.

"—which is completely false." I held my palms up, as if weighing the options before me. "But let's say I have the first clue. Why would I tell you?"

I raised an eyebrow, waiting for the information to sink in. I was in possession of all the cards here.

"Because we can help you find it." Squid's gaze flitted to the floor. "For a small fee of course."

"No way, dude." B rapped her knuckles against the table. "If we do this, we split it evenly."

Their earnest expressions made me blink first.

"Oh, sure. Yes. Let's split it evenly." Hysterical laughter spurted out of my mouth. I guessed now was my turn to mock them. But as my laughter trickled to a stop, I looked at Squid's earnest expression, at the hopeful gleam in Tanner's eyes. Even B looked at me with interest.

They were dead serious.

"It doesn't matter where I found it." I shot up from my seat with a heavy sigh, intent on putting them out of their misery. "Because there's nothing else there."

"You don't know that." Squid slouched in his chair, his fingers knotting together.

"I checked," I hissed.

"You did?" Tanner's mouth fell open. His eyes squinted in skepticism, but after a few moments, I could almost see he comprehended as his face relaxed. He slid the stack of papers over to his friends. "Guys, could you give us a sec? Maybe go try to find the old deeds from around the time that old photo was taken?"

He tilted his head over his shoulder, waiting until we couldn't hear B and Squid anymore, before continuing in a low voice.

"You went digging around in the rain last night."

"Of course I did. And I feel like a grade-A dummy." I bit the inside of my cheek and looked away from him. "Haven't you heard that I'm broke?"

"I didn't know it was that bad. I mean, you hear stuff, but..." He stepped closer, so close I could feel his breath brush against my forehead. "I'm not gonna lie. I need the money just as bad as you do."

His eyes were intent, earnest, and something shifted in me like a key in a lock. I believed him.

"Look, all I know is that I found the coin when the lake was low like ten years ago." My shoulders slumped forward. "On the embankment near my old dock, sort of underneath the willow tree."

"You won't regret this." He placed a hand on my shoulder and squeezed. "I have a good feeling about this."

Rustling in the corner snapped our attention to a nearby bookshelf. A book slid out from the middle shelf and fell to the floor. A large brown eye darted between me and Tanner, followed by a gasp. Fatima poked her head from behind a bookshelf and tumbled into the aisle, her eyes bulging.

"Shut the front door, I'm gagging! I totally knew it." She ran her fingers through her uncharacteristically disheveled hair, then wiped her mouth with the back of her hand, clearing away a bit of smeared lipstick. "Up here in the stacks. Together. *Noice.*"

"Um. We're doing research?" My voice ticked up, as if it were a question. I was getting tired of all the lying, especially after I'd just leveled with Tanner.

"Please. No one does actual work up here." She twisted her shirt back in place and ran her hand over the line of buttons, straightening out some of the wrinkles. "Everyone knows what the stacks are for."

It dawned on me that she too was not alone up here.

I craned my neck to see farther down the aisle of dusty bookcases just in time to see a retreating figure fumbling with their belt loops, the bottoms of their shoes scuffing against the carpet as they hurried out of sight.

"Um, hello. Who's your friend?" I cocked my head to the side, shocked to find Fatima with a rando in the stacks.

"Oh no, this is *not* about me. Stop trying to change the subject. So this," she said, swishing her finger in the air between me and Tanner. "This is happening?"

I sighed, ready to tell Fatima what we were really doing up here, no matter how dumb it sounded. I was in an honest mood, tired of lying.

"It's really not what you think. I found this—"

"You caught us." Tanner scooted closer to me and wrapped his arm around my shoulders.

My head tilted up, and I shot him a horrified look.

"Oh my gordness!" Fatima danced on the tips of her toes. "I'm totally vibing with your energies."

"Gahhh I know," I said through a tight, awkward smile.

"Prom?" She nodded, waiting expectantly for her suspicions to be confirmed.

I slid out from underneath Tanner's arm and stepped toward Fatima. "No, I thought we weren't bringing dates. You know, we were gonna be our own women."

"Like Dylan was ever going to go solo. She's essentially holding tryouts with the football players to be her date. I bet she's in the courtyard chatting up Pierce right now. He's asked her to go with him like five times already."

My jaw fell open—I was truly at a loss for words. I couldn't backtrack without telling her about our treasure hunt. And clearly, Tanner wanted to keep that on the down low. But I couldn't exactly foist myself upon him. Feeling like I was stuck between a rock and a hard place, I froze.

"What do you think?" Tanner nudged me with his shoulders, thawing me with a genuine smile. "Want to go to prom together?"

My breath caught, and for several very uncomfortable seconds I considered it. I nodded slowly in agreement.

"What is happening right now? What the *eff* is happening right now?" She said it over and over again, so fast that the words started to sound like a jumble of nonsense. She paused, taking a deep breath before raising her arms above her head in the shape of a goalpost. "I'm stanning this in such a big way. Fill him in on all the deets?"

She wiggled her fingers in farewell, as if sprinkling fairy dust in her wake, and then nearly skipped down the hall on the tips of her toes.

"You didn't have to do that." I covered my face with my hand, too mortified to even look at him.

"Oh, yes I did. What are the deets?"

TWELVE

Fifty-two days until we lose the house

Mercury was definitely in retrograde. I hated to adopt Fatima's astrological musings, but there was no other explanation. The universe was clearly intent on turning my world upside down. I spent the rest of the day and night running through every detail of my time in the stacks, my cheeks heating every time I thought of the way Tanner had looked at me, the way a dimple formed in the crook of his mouth when he'd smiled. It was like he actually wanted to go with me.

And I was okay with that.

When I stepped onto Dylan's porch and rang the doorbell late Saturday afternoon, I was buzzing, even though I was still wearing my uniform for the club. In a last-minute attempt to appear more casual, I untucked my white collared shirt and loosened my high bun. I was checking myself out in the window's reflection when Dylan's mom answered the door. The sight of her knocked the breath out of me, snapping me out of my primping. Her face was pulled taut, her eyebrows frozen in place. Plump with filler, her cheeks didn't move as she somewhat smiled at me.

"Casey, baby, hi." She had the voice of a gerbil, strained through lips that didn't move. She held her phone away from her face and leaned forward, her lips smacking as she gave me air kisses on both sides of my face. She opened the door wider. "Come on in. They're upstairs."

My sandals clapped against the marble staircase. Laughter reverberated off the walls of the upstairs corridor, growing louder as I walked to Dylan's room.

I kicked my shoes off before walking across her off-white, faux fur rug. Her room was massive and plush, accented with pink jewel tones and soft creams, smelling of expensive perfume—and something else. My nostrils perked up at the smell of smoke. I made a beeline for her closet across the room. A haze hung in the air, smoke refracting off the glow from the skylight above.

Dylan stood in front of a floor length mirror by the window, wearing a long, puffy-sleeved dress, a silver scrunchie holding together a messy bun on the crown of her head. She stabbed her one-hitter pipe into a grinder sitting on her accessories table and brought it up to her lips.

"Thought you were gonna stand us up," Dylan said before bringing the pipe up to her lips. She lit the end with her lighter, inhaled, and stifled a cough by holding her breath. She held it out in Fatima's direction. "You want a hit?"

"Ooooh, yes please." Fatima wiggled her fingers and grabbed it. She sat back in Dylan's faux fur beanbag and took a couple of puffs before flicking ash into a Diet Coke can on the vanity countertop. She looked apologetically at me. "Sorry it's cashed. But don't worry, I'll load another."

"I'm good." I shook my head, feeling slightly light-headed. I was still on a high from yesterday—that dizzying feeling of a developing crush.

There was a rack of dresses in front of her tweed chaise lounge, the tags still dangling off all of them. I walked slowly along the line of hopefuls, my fingers grazing the chiffon, silk, and tulle. Dylan had outdone herself.

How many dresses did one girl need?

I untucked a price tag from the armpit of a chartreuse strapless dress, and my eyes bulged at the four digits. Langston was a ritzy retreat, but it didn't offer the designer stores to satiate Dylan's tastes. She had done what any self-respecting charmie would do and ordered dresses from Neiman's, Saks, and Bloomingdale's with her credit card—with the expectation of returning most of them—bringing the fashion mountain to Mohammad.

But still. The money spent for one of these dresses could buy my schoolbooks for my entire freshman year—and then some.

I slumped into her Lucite bucket chair, wistful about the times when I used to be able to dip my toe into the fashionista waters.

"My sister's in town and going on a cleaning spree. That's why I'm late."

"Ugh, I love Lucile," Dylan said, smoke trailing out of her nostrils. "She's so spunky."

"And has great style," Fatima added.

"You should have brought her over. She has a good eye, and I'm pretty undecided on what I should wear to prom. At least I picked a dress for the centennial." She whipped around, holding her arms out wide to invite our inspection. "Guys, tell me the truth. Do I look fat in this dress?"

"Girl, stop." Fatima's face turned serious. "Your body negging is so triggering."

"You kinda look bony," I said. Despite all the overflowing fabric, she looked small. I looked at her backbones jutting out and could count almost every single vertebrae.

Dylan beamed like she was taking it as a compliment, but I'd meant just the opposite. I was concerned.

"It's just all this material. I mean I know puffy is a vibe right now, but come on." Her arms flapped at her sides, sending ripples through all the layers of taffeta. "I kind of wanted to show off this time. It is my last prom, after all."

"Personally, I think the Pilgrim-sleeve thing is a little played out right now." Fatima brought the one-hitter to her lips.

"Plus, Pierce is weirdly an arms guy." Dylan grabbed her phone off an end table and held it in front of her, puckering her lips. She snapped a selfie, then frowned. She held the phone farther away from her, and slid one of the straps off her shoulder, exposing her lacy bra.

"Uh, should we give you some privacy?" I laughed.

"What? A little tasteful side boob never hurt anybody."

"So, you caved?" I asked. "You're going to prom with Pierce?"

"Called it." Fatima stomped her foot on the ground. She wiggled her fingers, inviting us to give her some props.

"I mean, how am I supposed to live under that amount of pressure?" Dylan's brows upturned in her pretty pout. "If I'd said no, he would have started asking me every day. I had to put him out of his misery."

"Guess the dude's never heard of consent and boundaries," I said it low so that only Fatima could hear me.

"Yeah, no means no." She laughed and caught a stink-eye from Dylan.

"I'm not the only one. Dev's been poking around Casey. And Captain Speedo was creeping around our table yesterday while you were MIA." She frowned at Fatima through the mirror. "But you two can still go together though. I'm sure it won't be weird."

"Actually, Case here already has a date." Fatima grinned. "I found her sealing the deal up in the stacks."

"Oh?" Dylan peered at my reflection in the mirror.

"We were just *talking*. That's all."

"No one just *talks* in the stacks." She rolled her eyes.

"That's exactly what I said!" Fatima stomped her foot again, clearly feeling vindicated. "Dish the deets, bitch."

"Please tell me it's not creepy Captain Speedo. I can't imagine why he'd think he'd ever have a chance."

"Why's that?" I asked.

"Yeah, the dude is stacked." Fatima nodded vigorously. "He's definitely prom photo material."

Dylan searched my face, watching the blush creep across my cheeks, and her smile curdled.

"Dude is not unfortunate looking, I'll give him that, but come on!" She tilted her head to the side, reminding me of my mother when she was in one of her scolding moods. "I mean, seriously. How would he fit into our crew?"

"Oh, because he's from the other side of town?" I raised a defensive eyebrow. I lived on the south side, too.

"Because he hangs out with freakin' public school dropouts in an old mine."

"They're not dropouts. They just . . . skip Fridays," I said, remembering Squid's truancy confession. As for the mine, I knew they hung out up there—there was no denying that. But that wasn't a deal breaker. Not anymore.

"Um, how about because he sells tchotchkes at a pawnshop. You can't sit someone like that across the table from Pierce, whose dad manages a billion-dollar hedge fund."

"I'm sure he'll be able to keep up with your date. A toddler could run circles around Pierce."

"Sick burn." Dylan hissed under her breath, making a searing sound.

I flipped her my middle finger. My cheeks burned with anger as my phone buzzed in my back pocket, and I leaned to the side to fish it out. There was a text from Tanner.

Found something cool. Can you talk?

I squinted, reading through the text several times. My interest was piqued. I fired off a text in response.

Can't right now. Busy. But do tell.

I was prepared to put my phone back in my pocket. In my experience, guys never texted back right away. But to my surprise, he did.

I'll explain it all later. Meet in an hour? I'll drop a pin.

I couldn't help the smile that forced its way onto my face. It caught the attention of Dylan, and before I knew it, she'd snatched my phone out of my hands. I leapt from my seat, pawing at her clutch around it.

"Give it back." I finally managed to snatch it back.

But Dylan had seen our texts—I could see it in her wide eyes. She lifted he fingers in air quotes. *"Meet in an hour?* Jesus, Case."

"You're such an asshole," I grumbled under my breath, gathering my purse off the floor.

"My mind is blown right now. You could go to prom with Dev, but you want to slum it with pawn bro?"

"Dylan, stop." Fatima finally jumped in. It was a low blow.

"No, it's cool. I'm leaving." I banged against Dylan's shoulder on the way to the door. "And for the record, Tanner did ask me to go to prom. And I said yes. So, suck on that."

"My bad. Look, I'm happy if you're happy. You can borrow one of these dresses. This one would look great with your neckline."

And she held up none other than the puffy-sleeved dress she'd discarded moments before. Her reject.

"I'd rather slum it, thank you very much."

I turned on my heels and stormed out.

THIRTEEN

I rolled to a stop where the GPS told me I'd reached my destination. I frowned, pinching outward against my phone screen to enlarge the map. I didn't see a house through the thick clump of trees. I eased down the lane to my right, my car's tires crunching on branches and pine cones. I crept along, searching through the woods, wondering if maybe Tanner had given me the wrong address. The trees gave way to a grassy inlet. A small house came into view.

I stopped just before the cracked asphalt sloped down to the lake, disappearing into the water. I put the car in park and unbuckled my seat belt, grabbing my backpack on the way out.

Squid lived on the edge of the lake near the dam, where the roar of the water rushing through the dam dominated the air along with the purr of the cicadas in the high grass. His house was comprised of a patchwork of sidings as eclectic as the front yard. The bottom half of the house was whitish brick. The second half was turquoise vertical siding. And the second story looked like a later addition with its khaki horizontal siding in a fresher coat of paint. It looked like it was cobbled together over time—and judging by the slant of the roof near the rear of the house, it wasn't exactly permitted work.

But I guessed that was Squid's style—a true DIYer. My dad could learn a thing or two from him to apply to our house. He hopped off an outdoor couch riddled with holes and loose stuffing.

"Welcome to Squid's Hollow." He opened his arms, proudly showcasing his domain. The inlet was set against the craggy cliff of the hillside—his own little Hobbit hole.

A ragged-looking truck eased to a halt behind my car. The paint was dull, almost like the weather had stripped the shine from the surface, and the hinges creaked as Tanner opened the driver's side door and stepped out.

"All right, who took my parking spot?" He slammed the door shut, wearing a playful smile. He saw my worried look and jogged to my side. "I'm kidding. What's mine is yours."

I blushed.

"I like to park on the street anyway, just in case I need to ditch the Hollow in a hurry."

"What makes it 'The Hollow'?" I asked.

"We call it that mostly because we went through a Lord of the Rings phase in middle school. But you have to admit, it's kind of the perfect hideout."

There was an upside-down bike frame with no wheels. An old car with the hood propped up, rusty hubcaps strewn about. An extension cord snaked across the lawn and connected to a table saw with sawdust scattered on the ground beneath it. A million ongoing projects, haphazardly laid bare for all to see. Maybe Squid was handy. Or maybe he had more starts than finishes.

B dismounted from her motorcycle and propped it up against the busted car.

"Sorry I'm late. Ms. Harold wanted me to pull a double, but I reminded her of child labor laws," she said, collapsing onto the pockmarked couch in the yard. "Also, the throttle on the bike is still sticking."

"I can fix that." Squid held up his finger and rummaged around in a case on a folding table.

"That's what you said last time." B rolled her eyes, biting the skin around her nails.

"Did you bring the stuff from the library?" Tanner asked Squid and B.

"Oh yeah, we couldn't find the deeds." Squid shrugged apologetically.

"Seriously?" My voice hitched up. There was a whole section devoted to the town's history. "How is that possible?"

"I don't know. It's an old town. What do you expect?" B shrugged. "We can always look at the deed to Langston hanging in the hall of the club."

"That's actually a good idea." The framed deed to the land parcel hung above the reception desk at the country club, and it had black-and-white pictures of the town's construction lining the halls. Her eyebrows shot up at the sound of my compliment.

"But we have something even better than old deeds," Squid said. "An old property map from Toulouse."

He dug in his backpack and pulled out a large piece of rolled paper. He unfurled it, revealing an old map of the main tracts of land.

"They let you check this out of the library?" I asked.

"We borrowed it." B smirked, but her smile fell when she saw my horrified expression "What? We'll give it back."

"Scout's honor." Squid held up a three-fingered Boy Scout salute, then returned his attention back to the map. He spread it out wider, setting rocks on the corners so that the curled corners would lie flat. He pointed to a location off-center. "Okay, so you found your coin here."

I leaned forward so that I could see the faded letters under his fingertip. My breath released in a rush, he was pointing to my house. Even seeing it on the map made me flustered. I blinked away and stood back up.

"There's nothing else there." I gulped, unsure of whether I was talking about the treasure or remnants of my old life. "I already checked, remember?"

"And I believe you." He looked up at me through his eyelashes.

"Really? Just like that?" I asked, surprised. I thought he would put up a bigger fight, maybe even suggest that we dig in the mud around my old house. That was something I really didn't want to do.

"Aww, tell her Squidy." B cocked her head to the side, batting her eyelashes.

"I kinda went there last night and poked around with the metal detector." He flicked his head to the shed where a long pole with a circular sensor on the end stood propped against the door. I recognized it as one of the metal detectors from the Dive—yet another thing that these guys *borrowed*. Squid smiled sheepishly. "Found some good dig spots."

"Unbelievable." I grumbled under my breath. "That's the plan? To dig up my old backyard?"

"There's also a backup option." B traced her finger along the map and stopped almost directly in the center of it. She gave a sly smile. "We should also check here."

I craned my head to the side, reading the word *Bank* on the page. But I didn't recognize that location. There wasn't a bank behind my house—I would know that. All the banks were by the interstate on the other side of town. Yet there were clearly marked roads snaking across the map, a layout I'd never seen before. Then it slowly dawned on me that she was pointing in the center of Langston Lake.

"You want to search in the lake?" My breath rushed out of my lungs, inflating my cheeks. This hunt was getting complicated. "How is that even going to work? We can't dig underwater."

"We won't have to." B elbowed Squid. "We snagged an underwater metal detector from the Dive."

"Which I will also return," Squid added, raising two three-fingered salutes.

"It's not going to work." I said confidently. If I was reading the map correctly, the bank sat just below the dive point. That was a high traffic area, picked apart by tourists. "Every diver has searched that area."

"Then we found a backup." She trailed her finger across the map in the direction of where the valley narrows—closer to where the dam was. "This is the Anderson house."

"From the picture I showed you in the library." Tanner spoke over my shoulder as he looked at the map. "They owned the Toulouse Bank."

"Sure, but it's not like they kept the money in their house. That's what the vaults are for."

He shrugged. "Couldn't hurt to look."

At his touch, a tingle rolled up my spine and my eyes unfocused. In that moment, I would have agreed to do anything. Squid clasped his hands together.

"So we just follow the road that leads to the center of town, then hang a right to get to the Andersons' place."

I blinked out of my trance, and turned to Squid with disbelieving eyes.

"It's not going to look like an actual town when we get down there. There are no street signs." I remembered diving in the lake years ago when we were getting certified for a family trip to the Caribbean. Aside from the intact church steeple, everything else was in ruins, chunks of concrete and brick covered in silt. And it was almost completely dark down there, the light barely reached its eighty-foot depth. "Haven't you ever been down there?"

"No. I just work the dock. But I've *wanted* to go down. And I've listened to the diving instructors like a million times, so I think I'm ready."

"Not even close." I shook my head, feeling the shock make the hairs on the back of my neck stick up. Diving took training and study. It didn't exactly come naturally to people. And then there was the number-one rule: Don't dive without a buddy.

Never, ever dive alone. Which meant that someone here would have to dive with me.

"Anyone else know how to scuba?"

"I got certified." Tanner offered. "But I only dove in a pool."

"Oh, that's just perfect." B sniggered from the other side of the map.

"I don't see your certification."

"You know . . ." her voice trailed off. Her eyes darted from Tanner to me then to the ground. "You know I'm claustrophobic."

So she did have her limitations, a chink in her armor.

I sighed into my hands. This did not bode well for the underwater search. But it seemed to have the opposite effect on Squid. He bounced on the tips of his toes, his smirk widening into an unmistakable smile.

"So we're really doing this?" He raised his eyebrows expectantly, waiting for us to nod in agreement. When each of us slowly bobbed our heads, Squid pumped his fist in the air. "You know this makes us pirates, right?"

A loud blast rocketed from above, louder than I had ever heard it. I flinched, ducking to the ground and looking up to see the others standing unfazed by the gunshot. I peered up the cliff side, recognizing that we were just below the old mine.

The screen door to the back porch swung open, and a shirtless guy with long, stringy hair bounded out. The door slapped against the siding, rattling the panes. He cupped his hand around his mouth and howled like a wolf up toward the mountain. After a brief moment, another howl called back.

"Call of the wild." He flared his nostrils and looked in the direction of the distant howler, gripping the belt loops of his jeans.

I leaned over to Tan, whispering hurriedly, "I always wondered who fired shots from the mine. I was kinda afraid you guys hung out up there."

"No way." Tanner slapped his thigh. "That's totally not our speed. We try to stay away from Seb and his friends because they are pretty bad news bears."

"Seb, keep it down already." Squid's jaw tightened in frustration. "You better not wake Grandma up again, or I swear to God I'm going up there this time."

"Relax." He rolled his eyes then set his gaze on me. "Who bagged the charmie?"

"Tanner," Squid said, but then he quickly shook his head. "No, I mean not bagged. I mean only if she wants to but—"

"Jesus, Squid," Tanner said, cussing under his breath. His cheeks turned a bright pink.

"No one bagged anyone." I put my hands on my hips. "So you're the one who's been firing off the mountain?"

"Oh, he's not the only one." B's nostrils flared. "There are a whole bunch of them up there. Giving *us* a bad name."

"It's a free country. Gotta keep the charmies on their toes." He walked toward me, his bare feet crunching over fallen pine needles. "It's actually kind of creepy cool. Now that the water line's fallen, you can hear your voice echo all the way down the shaft. I can show you, if you're game."

"Hard pass." I held a hand up, stopping him in his tracks. "I don't want to see your shaft."

He froze and then after a moment, threw his head back with a hearty laugh. He slapped Tanner on the shoulder and wagged his finger at me.

"I like her," he said, then snatched an old pair of boots near the couch. He waved over his shoulder, hopping on one foot and then the other to slip on his boots. Then he broke out in a jog, disappearing through the trees.

"Sorry about my brother." Squid lowered his head.

"Sebastian is like king of Burnout Mountain up there." Tanner leaned closer, lowering his voice so that Squid couldn't overhear him. "They don't really get along."

Squid's head popped up like he'd heard Tanner.

"He's gone fully rogue since our parents started long-haul trucking and left us with my grandma." He sniffled, hiding his face in the bag of supplies. When he resurfaced, I could tell he was more upset than he let on. There was some underlying trauma there, the sting of abandonment, but I didn't feel like it was my place to pry.

"Look don't tell anyone, okay?" Tanner reached out, squeezing my hand. "He's on probation. And if the cops found out..."

"I won't tell." I held three fingers up in a Girl Scout salute. It earned me a toothy grin from Squid. Tanner reached for my other hand and squeezed. I looked into his green eyes and squeezed back. "Your secret's safe with me."

And this time, I winked at him.

"See? We're building trust already." Tanner wagged his finger at me, his smile widening.

"Maybe a little." I bobbed my head from side to side, covering my mouth with my hand to hide my smile. I didn't want to encourage him too much. I looked back at the map of old properties, at the spot in the middle of the lake. I wasn't sure I trusted him enough to go all the way down there. My gaze fluttered back to the spot on the map where I found the coin. "I guess we should start at my old house."

"Right on." Squid pumped his fist in the air.

FOURTEEN

B's head tilted back as she scanned my old home from the hedgerow out front all the way to the dormer windows on the third floor. She released her breath so quickly, it sounded like a whistle.

"So this is where you're from?" She lowered her head and looked at me over her shoulder. She barked a laugh. "Seriously, this is insane."

"Shh!" I gripped her sleeve, tugging her closer to me. Her eyes widened, probably mirroring my panicked expression. "Keep your voice down. There are security guards on patrol all up and down these streets."

"Must be nice," B grumbled under her breath.

We waited for Squid to unpack the metal detector from the trunk of my car, holding our breath as he gently lowered the door and leaned against the top until we heard a soft click. Then we scurried across the yard, our shoes quietly shuffling through the grass.

"Okay, we're in." Tanner leaned against the back of the house and caught his breath.

"Let's see." Squid squinted at his phone screen where he'd saved a picture of the old Toulouse property map. He turned his phone to the side and then around again, trying to orient it in the right direction.

"We should check there first." I pointed to the shoreline to the left, just below the willow tree. "That's where I found the coin."

"So, uhh." B pointed behind her shoulder as we walked toward the dock. "Mind if I ask where y'all got all the dough to buy this place?"

"It was in my dad's family." I shrugged, feeling a slight pang in my chest at the thought of losing the house. I couldn't help it—it was painful coming here, reliving the past. But if it could help me get back on top, it was a price I was willing to pay.

"That's even weirder. To be Black and have a house on Violet Drive...there aren't many of us standing toe-to-toe with the Founding Families over here."

"And now there aren't any." I bit down on my lip then shook my head, trying not to think about it anymore.

From the edge of the deck, I flicked my head in the direction of the tree. Tanner's jaw fell open and Squid gasped beside him.

"Someone's been here," Squid whispered. He hopped off the edge of the dock and sloshed through the shallows. Tanner lowered himself then held his hand up to help me and B down. I splashed down and trudged behind Squid, fighting against the pull of the shifting silt beneath my feet. Squid crouched next to a pile of disturbed dirt and a corresponding hole, half-filled in with water brought in by the morning tide.

"Looks like someone beat us to it." Tanner stroked his chin, his eyes tight. He peered down the shoreline. "There's another dig spot up there."

"Fuck, dude." B slapped Squid's back. "Were you followed?"

"Uh...no?" He held both of his hands up in an exaggerated shrug. He balked at all of our expectant expressions. "I mean...at least I don't think so. I don't know, I wasn't really looking. Who would possibly tail *me*? No one else knows about the treasure except for us."

"That's not exactly true." Tanner planted his hands on his hips and bowed his head. "Ron knows. Or at least he's suspicious."

"Guys?" I squeezed my eyelids shut, debating whether or not I should tell them. "Does he drive a silver Chevy?"

I pried one eye open and found Tanner's lips drawn in a taut line, the color drained from his cheeks. After a moment he took a deep breath. "You saw him that night? After you left the pawnshop?"

"I didn't think anything of it at the time. But yeah. He was there." I shook my head, afraid to look him in the eyes. "I'm so sorry."

"He couldn't have gotten more than a few coins, if that." Squid held his hands up. "It's not like the metal detector was going berserk."

"Look, we need to be careful." Tanner pointed to each of us. "Make sure you're not followed, and keep whatever research you have tucked away."

"Come on." B scoffed. "It's not like Ron's a criminal mastermind."

"I'm for real," Tanner said. The usual playful glint in his eyes had evaporated. He was dead serious. "Do not underestimate my stepdad. He can be ruthless when he doesn't get what he wants when he wants it. So steer clear. Agreed?"

"Yeah." I nodded, feeling the hair on the back of my neck stand at attention.

"So what now?" B stabbed the mud with the tip of her shovel.

I looked to the lake, its dark water appearing almost as black as the night's sky.

"I guess we go for the backup search in the lake. One week from today." I gulped. I wanted more time to prepare for the dive. Diving was complex and had so many components to it, and I needed to refresh my skills. But time was not on my side. I needed to save my family's house. And I'd dive to the bottom of Langston Lake if that's what it took.

When I returned home, I was welcomed by a mound of black garbage bags spilling over the curb and into the street in front of our house. Lucile had clearly been busy sparking joy in my absence, purging my grandmother's old house of anything she deemed extraneous.

I opened the back door and it actually swung open all the way. My jaw dropped. I could actually fit through the door without shimmying to the side. I stepped inside, my jaw dropping even farther as I looked at the clean counters in the kitchen, and the clear walkway to the living room.

The stack of pictures that had been piled against the wall had disappeared. Family photos lined the small hall and the paintings decked the walls of the living room. For the first time in a long time,

I felt like my house was a real home. My mom lounged on the couch, her face flushed like she'd been working all day.

"Mom, the house looks freakin' awesome!" My voice came out louder than I'd intended, but I couldn't help it. I was too excited to have some breathing room. I'd felt stifled lately—from the pressures of paying for college, to dealing with bitchy friends, to dealing with my broken family, I'd felt kind of suffocated.

"Could you please not yell?" My mother grabbed her temples and sighed. She sank farther into the couch and grabbed the remote off the end table. She held it in front of her and turned the TV louder. Then she grabbed her glass of wine. It was only four in the afternoon. It was early for wine—even for my mother.

"Where's Lucile?"

"In the garage somewhere. I can't keep up with her three cups of coffee."

Lucile bustled into the living room, her silk scarf wrapped around her curly hair. Her hands were full of a stack of old, yellowing magazines.

"Why did Grandma keep so many old newspapers and magazines?" She shook the stack, rustling the pages.

"She was an eccentric. What can I say?"

"Nope, she was a hoarder." Lucile raised an eyebrow before dumping the entire stack into the already full trash bag.

"She held on to the past." My mom's gaze grew distant as she stared out of the window, and I wondered if she was thinking about all the things she herself was holding on to—the furniture, her list of grievances of all the wrong things my dad did. In a way, she was turning into her mother, and the way she tossed back the rest of her wine, she wasn't happy with herself.

"Let me show you the garage." Lucile grabbed my shirtsleeve and tugged me through the living room, past the kitchen and to the garage door. She called over her shoulder, "Have fun going through that stack of pictures I left in front of you. Maybe you could stick them in an album while we work on furniture."

"What's up with her?" I asked, huddling closer to my sister at the garage door.

"She's in a foul mood. You missed an epic fight between the parentals this afternoon." Lucile released a heavy sigh. A lot could change within the course of a few hours in this household. Now, Lucile had a taste of the whiplash I'd been feeling. "She ripped Dad a new one. I almost feel sorry for him."

"She was in such a good mood when I left this morning."

"So were you." She wiped hair away from my eyes, her perceptive gaze tightening. "Your eyes are a little puffy."

"Dylan was a jerk. I had to sit in her giant house, with her giant wardrobe. She has a dozen dress options for the centennial and for prom and compared to her, I'm just going to look like a bumpkin. And she hates my prom date."

"I hate to say it, but I told you not to go over there. She's always been a jerk. Just tell her to eat a you-know-what." She shoved open the garage door and placed her hands on her hips.

"Oh no." My heart caved as I surveyed the bevy of boxes and trash bags stuffed in the middle of the garage, cramming the small space. This was where all the bulky furniture had gone. And if Lucile had intended to rid our household of boxes, it seems that she had done the opposite. The boxes seemed to have multiplied.

"Could you stick this on that?" She handed me a sticker on the tip of her finger for the broken-down armoire.

"But this is Grandma's stuff." I stroked the polished wood, dust collecting on my fingers. These were my grandmother's treasures, things from long ago that she couldn't let go of.

"We don't have to throw it all away. The nicer things we can sell. But most of it is old junk. Let's face it, Grandma really was a bit of a hoarder." She put her hands on her hips again with a sigh and surveyed the piles of unnecessary stuff my grandmother had accumulated through the years. "What a waste."

"Maybe Dad can fix the armoire. And he can store his puzzles in it instead of leaving them sprawled out on the floor."

"Dad can't fix this. He can't fix anything. Here." She waved a pack of color-coded stickers in her hand. The ones she always used for note taking. "Put the yellow stickers for keeps. The green for sale. And ... well everything else must go."

An alarm went off in the kitchen, and my head popped up.

"Oh no. You didn't cook something, did you?" My lip trembled. As scary as I found the state of this room, it was nothing compared to my sister's cooking. Neither of us had spent much time in front of a stove—and why would we have needed to? We'd had a cook.

I cupped my hand and wafted the smell from kitchen, surprised that I didn't smell anything burning.

"Oh yes, I did." She shook her head with a chuckle. "Don't look so worried. I've been practicing."

"Still watching Food Network?"

"You know it." She bobbed her head from side to side, admitting to her guilty pleasure. "But I got this recipe book with stuff that takes only five ingredients. It's been a life changer. Have you figured out how to do laundry yet?"

The blood drained from my face—laundry had been a tough learning curve. I'd never done it before three months ago. But I was getting better at it.

"Who else is going to do it? I did wash something dry clean only by accident and Mom cried. I'm trying to learn quickly, but I'm so exhausted." I snorted out a laugh. "Dylan's housekeeper does her laundry *every day*."

"Stop comparing yourself to her. It'll drive you crazy. I learned that the hard way." She sighed. Then she scrunched up her nose as if something just occurred to her. "Why are you still friends with her?"

"We've been friends forever." I shrugged. "I always thought she would go back to normal."

I missed the Dylan who ate actual food, who stayed up late with me and painted nails during our horror-movie marathons. She was a friend then, who shared her hopes and dreams with me, who was honest with her fears about her parents' rocky marriage— her mom's coldness, her dad's indifference. But now it was like she'd hollowed all the realness out of her, and all that was left was just savage. "I think we're just growing in different directions."

"Yuh," Lucile said before diving into another box.

"But does she have to lord it over me? I didn't do that to people when we lived on the north side." And then in a softer voice, I asked, "Did I?"

"Maybe." She pursed her lips together. "Just a little."

"Yeah right." I shook my head—no way was I ever like that.

I tried to laugh it off, returning to the pile of my grandmother's newspaper hoard, but my chest tightened as I thought about Lucile's truth—that I'd acted like a snob before moving downstream. I cringed thinking about how Dylan turned her nose up at people, how she flaunted her wealth and status. She'd never deign to entertain a guy like Tanner Holmes, would never be caught dead at his family's shop. No, Lucile was wrong. I wasn't a thing like her.

Still, my stomach twisted into knots. Maybe I was engaged in a revisionist history.

What would happen if I really found Langston's treasure? Would I go back to the snob I used to be? I began to question why I really wanted this money. Was it really to save my family? Or was it to get back to the top?

I had much bigger problems than Dylan. Maybe I needed to work on myself.

I heaved myself off the floor and followed the aroma coming from the oven. Lucile knelt down and slid out a tray of roasted chicken and brussels sprouts.

"Wow, this looks edible. Like . . . *really* good."

"Hate to say I told you so." She bumped me with her hip, a smug smile tugging at her lips.

"No, you don't."

"Okay, let's eat quickly and get back to work." She tossed her oven mitts onto the counter and clapped her hands. "I promised Mom we'd have the house cleaned up before we leave for Atlanta."

"Wait, you're taking her back to Atlanta?" I gripped the counter for support. "You'll have to tell her about Bryant."

"Don't remind me. Let's just cross that bridge when we get there. But one thing I'm sure of is that our parents need a break from each other." She gripped her forehead with the tips of her fingers. "Sometimes, distance is much needed. The way those two are going at it, it's the healthiest option if we separate them. Temporarily. Nothing permanent."

That night we ate dinner as a family for the first time in a long time. At the table with mismatched plates and cups. Mom even drank wine out of a coffee cup without complaining. And for the first time in weeks, I saw my dad smile. It was a bit faded, a shadow of his former joy. But it was a step in the right direction.

I just hoped my mom would come back from Atlanta to enjoy more nights like this.

FIFTEEN

Fifty-one days until we lose the house

The wheels of my mom's suitcase creaked against the cement floor as I rolled it through the garage. Lucile had backed Bryant's Tesla to the edge of the garage to make loading easier. When I got to the trunk, I raised an eyebrow.

"How long did she say she was visiting?" I asked, counting the suitcases. There had to be three bags in there, and only one of them was Lucile's.

"You know she doesn't travel light. Look at this hat box." Her fingers strummed the lid of a circular case. "Where does she think she's going to wear that? She's so out of touch."

There was a pile of trash near the garbage cans. Nearly ten bags of Grandma's old things. My heart lurched—I hadn't checked all the things. Maybe in her can-do haste, Lucile had thrown away something important—like wet suits for the dive.

"Hey, when you were bagging stuff up, did you find any of our diving equipment from Jamaica?"

"Diving? You're not thinking about going diving, are you? That's an expensive hobby."

"It's for a friend." I said, trying very carefully not to lie to my sister while also trying not to divulge my secret treasure hunt. "Did you see any wet suits?"

"I think they're in one of the plastic bins up there." She flung her wrist in the direction of the floating shelf, which bowed under the added weight of Lucile's stowage. "They're super old. Like from middle school. I don't think any of us will fit into them anymore."

Mom came outside in oversize sunglasses with her oversize toiletry case. I resisted the urge to chastise her for bringing yet another bag. I took it from her and tossed it in the back.

My dad stood at the back door. He waved sheepishly. My mom approached him with hesitation, then oddly held her hand up to shake his. Just as he was going in for a hug. It ended in a stiff embrace, my mom's arms dangling at her sides as my dad hugged her. Her face turned away. His eyes wet with unshed tears. It was an awkward parting.

"Bye, Mom." I wrapped my arms around her, relief washing over me when she returned my gesture. It was definitely a better hug than the one I'd just seen.

"Bye, sweetie." She kissed me on the forehead, then pulled back, giving me a knowing look. "Take care of your father."

"Do you have to go?" I looked from her to my sister.

"I'll call when we get there, okay?" Lucile gripped my shoulder and gave it a friendly squeeze.

Lucile tried to close the trunk of her car, but it was so full that it didn't close. She reopened it and rearranged the bags. Then she shut it and leaned against it, hopping up and down until the lock engaged with a *click*.

I stepped back, standing next to my dad. Her car whirred to life, the electric motor barely audible. We waved goodbye to them as they turned the corner. Then the garage fell silent, except for my dad's slippers shuffling against the cement. He tapped the old armoire Lucile had carried out there.

I said, "Lucile wanted to throw it away, but I thought maybe you could fix it. Use it for your work." My eyes scanned the pallet of pillows and moving blankets on the floor, at the mass of puzzle pieces haphazardly strewn across it.

"Want some pancakes?" My dad pointed in the direction of the kitchen with his thumb. "It's brunch time, right?"

"*Every* time is brunch time." My chest thawed as I saw a flicker of playfulness in my dad's eyes. But then I shrugged, my shoulders touching my ears. "I actually have a thing with friends, so I have to get going."

"Sure thing, sweet pea." His smile waned. He wanted to take care of me. He just didn't know how anymore.

I comforted myself with the knowledge that I was leaving him to find the rest of the treasure.

It was my turn to take care of him.

SIXTEEN

Forty-eight days until we lose the house

Underneath the four-faced clock of the school library, I stood in front of the circulation desk with an armful of books. For days, I'd scoured the stacks for more information about Toulouse, but the information was sparse. And if I was really going to dive to the bottom of the lake, I needed to know what to look for—something more than a hope and a prayer. There was a lot of information on Langston from conception to the building of the dam to the modern era. But the information about Toulouse was sparse—almost nonexistent.

"Excuse me," I said to the librarian behind the counter. He continued to stare at his computer, the blue glow of the screen reflecting off his glasses. "Um, hi?"

"Hi." He looked over the top of his monitor. "Was there a question somewhere in there?"

"I wanted to look at some more town records." I shifted the wobbly stack of books in my hand, hoping that they wouldn't topple over. "Do you have any other books about Toulouse?"

"Go upstairs to the third floor, turn left at the double doors." He tilted his head toward the section on the third floor that was devoted to our town's history—the section I'd already combed through. "There's the section on town history."

"I've already looked there and there's nothing. Can you double-check to see if you have the book *The Times of Toulouse?*"

"Whatever's up there is all we have." He shrugged, then returned his gaze to his computer. I thought that was all the help he was going to offer me, but after a long pause, he clicked his mouth and muttered, "Let me check the system for you. . . . Nothing on *The Times of Toulouse.* What else are you looking for?"

"I don't know, something that could tell me more about the town around the early 1900s." I chewed on the inside of my cheek, bobbing my head from side to side as I thought about the old pictures Tanner had shown me. "Maybe 1920s or even the 1930s."

"Well, *that* narrows it down." The librarian pursed his lips. "I'd suggest searching microfilm from around that time. It's just down that hall."

I followed his direction down the first-floor aisle, past the display cases of rare books and the study nooks where a few students sat under the glow of reading lamps. In the corner sat a massive microfilm terminal that looked older than I was. Whatever money the school was pumping into renovations was definitely not being spent on this part of the library.

A diagram on the side of the bulky machine illustrated how to use the terminal. I pressed the power button and it whirred to life. While it booted up, I scanned the shelves of film behind it, plucking out one from Atlanta 1903. It was the nearest city in the volumes from around the time of the picture. It was my best shot.

Carefully, I inserted the spool on the spindle, making sure the film was facing the right direction. I flipped through the screens, looking for any mention of Toulouse.

The articles were predictably dominated by Colonel Langston and the expansion of his relatively new town. I expected that. But these articles were different. They painted Langston in a different light than town legend, which tended to downplay his confederate ties. There were pictures of him in his Confederate uniform, articles regaling stories of his brave fight in a lost-cause war. In one of the pictures, he proudly waved a dark flag with a white star in the middle of it. The caption read:

For Bonnie Blue

I recoiled at the sight of it and quickly scrolled past it. That was one of the names for the Confederacy. His alignment with the wrong side of history was this open secret—something we collectively chose to forget.

This photo of Langston touting the Confederate symbol would never hang in the hall at the club. I'd never seen it, and maybe that was by design. It dispelled the image of the benevolent benefactor, the fairy tale this town thrived on.

We were taught about *the war of northern aggression*, spoon-fed a sanitized history of the South fighting for states' rights, not to protect slavery. We were told to focus on the good old days of the south, the ones where everyone took care of one another. The mayor always said it—that this town was founded on friendship and camaraderie.

But that was a bunch of bullshit, wasn't it? The colonel's personal history was problematic.

Why were we so afraid to confront our history?

I inserted another roll and then another, my frown deepening as I was confronted with more unsettling articles about the founder of our town. I dug deeper, working my way back in time, going from 1902, to 1901, and then to 1900. My gaze flitted to my phone, noting the time. I only had enough time to view one more roll of microfilm before the lunch bell rang. I slid in the slides from 1899 and scrolled quickly through the articles, expecting more of the same. But then I finally saw something—a small column in the right corner of the *Atlanta Tribune*.

CITY DESTROYED IN BLAZE

I leaned forward, devouring every word of the short article. It didn't say much, only that the thriving Negro city of Toulouse burned to the ground with many casualties. Many were forced to flee their homes.

"What?" I said under my breath. I'd never heard of a massive fire in Toulouse. Slowly, I scrolled through the reel, hoping there was more information than what was on this tiny sliver of a page. "That can't be it."

But it was. As I meticulously sifted through the rest of the microfilm, I found no mention of the cause of the Toulouse fire, no culprit caught in the aftermath. Toulouse was a mere footnote in the news of 1899, its mass destruction chronicled between ads for old-fashioned suits and miracle snake oils. I rolled back the film and reread the small article, getting tripped up on the word *thriving*.

Toulouse was a thriving city in early 1899? That was a mere year before construction on the dam began. And construction only commenced because Toulouse was abandoned property. *Thriving* was a far cry from *abandoned*. This didn't add up. The state wouldn't flood a valley when people were trying to rebuild their homes. Right?

I pried my eyes from the page and leaned back in my chair. There was still more film to review, but I had a sneaking suspicion I wasn't going to find anything else on Toulouse—not in these newspapers. Whatever secrets that old town held lay at the bottom of Langston, buried under eighty feet of water for over a hundred years.

A rustling of papers and faint giggling drew my attention down the row of bookcases, where Fatima was handing out flyers in the library to anyone with a pulse. She rounded a bookshelf, startling an unsuspecting reader as she shoved a flyer in his hands.

"Don't forget to vote for prom queen." She sidled up next to me and bumped my elbow with her hip. "You too."

"What is this?" I scanned the page, reading one of Dylan's campaign flyers. Scrawled in ransom letter font, the page was chock-full of a list of attributes Dylan possessed that would make her an excellent queen. The top of the page read:

Did you know, Dylan, your future queen...

IS the OG Goldilocks.
Roundhouse kicked Brian Kemp in the face—twice!

Climbed Mt. Everest and K2 in the same day,
Has a positronic brain.
Can Dolittle your doggie.

"She definitely did *not* put this together. You wrote this." I laughed out loud on the last one: *Can Dolittle your doggie.* I pointed to it. "What does that even mean?"

"Okay, I ran out of things to say about her." She burst out into giggles, slapping the table.

"Why are you helping her? *You* should run."

"It's not really my thing. I don't really get prom court. It's so binary." She shrugged. "I still think you have a shot. I've been handing flyers out to everybody I see, and I've gotten a lot of questions about you. Are you going for it?"

"No, Dylan wants it more," I said, shaking my head. Those days of me courting the school, of worrying about things like this, were over. I obviously had bigger things to worry about. What I cared about was spread across all the books and microfilm in front of me. There might be something here. There had to be. "Maybe she even *needs* it."

"Shh!" a boy at an adjacent table hissed.

Fatima sighed. "We can't keep meeting like this, in the library. I need to be at full volume. What are you working on?"

"Research." It was such a tired excuse. I almost didn't believe it myself—but I really was doing important research. Research that could help me save my family's house.

"Another research project? Or the same one you've been *working* on with Tanner?" She sifted through the papers and books in front of me. My heart rate quickened. What if she pieced the puzzle together and found out what I was researching?

I nodded, not wanting to give too much away. She was giving me a way in, an opportunity to unload. But this wasn't my secret to tell. It was jointly owned by me, Tanner, Squid, and B. Even though I wanted to bring Fatima in, I couldn't.

But I could let her in on something else.

"I winked at Tanner." I grabbed the stack of prom queen flyers off the table and covered my face with them, hiding my shame. I still couldn't believe I'd done it. And in front of the whole crew, too.

"A wink? That's it?" She sank to the chair next to me. "I was expecting something saucier."

"I know, but he's different." I slid the flyers down so that I could look at her over the pages. "I think I really like him. Ugh, why is this happening at the end of school?"

"I was reading your chart the other day, and it did say that a kindling of affection was on the horizon for you."

"Eh, do you do that a lot? Look up my astrology chart?"

"I do that for literally everyone I know. Why do you think I know the exact time and location of your birth?"

"Okay, weirdo. You heading to the courtyard?"

"Nah. I'd rather stay here and finish my problem set." She threw her calculus textbook onto the table. It hit with a loud thud, earning her another glare from the boy at the neighboring desk. But Fatima ignored him.

We whisper giggled over the table. It felt so good to have a light moment after all of my heavy reading and speculation about Toulouse.

"I don't wanna do this." She slid down to the math textbook, groaning into the diagrams. "I don't understand why teachers are assigning things a week before the end of the year. Don't they know we've already gotten into college?"

For a moment I got wistful. Next year, Fatima would be at UCLA, on the complete opposite side of the country from New York. I gulped. I still didn't have a way to pay for school. And even if I did get funding, that would still leave my parents without a home.

But the answer could be here, right in front of me in all this research. I just had to find it. I smiled, remembering what my world history teacher always said. "Mr. Brown says the best people learn something new every day." The thought buoyed my mood.

Fatima pursed her lips, obviously not convinced by his words of wisdom. "Yeah? Well then *he* can finish this calc homework."

The house was quiet all week. The space felt larger, partly because of Lucile's purge of clutter and partly because my mom's resentment wasn't seeping out of every nook and cranny. By week's end, the house had been exorcised of some of its demons, but the threat of our home being seized still hung over our heads.

I knocked on the door leading to the garage and listened closely for signs of life from the only person left in the house.

"Dad?" I called, knocking again. I gripped the door handle. "You in there?"

The hinges creaked as I cracked the door open. My dad was sitting on a palette of pillows with his back turned away from me. When I approached him, I could see that he'd started a new puzzle, one with the tiniest pieces I'd ever seen. There had to be thousands of them scattered across the concrete. I leaned over his shoulder, studying the developing picture. He'd managed to piece the edges together, but the middle remained blank.

He must have seen my shadow, because he looked over his shoulder and gasped.

"Geez!" He grabbed his chest with one hand and plucked an earbud out of his ear with the other. "I didn't know you were here."

"Clearly," I grumbled under my breath, loud enough so only I could hear.

"I don't even know why I'm listening to this." He took his other earbud out and set it next to the other one on the floor. "Money markets and crypto and all that mess." He sighed, his gaze growing distant, and I thought I caught his eyes water, but then he cleared his throat, turning back to me. "Shouldn't you be at school?"

"It's Sunday." I clenched my jaw, trying to be patient with my absentee parent. In his garage retreat, he was insulated from everything around him. Our world was crumbling, and he'd curled into a ball.

"Right. Okay. You hungry?" He heaved himself off the ground with a huff. Dusting his hands, he said, "I can make us something, maybe scare up some pancakes. What do you think?"

"I already ate breakfast…and lunch." I nodded my head toward the kitchen door. "I left you a sandwich on the counter. Will you please eat it? All of it?"

"You sound like your mother."

My eyes tightened as I appraised my father. His brown skin looked gray under the fluorescent lights, and his sweatpants hung loosely on his hips, which was no surprise since he was barely eating. But I didn't want to nag like my mom did. He should be able to take care of himself. I wasn't the parent here. He was.

"I'm gonna go meet up with a few friends. Can you help me reach the diving stuff up there?" I pointed to the top shelf over the discarded armoire, where Lucile had put our least used items out of reach.

"Diving?" His eyebrows shot up. "You're not going out alone, are you?"

"No, I've got a partner." I wanted to promise we'd be safe, but I couldn't exactly do that. Tanner didn't have a lot of experience diving and neither did I. So, I offered the only thing we had in our favor. "He's practically a professional swimmer."

I left out the part about how he'd only trained in a swimming pool.

"Okay, because you never want to go alone." Dad shuffled to the shelves on the far side of the garage wall, then looked over his shoulder. "Why are you diving? I seem to remember you complaining about it."

"I don't know." I shrugged, avoiding eye contact. "Thought it might be fun."

"Well, be careful out there." He pulled out the bottom drawer of the armoire and used it as a step stool.

He strained to reach it and started jumping in order to make up for the deficit. He landed the wrong way on his overturned slipper and fell against the armoire. It groaned beneath his weight and then one of the legs cracked and broke. The cabinet fell to the side and all the drawers slid open.

"I'm sorry. I'm—just breaking everything these days."

"No, Dad, it's okay." I scurried to help clear the mess. As I was closing one of the drawers, the corner of a piece of paper caught my eyes. I pawed inside and found more paper. I withdrew a stack of old photos—older than the stack my sister had given Mom to sort yesterday. Lucile had not been as diligent cleaning out every compartment of the furniture as she'd thought. I held them up to my dad. "Look."

In the top photo, a mother smiled at the camera as she bent down and helped her child take what looked like his first steps. In the background, I could just make out the Toulouse Bank signage down the road. Scrawled on the bottom corner were the words:

Ava Anderson, Toulouse 1898.

My heart pounded. Ava Anderson was in the photo Squid showed me—a photo in the library—one with Eustice Hornsby, Ernest Anderson, Colonel Langston, and *Ava Anderson*. And here she was again, staring back at me with those wide eyes. But it didn't make sense. Why was she in a stack of old photos in our garage?

"Who is this?" I asked pointing to the boy in the picture. "Why would Grandma Bernie have someone else's pictures? Who are the Andersons?"

"Those are hers." He pointed to the boy. "I think that's her grandfather. I don't know. You'd have to ask your mother to be sure. That's her side of the family."

I blinked, still not understanding.

"Before your grandmother married and changed her name, her last name was Anderson."

SEVENTEEN

Forty-six days until we lose the house

The roar of the dam whipped through the Hollow. We crouched around the tree stump, our heads jockeying for a prime position to look at the picture. For a while all I could hear was the rush of water spilling over the ridge, the mutterings of Squid as we looked at the picture of Ava Anderson and the child. Finally I broke the silence.

"What do you think it means?" I asked, turning the picture so that it faced me. The corner of the photo snagged on a splinter and my breath hitched. This was old—probably the oldest photo I'd ever laid my hands on. And it was a missing link of my ancestry. I didn't want to damage it.

"It means you're from money." B shrugged. "And we've always known that."

"But not on my grandmother's side."

"So, now you're a double charmie." B raised her eyebrows and exhaled with a whistle. "Both on the Whitecroft side and now with the Andersons being one of the founding families."

"I hadn't really thought of it that way." I shook my head slowly, still trying to wrap my head around this new information. "But the

Andersons were part of Toulouse, not the founding of Langston. Right?"

"I don't know. There isn't much about it in the books we read." She shrugged then pointed to the map rolled up beside the stump. "It doesn't really change the plan, right? I mean, if anything it just confirms our suspicions that we need to hit up the old Anderson property."

Squid looked at my dive bag and snapped his fingers impatiently. "Let's see what you brought."

"Don't get too excited. They're old—like *really* old. They're from our trip to Jamaica a few years back." I held up mine—a junior size 13. It would probably be too small on me. And then I looked at my dad's, wondering if Tanner's long legs would also fit.

"These are honestly perfect. It'll get the job done." He held up my mom's old diving suit. "Maybe I can fit in this. Diving suits are mostly unisex, except for the chest area."

He looked awkwardly at my chest and then tilted his head upward, as if suddenly curious about a bird in a tree.

"Anyway, bathroom is inside, first door to the left." He shooed Tanner and me toward his house. "And try to keep it down. My grandma's taking her afternoon nap."

The screen door snapped shut behind us as we piled into the small foyer. The ceiling was so low it nearly grazed the top of Tanner's head. He nodded to the first door on the left, holding the bundle of my dad's wet suit in his hand.

"I can go first if you want."

"Sure. Hope it fits. You're tall." My eyes flitted up to him and then quickly away. "I mean not freakishly tall or anything. But you're the tallest swimmer in the district, right?"

"How did you know that?"

I'd seen him swim last year. I'd thought he was cute then. But I wasn't going to tell him that.

"It's common knowledge," I said, doing my best to avoid eye contact. Because if he looked into my eyes, he'd know I was holding back. He saw through me like that. I cleared my throat. "Go change. I'll wait here."

I waited in the hallway, fidgeting with my hands as I tried not to think about Tanner getting changed on the other side of the door.

I wondered if he got flustered when he thought about me, or was that just me? He hadn't mentioned prom yet. I wondered if he was just being polite last week and didn't really want to go with me.

The floor creaked beneath my feet, and a thud hit the floorboards. An older woman hobbled into view with a can, carting an oxygen mask behind her.

"Who the hell are you?"

EIGHTEEN

She coughed into the crook of her elbow, a scratchy wheezing cough, then wiped her hand on the side of her denim skirt. Her thin hair stood in haphazard wisps atop her head. She squinted, inspecting me through thick, smudged glasses.

"You must be Squid's grandmother." I waved awkwardly. "I'm Casey. Casey Whitecroft."

She grunted in response before hobbling over to the armchair in front of the television. Part of me wanted to help her—she looked so unsteady, like she could fall over at any moment. But there was something about her body language that told me she'd rather be self-sufficient. I resisted the urge to help.

She plopped into a floral upholstered armchair and repositioned her oxygen tank to sit beside her.

"Whitecroft, you said?" She looked at me from over her Coke bottle lenses. "You one of Berenice's?"

"Yes ma'am."

"Tell her I say hi." She coughed into her elbow again, this one sounding wetter than the previous one.

I didn't have the heart to tell her my grandmother had passed away. I kept my mouth shut.

"How do you know my grandson?"

"I'm a friend of Squi—Chris's. I work with him at the club."

That earned me another grunt from her. She turned the television on, and the sound blared through the house. It must have been turned all the way up.

"I'm going to watch my program now. Only hope Brenda's evil twin doesn't make another appearance. I don't like her much," she yelled over a loud infomercial. "Can you grab me a Crystal Light while you're over there near the fridge?"

"Um, of course," I said, walking to the fridge. She cupped her hand over her ear, signaling that she wanted me to repeat myself. Instead of yelling across the room, I grabbed a bottle from the fridge just as Tanner was coming out of the bathroom.

"Okay, it's all yours." He patted the spandex wet suit stretched tightly across his chest. It was clearly too tight, outlining the ripples of his pecs.

I wasn't complaining.

"How's that drink coming?" Squid's grandma yelled from the other room. Grandma wanted that drink to go with her stories.

"Coming, Mrs. Sciuducci." Tanner grabbed the bottle out of my hand and crossed the room in a few long strides. He handed her the drink.

I crammed myself into the hallway bathroom to change into my old wet suit. I changed quickly, my elbows knocking against the walls of the tiny bathroom as I squeezed myself into my childhood wet suit. It had to be three sizes too small. I tugged on the crotch, trying to make sure I didn't have a camel toe, before stepping back into the hallway.

"Oh." Mrs. Scuiducci's eyes widened as she surveyed me. "Who is that girl over there by the kitchen?"

Squid's grandmother clearly had memory problems. Maybe that's why he wanted to find the treasure so badly—so that he could give his grandmother the care she needed.

"That's Casey." Tanner raised his voice and spoke again. "KAY-SEE. She's my friend from over at the academy."

"You make us all so proud, Tan." She gripped his arm, her nostrils flaring with emotion. "You're going places, and remember to take my Christopher with you. Even to Yale next year."

My eyes kept darting over to Tanner as we walked to the water's edge. He was going to Yale, one of the most prestigious universities in the world. I couldn't believe it. All this time I'd thought he and his crew were burnouts and flunkies on a road to nowhere. But obviously, I was wrong—Tanner was going places.

What else had I been wrong about?

"Is it that bad?" Tanner asked, giving me a sidelong glance.

"What?" I blinked up at him. What I'd been thinking about hadn't been anything bad—quite the opposite.

"The wet suit." He lowered his head, then pinched the fabric of his diving leggings, making the neoprene smack against his thighs. "You keep looking at me like I've grown three heads."

"I don't know what you're talking about." I gulped and looked away. "You look fine."

When we reached the shoreline, Squid yanked a tarp off of a mound with a flourish, revealing a dented flat-bottom boat.

"I bought it off the local scrapyard for cheap. Fixed the motor. And the rudder. And banged out most of the dents. But she's fine. Totally seaworthy."

I was sure that it was scrapped for a reason. Still, I held my hand out. Squid gripped my hand and yanked me into the boat. It teetered and wobbled.

"Welcome aboard, milady."

Tanner sloshed into the water, a bag of scuba equipment slung over his shoulder. He swung it into the boat, then pushed it farther away from the shore and swung his leg onto the boat, then heaved himself up, his biceps quivering. I couldn't help but look. Dylan was right about one thing—Tanner was definitely not unfortunate looking.

He was *hot*.

He ran his fingers through his hair and caught my gaze. I quickly blinked and looked away, pretending to study the shoreline.

"That's my house." Tanner pointed to a double-wide nearby. He smiled sheepishly.

We neared my neighborhood. I could see my house poking out from behind a waterfront shanty, long abandoned. I did not reciprocate Tanner's openness about his house. I hid the fact that we were steps away from mine. I was still embarrassed at the house.

Even though I was now fighting to save it. It was my family's life raft, all we had. And we needed it to stay afloat. Kinda like Squid's boat.

"How many tourists do you think have been down there?" I asked. So many people had searched and failed to find the treasure. And let's not forget the lost diver who was supposedly looking for the same thing. What made us think we would be any different?

"They didn't have this map. Or a location for the coins."

"And no one will ever see the map again, if B has anything to do with it." I cringed, hoping that the map wouldn't get wet. I rested my hand on Tanner's shoulder. "Promise me you'll return it."

"I already took a picture of it. Returning it Monday morning before school. I promise." He drew an X over his chest, crossing his heart. "You ready?"

Squid eased the boat to a stop next to the buoy in the middle of the lake. The rope attached to the bottom of the buoy was just visible below the surface. I could just see about ten feet of it before it disappeared into the darker depths.

"Ready as I'll ever be. Do you remember the signals?" I asked Tanner.

The only way to communicate underwater was through hand signals—an okay sign for when things were good; a stop sign for a regroup. A thumb pointing upward meant it was time to head to the surface.

Clutching both of his flippers in one hand, Tanner jumped off the side of the boat, splashing into the water. He yanked his snorkel out of his mouth.

"It's colder than I thought!" He waved his hand. "Let's get a move on."

I leapt into the water off the other side. Wading, I struggled to keep my legs steady as I slid my flippers on. I submerged my goggles into the water, watching my feet kick around. Then I kicked them behind me, swimming toward Tan. He put his index finger and thumb together, his other three fingers wiggling above them.

Everything okay?

I returned his gesture, then pointed my thumb downward.

Good to go down.

I put my snorkel to the side and replaced it with my regulator, blowing bubbles to clear the water. Tanner did the same, and clouds of bubbles crowded the space between us.

I dipped my head under the surface and breathed in slowly, adjusting to the cold stream of oxygen coming through my mouthpiece. I waved my arms at my sides, pushing myself farther down. But Tanner gripped my arms, stilling them.

Through his goggles, I could still see his kind eyes. He shook his head, signaling for me to stop flapping my arms. He was right—it would only tire me out, and that would make me suck in more oxygen, which was not great for a deep-water dive. I wanted to have all my reserves when I reached the lake's floor. He held my hands, and we floated for a few minutes while we waited for my heart rate to slow and my breathing to normalize.

He patted his shoulder, right where his vest pressure valve was.

He tugged on the cord, releasing a few more bubbles, making his pack less buoyant. I did the same, sinking farther into Langston's depths. In the distance, I could just make out the outline of the Toulouse ruins. As my eyes adjusted, I could see the outline of the church steeple below—the only intact structure of the town.

We stopped after a few yards, allowing our lungs to adjust to the increased pressure. I fished in my pocket for my flashlight, and when I looked up again, Tanner had sunk lower, almost out of reach. Through the condensation in my goggles I saw Tanner tapping his mouthpiece. His fins kicked as he tried to slow his momentum.

Something was wrong.

I dove toward him, spinning him around to see what was pulling him down, and sure enough I saw it—a small hole in his oxygen tank releasing a string of tiny bubbles. He had a leak—a very serious one. I snapped my head toward the surface, estimating that we were about twenty feet down. At this rate he wouldn't make it to the surface with enough air.

I pointed a thumb upward. There was no way we could descend any farther.

Tanner unclipped his harness and tugged the straps of his gear off his back, casting it aside. It drifted away from us in a tailspin, picking up speed as it plummeted to the bottom. I reached behind my back, searching for my spare mouthpiece, and then the weathered strap of my secondhand goggles popped apart.

Water flooded my googles in an instant. I clamped my eyes shut. My heartbeat thudded against my throat. I was completely in the dark.

His arms enfolded me and propelled me upward, his strong swimmer's legs knocking against mine. He squeezed my arm hard as we stilled, and I stopped kicking so we could equalize. My hand closed around the secondary oxygen tube and followed it all the way to Tanner's mouth. He'd found a way to breathe.

With another squeeze around my arm, we kicked toward the surface.

We broke through the surface, and the first thing I did was rip open my eyes. I blinked rapidly, my eyes adjusting to the daylight. I could finally see.

I heaved myself onto the boat, Tanner hot on my heels. He hoisted himself onto the dinghy and leaned over the starboard side, coughing up a bit of water. B slapped her hands on her sides.

"What happened there?" Her jaw went slack as she looked from me to Tanner, sounding half horrified and half relieved that she'd stayed on the boat.

"We could have died down there!" I yelled at Squid. "Or busted my retinas, or collapsed his lung!" Squid had mentioned the equipment was secondhand, but I begged to differ. It was in worse shape than secondhand. My oxygen tank fell to the dinghy's floor with a thud. "This is *exactly* what I was worried about. I knew diving with amateur shit was a bad idea."

"This equipment is trash, dude." Tanner spit off the side of the boat. "It was either me or the tank, so I had to let it go."

"I'm sorry, y'all." Squid sank to the edge of the boat and ran his fingers through his hair. "That's all I had."

"So I guess that's it." B lowered to a crouch and looked over the bow, frowning at the ripples across the water.

I shrugged. This made two failed attempts. I was starting to think that this was a fool's errand, that we had no business searching for Toulouse's secrets. But we had to at least try. I mean—we had proof that the treasure existed.

"I know a guy who has plenty of equipment." I wiggled my fingers toward my backpack, and Squid slid it closer to me with his bare foot. I fished out my phone and texted the one person I told myself never to text again.

> Any chance you could spot me some diving equipment? I need your help.

NINETEEN

We edged the boat into a tiny spot along the dock. Sidled next to a dock post so that we could tie her up. The dinghy was dwarfed on both sides by much larger boats, with fresh coats of wax and deck loungers. We definitely didn't fit in.

I suddenly felt super out of place with my wet hair and small wet suit on. I tugged at the thighs, self-conscious about its tight fit.

Dev was seated at one of the benches along the waterfront boardwalk. It was in front of his shop. To the right of it was the terrace to the Langston Club. And beyond that was the golf pro shop.

He hopped off his seat and half-jogged down the dock, his leather boat shoes sliding against the wood.

"That was fast." He wrapped his arms around me.

"We were already out on the water." I waved my hand dismissively. "I hope that's okay."

"I'm chained to the Dive anyway." He laughed, flashing his signature smile. But the joy didn't reach his eyes. I wondered if he really felt chained, trapped into doing everything his parents wanted him to do this summer.

"You know Tanner from school." I gestured to Tanner. He stepped forward, extending his hand to Dev.

"What's up, man?" Dev slapped his hand—half high five, half swatting it away. He didn't look him in the eyes. Instead he kept his eyes locked with mine.

"And this is Barb—I mean B. This is Squid."

"Hey." He waved. Then frowned a little. "Can I talk to you for a sec?"

He jerked his head to the side and walked farther down the dock. He mussed up his hair, sending the tendrils into a whirlwind.

"This is a new crew." He gave a sidelong glance toward the dinghy, where B and Squid were untangling the regulator lines. "I guess I thought you'd be with Dylan and Fatima."

"Getting their hair wet isn't really their thing." I laughed, trying to imagine Fatima and Dylan in wet suits. I shook my head, then pointed over my shoulder at the crew. "They're cool. I promise."

"It's definitely *his* thing." He nodded toward Tanner. Then he raised his voice. "You're on the swim team, right? That's what I thought. So, let's see what you've got."

Squid pulled his bag of supplies off the dinghy and onto the deck.

"I've got these that I bought off the charter across the lake." He jangled the regulator cords. Then he pointed to the oxygen tanks. "And these tanks were going to the scrapyard, but I figured I'd get some use out of this."

Dev looked from the busted equipment to my wet hair and back again.

"I hope you didn't try to go down in these. This is *dangerous*. If my dad saw this . . ." He ran his fingers through his brown hair. "Yikes."

I knew it was dangerous when I saw the equipment. But I ignored my instincts because I was curious to see what was below. My mouth still tasted of lake water and dashed hopes.

"Would you be able to lend us a set?" Tanner asked, his eyebrows raised.

"Just one? You can't dive alone. That's like the number-one rule. Or you'll end up like that missing diver."

"You haven't found him yet?" I asked.

"It's been days. That guy is toast." B folded her arms. "No offense if he's a friend of yours."

"No friend of mine. I think my parents know him—or *knew* him. We've combed almost every inch of this lake and nothing." Dev shook his head. He looked confident that he'd conducted a thorough search. He pointed to the third-hand gear on the ground. "Is that what this is about? You think you're gonna find the diver?"

"No, we just wanted to go for a dive, that's all," I said, and I thought it almost sounded convincingly blasé.

"Case, what's going on? I know you. Something's up. You don't exactly love diving. I mean, when was the last time you went down? Middle school?"

"Geez, third degree." B stepped forward, squaring her shoulders like she was my bodyguard.

"B, chill." I snaked my arm through Dev's and ticked my head toward the boardwalk before looking to Tanner, Squid, and B. "Give us a sec."

"Casey..." Dev's voice trailed off. He ran his fingers through his hair, looking nervously at my motley crew. "What is up with her? With all of them?"

"Nothing, we're just—"

"Just going for a swim?" He frowned incredulously, folding his arms with a shake of his head. He clearly wasn't buying what I was selling. "Either tell me what the hell is going on, or we're staying on land."

"Seriously?"

"Dead serious." Dev gave a curt nod, making it clear that this was nonnegotiable for him.

Secrecy was the one thing we'd all agreed to—my downstream crew didn't want anyone to know about the silver. We already had competition and undercutting from Tanner's stepdad, and we didn't need more of that from yet another person. But if we wanted to dive in the lake, Dev was really the only person who could help us.

I stood there quietly, weighing my options. But Dev ducked his head down to my level, his eyes expectant. His patience was wearing thin. I had to make a choice—bring Dev in or stay out of Toulouse.

I hoped the crew would forgive me for what I was about to do.

"Okay, this is going to sound stupid." I took a deep breath. There was no way to get the diving equipment without telling Dev the truth. My cheeks heated. "You're gonna laugh."

"I'm waiting." He tapped his foot against the deck.

"But you have to promise to keep it a secret. Seriously."

"Still waiting." He nodded.

"We're searching for the Langston Treasure."

He threw his head back and barked a laugh. I *knew* he would laugh.

"Okay, I'll grab the drawstring bags, and we'll go." He pointed to the stack of treasure bags by the fish weighing station. His eyebrows scrunched up as he realized I wasn't laughing with him. "Wait, you're serious."

"I found a coin with the Toulouse rose on it." I leaned closer to him, whispering conspiratorially. "And we got a map of Toulouse from the library. Stop laughing."

"I mean, Dylan said things were bad, but I had no idea they were as bad as *this*." He blinked away from me, stroking the stubble on his chin. "Case . . ."

"Dylan's been talking about me?" I clenched my jaw shut, my nostrils flaring. "I knew it."

I'd had just about enough of Dylan and her big mouth. And she didn't even know the half of it. How my parents were fighting all the time. How my dad barely got dressed in the morning. How he crouched over five-thousand-piece puzzles in the garage every day. If she found out about any of those things, she'd ruin me.

"So you've been talking to Dylan?"

"She comes around sometimes. After she goes to the club."

"Thirsty much," I mumbled under my breath.

"It's nothing really." Dev shook it off. Then he looked over my shoulder, and his expression soured. "Shit."

Dev's mom was walking toward us. She gave Dev air kisses and looked down at me.

"Casey, I haven't seen you in a while." She pursed her lips, as if closing up the air kisses shop. She would not be stooping to my level.

"Hi, Mrs. Hornsby." I waved despite myself.

"Ha-ha, call me *Mayor*." She chuckled and slapped her thigh. But she said it in a way that made me think she was serious. "How are your parents?"

"They're fine." I didn't sound convincing, even I didn't believe the lie. "My mom's in Atlanta for the week."

"Good. She needs a retreat after . . . after everything. Poor thing." Her lip jutted out in that fake pout. Then she tugged on the sleeve of my wet suit, looking disapproving. "What are you doing in that tiny thing? Dev, you know better."

"Mom, I'll take care of it." He clenched his jaw.

"We don't want to be known as a lazy charter. All the tourists will flock to another. Got to keep up the optics."

She peered over her sunglasses at the motley crew behind us, her lip upturning a bit. She clearly did not like the optics of having them on her dock or anywhere near her shop. She turned on her heel and walked briskly in the direction of town hall.

"Sorry about her."

"It's fine," I lied. It really wasn't. I was getting tired of being talked about, gossiped about, condescended to, looked down upon. I looked at the water, willing the treasure to float up into my arms. I had a solution to all my problems, and it was a hundred feet below us. I set my jaw tight and looked at Dev. "Are you going to help us or not?"

"Fine. I will," he said. "But on one condition. I'm coming with you."

TWENTY

Dev's boat swayed with the shifting tides as we piled onto the deck, which was several times bigger than Squid's mudskipper. We had room to walk around without bumping into one another. It was much nicer, roomier. But even with the added distance, there was no way I could hide the look of guilt on my face for dragging him into our treasure hunt. B spat off the side of the boat, cursing under her breath.

"She told him about the treasure. What did I tell you?" She pointed an accusatory finger at my face, right in between my eyes— an indictment.

"We need his help." I sidestepped out of her finger's aim. "Do you have a better idea?"

She rolled her eyes then rounded on Dev. "So, are you going to let us keep the treasure? It's not like you need it. You being rich and the mayor's son and all."

"I've got stuff I want to do, too. Without their money." He jabbed his finger toward the shoreline, toward his demanding, unforgiving parents. "They're *this close* to cutting me off, and sometimes I wish they would so I could be free." His nostrils flared. He shook his head.

"Like we're really going to find the treasure. I've told you. I've seen every inch of Toulouse. There's no gold down there."

"Not gold. Silver." I pulled the coin out of my pocket and opened my palm. The silver glinted in the sun. "Where's the map?"

While Squid searched his bag for the map, I sidled up next to Dev. I nudged him with my elbow.

"Dev, I had no idea you were going through it."

"My parents are always threatening to cut me off if I don't do what they tell me to. Law school. Work at a firm. It's all so not me."

"What would you do with the money?" I admittedly didn't even think about Dev's hopes and dreams beyond the box his family kept him in. I was curious—what made Dev tick?

"Move to LA. Support myself while auditioning." He looked nervous as he divulged his secret. After a moment, he lifted his chin up, finding his confidence again. "I want to be an actor."

"That is fitting. You do have a flair for the dramatic."

Squid hopped over the pile of flippers, returning with the map in his hand. He unfurled it onto the captain's stand.

"Where did you get this?" Dev rubbed the old paper between his fingers. His eyebrow arched. "Do I even want to know?"

"No." I shook my head, hoping that he wouldn't press any further. We'd already broken so many rules. And he would not love the optics of that—he was on thin ice with his parents, after all.

"We need to go here." Tanner pointed at the map, tracing along the ridge behind the old Bank of Toulouse. He looked out onto the open water, trying to pinpoint what he was seeing on the map. "So that's um . . . over there?"

"No." Dev turned the map in the right direction. "It's down there."

"And I want to see this part of town." I pointed to the place I'd seen this morning in the picture of Grandma Bernie's grandfather. He'd taken his first steps outside of a residence on the main drag. It was part of my history.

"Why?" Squid scrunched up his face, confused about the slight change of plans.

"It was my family's. It's not far from the Bank of Toulouse, so it's no big deal."

"That's a lot to cover in one dive." Dev squinted at the horizon, watching the sun beginning to dip lower. "Are you sure you want to go out now? It's already late afternoon, and the sun will set soon."

"No. Now." I thought of my crumbling family, my impending year at Barnard, the empty bank account. And also my injured pride. I wanted it all to work out. We needed to go now.

"Okay, who's going with us. I have one more pack. Care to join, B?"

"I..." Her lips smacked as she lost the ability to speak. She looked at the dark water, her eyes growing wide with fear. "I can't do the equipment and be trapped in the dark. I'm claustrophobic."

"I'm going." Tanner stepped forward. "I'm a strong swimmer. And I won't get lost looking at every shiny object like Squid might."

"You know the signals?" Dev asked. "You've been diving before?"

"Yeah, sure." Tanner flicked his head up. "I've got it under control."

I could almost see Dev thinking whether he should check his diving license. But something distracted him.

"These tanks are not full. They have about forty-five minutes in them. So when I say we go up, we go up."

"Sir, yes sir."

"Ready to walk the plank?"

I put my flippers on in the water, just like I had in the morning. Carefully, I dunked my head underwater. I breathed into my mask, into my regulator, waiting to see if it would fill with water just like it had this morning. Thankfully, the equipment worked like it should.

I nodded toward Dev and Tanner and they both gave me the all-clear sign.

I pushed myself deeper and deeper with the buoy rope, descending farther into the darkness. We stopped about fifteen feet down to equalize our ear pressure. Then we pushed farther down the rope, repeating the checks every few yards. I knew it was for our safety—descending too fast could mean a ruptured eardrum or a collapsed lung. But it did take a long time. I figured we only had thirty more minutes before we had to head back up.

We headed toward the old church steeple. The old tower came into view with my flashlight. Rising eerily from the depths. How it still stood, I couldn't imagine. When the water flooded the valley, almost everything tumbled. But this still stood.

Bubbles trickled out of Dev's regulator pack as he descended expertly. We floated, waiting for our lungs to adjust to the increased pressure, hovering over the tower below. Dev pointed to the landing spot and slowly descended. I followed.

The silt on the bottom of the lake swirled around my flippers. I slowed my kicking, waiting for the sand to settle so that I could see where I was going. I turned on my flashlight and flooded the dimly lit depths with light. I trained the spotlight on the base of the church tower and pivoted slowly.

It had been years since I'd come down the rabbit hole of the Drop Point. The ruins of Toulouse were in much more disarray than I remembered. Tangles of iron twisted out of sand-covered shadows, a jumble of remains that fish swam between. Another beam of light crossed mine. I followed the trail of light to its source and found Tanner giving me the *okay* signal.

I signaled back then twirled, searching for Dev. He was a few yards away, just under the shadow of the tower. Tanner and I made our way down through a canyon of decaying brick, scattering sunfish in our path. Freshwater clams closed. The lake grass waved in the soft current.

I veered down a break in the debris, visualizing the Toulouse map in my mind. The bank was around here somewhere, not far from the tower. And somewhere deeper in the shadows was the Anderson house.

I came to the bank's crumbling walls, its blown-out bricks. When the town was flooded to make room for the dam, almost everything fell from the force of the waves. I had expected this. But I didn't expect to find pockmarks peppering what was left of the facade.

I traced my gloved finger along the brick. There was a hole in the wall. And another. And then another—all about the same size.

Were those bullet holes?

Dev swam closer to me and tapped his watch. We were short on time and hadn't yet found the Andersons' property. But we needed to keep track of our time or else we'd run out of oxygen.

He pointed to the floor beneath his fins at a cluster of metal balls, about the size of softballs. They looked like cannonballs. I brushed away the silt surrounding them to get a closer look. Why would artillery be in the middle of a residential street?

Was this damage from the Civil War? No, that would be too long before the town was flooded in 1900.

These streets had seen battle.

I tucked a cannonball into the side panel of my vest. The added weight pulled me farther down. It added at least ten pounds. But I could handle it. I stabilized my regulator with more oxygen and found equilibrium.

I wanted to see it in the daylight. And I had questions.

Tanner shined his flashlight down a row of rubble. With a nod to the left we headed away from what was the town square toward the Anderson property. Where my great-grandfather lived as a child.

The lake bottom sloped upward several feet. Their house must have been more elevated with a grand view of the town below. When I reached the top of the hill, I could feel the current change. It pulled me farther downstream, the water streaming toward the dam. I kicked harder, kicking up the rocky bottom. But it was either do that or be swept away.

The Anderson house was even more dilapidated than the bank was. There was nothing but old boards with rusty nails sticking out and the remnants of an old door. Dev grabbed one end, Tanner the other, and together they kicked their fins, stirring up the silt and sand on the bottom, making a whirlwind of it. They lifted it and threw the board down the hill. It slid slowly out of view.

I swam closer, my flashlight pointing at what would have been the interior of the house, judging by the scattered beams on the ground. It was amazing how the old wood had survived. Something shiny caught my eye. I turned my flashlight away from the wrecked barn. There was a light on underneath another panel.

I waved my arm, trying to get the guys' attention. They abandoned the door and swam to me, looking to where I was shining my light.

They saw the light, too. Dev tapped his watch again and flashed two fingers at me, holding it close to my goggles so that I could clearly see it in the murky water we'd created by stirring up the dirt. He did the same to Tanner. We had two minutes to lift the other panel.

There was light where no light should be. I had to find out what was there. We hurried to the other panel. I gripped underneath one side, waiting for the guys to grab hold of the other side. When they had a firm grasp on it, I tugged upward, kicking my fins to help me lift it higher.

We discarded the door to the side, then stilled. I looked beneath me at the source of the light. There was another diver, floating still just like us. I dove closer, turning his shoulder. And then gasped, sucking in a healthy amount of oxygen.

The cold, dead eyes of the missing diver stared back at me.

Tanner kicked back, and his suit caught on a piece of the jagged metal. A plume of blood formed around his thigh. And a stream of bubbles spewed out of his mask and I thought I heard a muffled cry.

Dev urgently pointed to the surface.

But I couldn't leave—not yet. The diver had been searching exactly where we were. What were the chances of that? Unless he was searching for the silver. Unless he had looked at the same land map we had.

Dev swam closer and yanked my arm, pointing to the surface. Then he tugged the diver's oxygen, trying to slide the pack off his shoulder. It was caught on one of the rusty nails. In a struggle to unhook himself, he must have disturbed the precarious walls of the Anderson house and gotten trapped underneath.

He pulled the cord on the man's regulator and the vest filled with the little oxygen left in his tank. His limp body rose gradually, floating to the surface. Dev guided his arm. But I could tell he was grossed out because of the way he kept jerking his hand back.

Then I looked next to the diver's light. Beside it was a small lockbox with a dull brass clasp set against a silver shell.

The diver had found a safe. But it was smaller than I thought. Certainly couldn't contain millions of dollars' worth of silver. I grabbed the handle and lifted it. It was thankfully lighter than the cannonball.

I kicked as hard as I could, following Tanner and Dev to the surface. They floated above me, already at their first equalizer check. The body of the missing diver floated lifelessly above them, slowly making its way to the surface.

My oxygen was critically low, so I needed to get back to the surface quickly, taking only a few minutes to depressurize every dozen feet. But I was weighed down by extra cargo, and I still had to periodically stop and equalize my ears so that I wouldn't get a ruptured eardrum or the bends.

I kicked harder, fighting against the dam's current, and the weight of my findings. It was hard work, but I tried to hold my breath and conserve oxygen. My lungs spasmed. My vision blurred. And I slowed to a halt, in limbo between the surface and the bottom of the lake.

My fingers fumbled with the front pocket of my vest as I freed the heaviest thing on me—the cannonball. It rolled off the tips of my fingers, plummeting back to the shadowy depths below. But that wasn't enough to lift me to the surface.

A blurry mass swam toward me and engulfed me, pulling me toward the ripple of light above. I pushed through the surface, my regulator ripped away from my mouth. I regained full consciousness with a gasp.

"What were you thinking?" Dev cried from the railing of his boat. "I said go up. You could have died!"

"I'm sorry. It's just…" I dropped my head and spit up a mouthful of water.

"Guys, who is that?" B covered her mouth with her hand, her black hair whipping around her in the wind. "Why aren't they moving?"

Her cheeks ballooned as she doubled over the starboard side with deep, dry retches.

"Oh, my God!" Squid screamed from the bow, pointing to the facedown body floating a few yards away. "Is that who I think it is? That's the missing diver guy, right?"

Tanner reached out his hand to pull me up, but I placed the lockbox in his hand instead. Then I heaved myself up, Tanner and Dev grabbing underneath each of my elbows in order to hoist me onto the boat.

"What do you think is in there?" I asked Tanner, still panting from all of my exertions.

"Whatever it is, it's not millions of pounds of silver." Tanner lifted the handle. "It's not heavy at all."

"Let's head to shore! B, call the cops." Dev barked the order at B, who was slumped over the captain's chair. She fumbled with her phone, her shaky fingers dialing the police while Dev eyed the lockbox in Tanner's hands. He reached over and grabbed it, blinking frantically around the deck.

Then he shoved the box into my dad's dive bag.

TWENTY-ONE

The night sky was awash with red and blue flashing lights. A swarm of patrol boats escorted us to shore. And in the distance, we could see the police lifting the body from the water.

The red and white lights of an ambulance lit up the sky. A paramedic bundled me with a lightweight blanket. And then placed a stethoscope against my chest.

"Breathe in for me." She looked at the pavement as she listened to my breathing. "And again."

Her partner bent over the stretcher where Tanner was lying.

"Really, I'm fine." He propped himself up on his elbows, wincing as the medic poured alcohol on his cut. "Ouch."

"Don't be such a baby." B smirked, but the smile didn't reach her eyes. She pushed his shoulder, making him lie back down. She was clearly worried as she busied herself with his blanket, tucking it around his arms so that he had less mobility.

"Looks like just a scratch," the paramedic over Tanner said. Then he yelled over to his boss, "Captain, they all check out."

Dev shuffled over to my perch, wrapped in an identical warming blanket. It was oddly cool for a May evening, and the breeze against my skin chilled me. But that's not why I was shaking. I was still in shock from the dive, from finding a dead body, from almost suffocating on my ascent.

"You okay?" He sat on the edge of the ambulance, scooting over so that his arm grazed mine.

"I guess so." I shrugged, hugging my blanket tighter around me. I couldn't get the diver out of my mind, no matter how hard I tried. I kept imagining him getting trapped underneath that wall, screaming into the watery void for help—drowning in the darkness of the lake. I didn't know the guy, but I felt so sad for the pointless waste of life. I shivered. "I've never seen a dead body before."

"I have. My grandad's funeral." His eyes grew distant as he looked at the water, and for a moment I let him lose himself in his memories. His grandfather was the son of Langston's right-hand man. I wanted to know more about him, but I was afraid to ask, especially in this moment.

"He opened the Dive back before there was even a boardwalk. He was always fascinated with the water. He loved the tales of treasure and Langston's gold. He was the one who came up with the idea of giving the amateur divers little mesh bags for any treasures they found. It just kinda stuck."

"But it's not Langston's treasure." I shifted to face him. "It's Toulouse's."

"You sound like them." He lifted his chin in the direction of B, Tanner, and Squid. "But seriously, Toulouse and Langston—aren't they one in the same?"

"I'm starting to think that Toulouse was more than what we were led to believe."

We sat there quietly for a while, finding a moment of peace in a chaotic day. I was the one who broke the silence.

"Toulouse and Langston aside, I am really sorry to hear about your grandad. I know you were close." I hitched my knee onto the lip of the ambulance and faced him, reaching a tentative hand out to pat his forearm. His eyes fluttered, and he turned away from the water, as if coming back to the present.

"It really shook me. I almost blew up my freshman year over it."

I nodded slowly, putting the pieces together of his mangled first year at Dartmouth. He'd almost failed out last year, squeaking by with barely passing grades. It made sense now why he'd lost himself to parties and too much drinking. He'd filled his days with distraction instead of actually processing his grief.

"I promised myself after his funeral that I'd never go to another one. It was too weird seeing him like that. I—I think the whole funeral industry is weird. But then today happened, and it all came back. But this was different. Finding the diver. His face." His breath hitched and his cheeks ballooned as he stifled a gag.

I squeezed his arm, a plea for him to stop gagging. His retching was making me queasy.

Just when I thought he was recovering from his bout of sickness, his face soured, as if he was feeling another wave of nausea. His eyes tightened as he looked over my shoulder, and I turned to see what he was seeing. It was his mom booking it down the boardwalk, her arms pumping at her sides as she made a beeline toward us.

A couple of local reporters held their microphones out into her path. Mayor Hornsby gave them a tight smile, and deftly dodged their questions. Then she flicked her wrist at the medics, half waving at them, half dismissing them from her presence. She kept that tight smile locked to her face.

"What were you thinking?" she said out of the corner of her locked lips.

"We thought it would be … fun." Dev lowered his head, avoiding her sharp gaze. "We weren't even under for an hour."

"I don't care how long you were down there. You are not here to have *fun*," she said. It seemed like she didn't care what her son did as long as it didn't drag him under. "Did you even *think* about how bad this would look for me? 'Mayor's son finds dead body in the lake.' Ugh."

She shuddered at the made-up headline, as if that was the worst thing that could have happened. But it wasn't the worst thing that could have happened. He could have drowned. We all could have. And the least she could have done was look relieved that we were safe. In that moment I saw what she truly was—a politician more concerned with optics and polls than her own son's safety. My eyes tightened at her. Dev's neck was turning red. I could feel the shame radiating off of him.

And for the first time ever, I felt sorry for him. No wonder he wanted to search for Langston's treasure.

Correction—Toulouse's treasure.

The media pushed in around us, and their cameras flashed as they captured what appeared to be a tender moment between the mayor and her son. My eyes squinted under the onslaught of bright lights. Reporters shouted questions, begging us to answer, but we were all a bit numb, frozen from shock.

"Madame Mayor? Ma'am?" The reporter from News Nine held her recording device in front of Mayor Hornsby. "If we could just ask a few questions."

She transformed her irked brow into a worried one and wrapped an arm around Dev's shoulders, hugging him closer. Her nose pinched, as if she was fighting back tears.

"This has been quite a night, hasn't it? Langston has not seen a tragedy like this in decades. But even in the midst of such a heart-breaking loss of life, we do have something to be grateful for. And that's the safety of these kids right here."

She gestured triumphantly at our battered group huddled around Tanner's stretcher and the rescue boat with the dead diver behind us, unleashing another torrent of flashes. Then she stepped confidently up to the bouquet of microphones.

"These kids were very brave to bring Mr. Boylston to the surface. Some might call them heroes. And they will all have seats on the stage at our annual Founder's Day celebration, an honor that they deserve. That's what Langstonians do. We take care of our own." Her eyes were bright and intense as she commanded the attention of the small crowd that had gathered around her. "This great city was built on the promise of a better tomorrow. It was built on the fellowship of neighbors and friends. It was a shining example of what this town could be. Which is why I am pleased to announce that after my may-oral term ends, I'll be running for the open senate seat. And I'll bring the spirit of Langston straight to the capital." She held her hands up, backing away from the reporters. "My family would appreciate some space and privacy as we navigate this difficult time."

Her upturned eyebrows were a convincing display of sadness— even for me. The reporters thanked her for her time and backed away from us. Ron slinked through the crowd, nodding toward Tanner without a single word. Then he turned to face the strangers, his arms outstretched.

"All right, folks. Show's over." He stepped forward, waving his arms for people to back away.

With sufficient distance from eavesdropping microphones and cameras, the mayor relaxed her face, her worried brow sliding out of sight. Her lip curled as she turned to Tanner and B.

"Why don't y'all give the police everything you found on his person?" She blinked expectantly.

"We did." Squid stepped in front of the stretcher, his hands fidgeting in front of him. His eyes darted to the boat and then back to the mayor.

"You didn't find anything else around the bank?" she asked, cocking her hips to the side. Squid opened his mouth and stuttered. Mayor Hornsby rolled her eyes and turned to me, raising her eyebrow expectantly.

"Nothing." I gulped, scared that she would catch me in a lie.

"I reckon we should search every last one of them and both of the boats." Ron sidled up next to her and folded his arms.

"I can't be seen raiding the possessions of children I just proclaimed the town's heroes." Mayor Hornsby's lip curled. She was clearly annoyed as she watched Ron lift the Velcro pocket of Squid's backpack and peek inside. "Oh, leave them alone, Ron, and go find something better to do."

I leaned over toward Dev while I watched the mayor and Ron bicker under their breath. "How does your mom know Ron?"

"She makes a point to know everyone in this town." He shrugged, looking at the ground instead of at my eyes. "I'm not surprised."

"A deadbeat stepdad turned town watchman? I'm sure the mayor loves that kind of story." Tanner propped himself up on the stretcher. This time B didn't stop him. She too was looking at the odd pair.

"I'm gonna take Casey home," Dev called to his mom. Her eyes narrowed at him, then at me.

"You're not going anywhere but straight home. Do you hear me?"

"But—" Dev started, but I grabbed his arm.

"It's okay." I squeezed his arm. "My car is parked on the other side. And I don't live far from Squid."

"Yes, they belong on that side of the lake." She cocked her head to the side. "And you belong on this side—at home and in your room until further notice."

That side of the lake.

She'd said it with thinly veiled contempt. As if we didn't count as part of the *fellowship of neighbors and friends* that comprised Langston—the one she'd so fondly talked about in her speech earlier. My grip on Dev's arm loosened.

The rescue boat pulled up behind Squid's dinghy.

"I think it's best you kids go home." Ron opened his arms, wide, shepherding us toward the boat and away from the mayor. "You've seen enough."

The mayor nodded at Ron, and there was something about it that seemed off—like Ron was her guard dog and we were unwanted trespassers. This was more than the mayor knowing *of* Ron as one of her many constituents. She *knew* him.

In a sudden burst of resolve, I wrapped my arms around Dev's neck and brought him into a hug. I mumbled in his ear, "Meet us at Squid's Hollow."

Then in a lower voice, one that would surely not be overheard, I whispered Squid's address on Lakeside Drive, hoping that he'd be able to ditch his mom and her guard dog and join us on the other side of the lake.

Because he was one of us now—no matter what his mom said. And we had a lockbox to crack open.

A bonfire roared in the Hollow, the wood crackling, the flames licking the night air. The fire cast spindly shadows against the weathered sofa. B jumped onto the center cushion, holding a bottle of Olde English malt liquor above her head. She cackled toward the moon then shook the bottle before unscrewing the cap. The bubbly amber liquid spewed out of the spout and onto Squid and Tanner, who were standing around the fire. They raised their bottles and returned primal howls in B's direction, stoking the flames of their hedonistic ritual.

My bottle remained unopened at my side. I didn't want to open it until Dev was here. It felt wrong to start our celebrations without him here to share in our victory. After all, it was because of his equipment and his expertise that we even got the lockbox.

I watched them revel in victory with mild amusement. We hadn't won anything yet. The lockbox still remained closed.

Squid's eyes kept darting to a tool bag he'd retrieved from the shed on the waterfront. It was filled with screwdrivers and lock-picking equipment. And a sledgehammer, just in case we got desperate. I stepped in front of the bag, blocking it from view.

"We agreed to wait for Dev, remember?" My voice hitched up. I turned back to the placid water, cupping my hands around my eyes to see any boats on the horizon, and ripples from waves approaching. But there was nothing. "Just give him five more minutes."

"He's not going to show," B said. "I already told you—he doesn't need the money anyway. Let's open this bad boy up."

She hopped off the couch and slapped the top of the box. Tanner waved his hand toward me, beckoning me to join them by the fire.

"I hate to tell B she's right, but I think she's got a point."

"Yeah, didn't you hear his mom?" Squid said, sidestepping around me to get to his tool bag. "He's not coming to the south side."

"Mommy mayor—sorry, *senator*—can suck it." B put her bottle to her lips and took a swig of malt liquor.

"Did anyone else think she knew what we were doing in Toulouse?" I stepped closer to the fire, feeling the heat on my face. There was something about our conversation with the mayor that raised a red flag, but my mind was a jumble. After two dives in one day and a string of sleepless nights this week, I was exhausted. Maybe someone else picked up on it, too.

"She doesn't care what we were doing as long as it doesn't make her look bad." B waved her hand dismissively and plopped onto the couch. "Folks on the north side are all like that. Now, can we please open the dang thing?"

"What do you say?" Tanner nudged my shoulder with his elbow, and looked down at me with wide green eyes. My breath caught, and for a second, I forgot my worries. I stepped closer, like a moth to a flame. He had that kind of effect on me.

"Okay, yeah," I breathed, still looking at Tanner. I blinked, regaining my senses, and then nodded to the lockbox sitting on the tree stump. "It's time."

"Right on." Squid whipped out a thin screwdriver-looking thing from his tool bag and knelt in front of the lockbox. We gathered around him. He took a deep breath before wedging the metal rod into the rusted key slot on the front. Slowly, he wiggled the screwdriver. After a while he frowned—nothing was happening. "This one's tricky."

He leaned closer—so close his ear was almost touching the box. He poked around in the keyhole, listening carefully for the lock to click. I leaned forward, too. I was anxious to see what was inside it. There wasn't a sound except for the crackling fire, the distant roar of the dam. Almost as if we were all holding our breath.

"Step aside, bro." B flicked her head to the side, signaling for Squid to get out of the way. She swung the sledgehammer at her feet like a golf club. She hiked up her leg and stomped on the top of the box with a muddy black boot. Then she swung the heavy mallet at the screwdriver sticking out of the slot, bludgeoning it farther into the lock.

The metal caved inward and something inside shattered. We leaned forward, our shoulders banging against each other. Slowly, the lid creaked open.

My breath caught.

"Case, you want to do the honors? Since you started this," Tanner whispered. "What do you think, guys?"

Squid nodded vigorously and stepped aside. So did B.

My hands were shaking when I grabbed the lid. I felt all of my hopes and dreams for the treasure surging through my palms. This was the moment we'd been waiting for. I dove into the box, my fingers frenzied as they pawed through the contents.

"What is it?" I was panting when I pulled out a handful of sludge, which I dropped onto the tree stump. I reached in deeper and pulled out another handful of slop.

I studied the contents of the box, slowly piecing together what it was—a useless hodgepodge of disintegrated paper and rusted broken metal, probably broken from the lock when B busted it open with the sledgehammer, and a round, circular ring about three inches in diameter. In the mash of sludge there was a piece of paper money. The deeper I sifted, the more coherent the bills were.

Paper dollars from the Bank of Toulouse.

"So we're rich?" B asked, bouncing on the balls of her feet.

"These were issued by the Bank of Toulouse. Not the US

government." Tanner ripped his gaze away from the box, clenching his jaw tight.

"Why?" B scrunched up her face, confused.

"Don't you know the history of Toulouse?" Tanner cocked his head to the side. "No one would loan money to Black people, so they made their own bank. And that's how they thrived."

"Unlike what the mayor keeps saying about the founding of Langston." Squid spat on the ground, putting his hands on his hips. "There wasn't much fellowship between the city of Toulouse and Colonel Langston, according to my grandmother. And she knows everything about this town."

"So then why do we call it Langston's treasure?" B raised a critical eyebrow. "It should be called the Toulouse Treasure. Because they made it. It belonged to them."

Tanner opened his mouth to say something but then thought better of it, tucking his lips between his teeth as if he didn't want to admit that B was right, but she did have a point. Langston didn't seem to have any claim to the treasure. It was all Toulouse.

I turned my attention back to the lockbox and sifted through the slop. More loose metal rattled at the bottom.

"Look." I opened my palm, revealing several familiar looking coins. "At least it's what we were looking for."

I sat back on my heels, feeling the adrenaline subside. The lockbox was a colossal disappointment. My frustration weighed heavily on my shoulders, they drooped forward as I settled into a defeated slouch.

"So, *this* is the Toulouse Treasure? A handful of coins and some busted bills?" B snatched up one of the coins from my outstretched hand. "There has to be something that we're missing."

"I don't know what to tell you, B." Tanner threw his hands up, his nostrils flaring. "It's better than nothing, I guess."

"That diver was in the exact place that we'd pinpointed. That couldn't just be a coincidence." B paced in front of the fire, her eyes wild. "He knew what he was doing. Maybe he—"

"Maybe he could tell us where to find the rest?" Squid cut her off. He chuckled softly. "Whatever secrets that dude had are dead now."

"Look, y'all. It is what it is." He pointed to the clump of paper money and coins on the stump. "One coin for each of us. That's worth *something*. My mom sometimes works with this coin collector guy out in Nashville. I'll take it to him and see if I can sell it. It'll be hundreds of dollars for each of us at least."

"Just enough to buy a couple cups of coffee." B snatched her drink off the ground and hopped over the arm of the couch. She took a swig of it as she headed up the gravel drive, calling over her shoulder. "I knew this was a waste of time."

"B, don't be like that." Squid yelled after her, but she was already at her bike.

The motorcycle sputtered to life, and she tossed her bottle onto the grass. She revved the throttle and skidded around my car and was gone in a flash.

After a while, the crickets started murmuring again, but their song was short-lived. A branch crackled in the woods behind the shed by the water. My head snapped up to where the crickets had fallen silent in that corner of the Hollow.

"Someone's here." I pointed to the shed then held a finger to my lips. We needed to be quiet.

"That you, Seb?" Squid peered through the trees. Another branch cracked, and a silhouette emerged from the shadows.

He walked slowly, his cautious steps cracking, rustling the leaf litter beneath them. Another shadow emerged behind him. The two figures stalked toward us. As the first drew near the fire, I could see that his face was covered with a ski mask. I scrambled to my feet and backed away from him.

"Stay where you are." Squid grabbed the sledgehammer off the ground and held it in front of him, his arms shaking. He was scared and rightly so. There were masked men in the Hollow. And they'd come uninvited.

"We know y'all found something down there." A man's voice boomed as he stepped closer to us. He slapped a baseball bat against his open palm like he was ready to use it on anything, including us. Branches and leaves crackled under his feet. "Come on, hand it over."

"Just hand over the box." The masked man took a step forward. His hand hovered near his belt loops, just above his pocket. Slowly, he pulled out a gun, its silver handle glinting in the firelight. He pointed it at our huddle, the pistol clicking as he cocked the hammer. My breath hitched as I stared down the barrel of the gun.

He stalked closer, his hand outstretched as if to pluck the box off the tree stump. "Listen here—that's all we want. Don't do anything stupid. You hand it over, and that's that."

"Wait. I know that voice," Tanner said under his breath. He stepped forward, standing shoulder to shoulder with Squid. "Ron?"

I gasped and covered my mouth. I recognized the deep tenor, the slight southern twang of that voice. Even the way he carried his body. It was Ron.

"Get lost, Ron." Tanner stepped in front of the tree stump, blocking the banged-up box from view. "Take a hint when you're not wanted."

"I've had just about enough of your lip, boy." Ron brought his hand back then hit Tanner on the side of his face.

Staggering backward, he tripped over the edge of the tree stump and fell to the ground with a muffled grunt.

"Now, I'm only going to tell y'all one last time. Give me the key." He flicked his fingers, awaiting our compliance. When we didn't respond, he swung the gun in the direction of Squid's house. He took a menacing step forward, his finger trembling against the trigger. A bullet blasted through one of the downstairs windows, dangerously close to where Squid's grandmother slept. Squid's jaw slackened as he looked in horror at the shattered glass.

"I swear to God, if you hurt her—" His hands balled into fists as he scrambled and ran to check on his grandmother.

Ron raised the pistol over his head, his eyes wild. His finger pulsed against the trigger, as if he was unsure whether or not to actually pull it. Tanner groaned on the ground and rolled over, his expression horrified as he looked at the gun above Ron's head. Tanner kicked his shin, throwing Ron off balance.

The gun fired, crackling in the night sky.

"Dagnabit." Ron paced, cussing under his breath.

"Are you okay?" I crouched down to Tanner on the ground. He rubbed his cheek, his expression a mixture of shock and fright.

"You forced my hand. I told you—I *told* you not to do anything stupid." Ron's voice was getting consistently louder. I turned back to Tanner.

"Run."

I scrambled to my feet and looked around. In the commotion, I couldn't find my backpack with my keys. They were inside Squid's house or maybe on the boat. I couldn't remember, but I didn't have time to search. The only thing I could think to grab was the lockbox. I quickly snatched it off the stump before Ron could grab it and took off in the direction of the highway.

The beam of Ron's flashlight scanned the tree line, casting spindly shadows against the dark woods. I held my arms close to my chest, trying to make myself as small as possible as I hid behind a large spruce. My chest rose and fell in short spurts, my breathing harried. The sound of water thundering through the dam dominated the air, but I still covered my mouth with my hand so that he couldn't hear me.

I crouched there for a while, waiting for the searchlight to shift focus to the other side of the woods. Then I sprang up and took off in the direction of my house. The old coins clinked in the lockbox, making me sound like a rattled piggy bank. I pressed it into my chest, praying it would absorb some of the sound.

"Get back here, Casey!" Ron howled.

His footsteps came quickly behind mine as I ran through the

patch of trees, his flashlight in a tailspin as he matched my hurried steps. Leaves and twigs snapped and snarled beneath his swift footsteps. The light grew brighter. He was faster than me, and he was getting close. Too close.

I shoved my hand into the box and grabbed a fistful of coins then tossed them over my shoulder, praying that it would slow him down—that he would drop to his knees and search the forest floor for my treasure.

But he didn't stop. It was almost as if he didn't want the coins. He wanted to know what else we'd found buried in the depths of Langston. But we didn't have anything else—this was all we had.

"Casey! Casey, get back here!" Ron boomed.

I doubted I could reason with him. He was so angry, so determined.

A gunshot sliced through the noise of the dam, through my ragged breathing, through Ron's footsteps. My feet faltered and I stumbled to the ground.

TWENTY-TWO

I propped myself on my elbows, panting heavily as I checked my body for gunshot wounds. I was so wired, I thought I might have been shot. Then a rustling from behind a tree beside me snapped my attention to the side. A quivering wail escaped my lips just as a hand snaked around my mouth.

"You're okay. Shh," Tanner said in a low whisper. He pointed his index finger up, and at first, I didn't know what he was indicating. Another shot ripped through the air, and I flinched. But as I held Tanner's firm gaze, I followed his finger up above the tree line, up the cliff to where the old mine was.

A distant howl pierced the night followed by another shot in the dark. I recognized that howl. It wasn't Ron and his cohort firing the gunshots. It was Seb firing off from the cliffs above us.

I'd never been more thankful for the burnouts at the mine than I was in that moment.

"Let's go while they're distracted." He crawled to his feet and nodded in the direction of the road. "This way."

I tucked the lockbox underneath my arm and hurried after him, looking at the ground as I took every step, trying to miss twigs and branches—desperately trying to avoid too much crunch under my feet. The roar of the dam was our friend. It covered our tracks as we slunk farther away from Ron.

Tanner's truck was parked at the top of the hill. He fumbled for his keys.

"Hurry," I hissed. "I think someone's coming."

"Get in." The door unlocked, and I swear it was the loudest thing around us. I ripped the door open just as the engine boomed to life. I slammed the door, figuring the noise wouldn't matter at this point.

The tires screeched as the old Toyota lurched forward, down the gravel road, the trees whipping past the windows. My feet dug into the piles of school papers and books on the floor.

"Is anyone following us?" Tanner adjusted his rearview mirror, his eyes darting to and from the road as he searched for signs of his stepfather.

"I don't know." I hitched my leg onto the seat and craned my neck to look behind us. "I don't think so."

"Did you see that guy Ron was with?" His voice cracked, and he wiped his forehead with the back of his hand. "Big meaty dude. He looks like Merrit, that cop who sits at the speed trap near school."

"What about B and Squid? Do you think they're okay? And what if Dev came? What if they got him, too?"

"B was on her bike, remember? She was too mad about the lack of treasure to return to the Hollow." He shook his head, trying to convince himself that he was right. "Squid went to check on his grandmother. And I know she's got a pistol in her nightstand, so they'll be safe if anyone tries to enter. And Dev . . . Casey, Dev's on the north side. He was never going to come."

"They're not picking up." I dialed Squid's number again, and it went straight to voicemail. Then I tried B for the third time. The phone just kept ringing. "No one's picking up!"

Headlights rounded the bend in the road, growing larger and brighter as they inched closer. My jaw dropped open, and I pawed against the dash until I reached Tanner's elbow. I tapped quickly, my eyes on the fast approaching car.

"There's someone behind us!" I grabbed my headrest, heaving myself upward to see more clearly. "They're definitely following us."

Tanner's eyes darted to the rearview mirror and then back to the road, the car swerving as he slipped back into our lane.

"That's not Ron's car." He clenched his jaw, taking another look in the mirror.

"Who cares whose car it is?!" My voice cracked as I yelled. "Go faster!"

"I'm trying!" His foot pressed down on the accelerator, and the pedal hit the floor. The old engine wheezed as it tried to comply, but the needle on the speedometer only ticked up slightly. "It won't go any faster!"

The black sedan edged closer, so close that I could see the insignia on the chrome grill—a Mercedes hood ornament. It lurched forward, ramming the back bumper. Our tires screeched as we jolted forward. Tan tapped the gas pedal again, but we didn't pull forward anymore. The Mercedes sped up again, closing the distance between us.

"They're coming again!" My breath was harried as I wrapped my arms around my seat, bracing myself for another impact.

"Turn around, and put your seat belt on." Tanner's jaw pulsated as he gritted his teeth. I looked at him incredulously. He said louder, "I'm serious, Case! I'm gonna do something a little crazy."

I scrambled to do as he said, my fingers trembling as I buckled up. I gripped the seat belt and pulled it taut as we emerged from the forest road and careened down Lakeside Drive, hugging the tight turns. Over the guardrails was a steep drop-off, where the ridge tumbled toward the lake. The town came into view below, and as we approached the final turn, Tanner gripped the steering wheel tight—so tight his knuckles went white.

"Hold on!" he yelled before slamming his foot on the brakes and spinning the car away from the guardrail. I jerked forward, the seat belt digging into my chest so hard it knocked the wind out of me. Tires screeched behind us, and the Mercedes swerved past us so that it wouldn't collide. It skidded to the side, the air smelling of burned rubber as it careened toward the guardrail. Tanner pumped the brakes, and in the glow of the taillights I could see Ron's face, his arms twisting and turning as he struggled to regain control of the car.

But it was too late.

The airbags deployed as the car crashed into the railing, filling the quiet night with the sound of twisted metal. Steam wafted up from the mangled hood. We waited in silence.

"Is he..." I gulped. "Is he dead?"

"I...don't think so. Look."

The driver's side door cracked open. And a hand reached over the ballooned airbag. Blood trickled down Ron's forehead. But Tanner didn't wait to see the rest. The tires of his old truck screeched as it picked up speed. We barreled toward my house, leaving Ron and his henchman to lick their wounds.

My house came into view. I tugged on Tan's sleeve, thankful for the first time in a long time to be home.

I leapt up the porch steps two at a time and shoved my key in the lock. The door swung open, and without the credenza blocking its path, it slammed hard against the wall. The drywall crunched underneath the blunt force. I'd have to pay for that later, but for now, I didn't care. Tanner scrambled inside right behind me, and together we slammed the door shut.

I backed against the door, my chest heaving as I tried to regain my breath. I hugged the lockbox as if it could plug up the hole I felt in my chest.

With my sister and mom gone, the house was dark—as if they'd taken all the light with them. It was quiet, except for my ragged breathing and the sound of the blinds rustling as Tanner peeked through—watching and bracing for Ron to show up. I tried to call B and Squid again, but there was no answer.

Tanner took a cautious step forward, and then another and another until he was standing in front of me. He reached a hand out to rub my shoulder. At his touch I crumpled into his arms with a sob.

"I don't understand." My voice was muffled through his T-shirt, thick with tears. "What the fuck is happening?"

"Ron knew about the coin. I thought I tricked him that day at the shop, but I guess not."

"And now we don't have anything. I threw it all at him. The coins, the paper." I groaned, remembering the chase through the woods, the gunshots and screaming. A fresh wave of tears ripped through me. "We have nothing. He got everything."

"Hey, we're safe. That's something." He rubbed my back in slow circles until my tears slowed to a trickle. His body stiffened, and he pulled away from me. "I've gotta go call my mom. Warn her about Ron."

He fished his phone out of his back pocket and strode across the kitchen to the living room. I stayed behind, intent on giving him privacy. And then it dawned on me, I had to warn my dad, too.

The garage light peeked through the bottom of the doorframe. I knew just where to find him.

I scampered down the concrete steps, skirting around the boxes and trash bags Lucile had piled into the garage. My dad was crammed into one of my grandmother's old armchairs, his slippered feet tucked underneath him, his head resting on the floral fabric of the headrest. A light snore blubbered past his lips. For a second, I hesitated. I was almost sorry to wake him. He looked so peaceful. But this was an emergency.

"Dad." I shook his shoulder softly. "Dad, wake up."

"What is it?" He jolted awake, blinking his sleepy eyes.

"Dad, you have to get up." I tugged on the sleeve of his robe, jerking him to the edge of his chair. "We need to call the cops."

"The *cops*?"

"Yes! We need to call 9-1-1 right now, okay?" I knelt down to the ground, standing on my knees so that I could be at eye level with him. I gripped the collar of his robe, and the words just tumbled out of me. "There are men after us. They chased us through the woods and said they want some key—it doesn't make any sense. I don't have a key! And then they like … they tried to drive us off the road. And they have guns. Did you hear the shots by the mine? That was them. Well it wasn't only them, but they started it. But we have to go to the police station right now. *Come on.*"

My dad's desperate eyes searched me. His mouth scrunched up as he studied the dirt on my arms, the scrapes on my fingers. His eyebrows turned upward. And for a moment, his muscles tensed like he was about to leap up from his chair. But then he relaxed, slumping back into the musty cushions.

"There is always shooting up the hill. You know that." He gave a heavy sigh. "The cops won't do anything about it."

"There were men *chasing* me and my friends through the woods." I shook his robe, hoping to shake some sense into him. "Aren't you listening to what I'm saying? I need you right now."

"If you wait here, it'll all die down." He looked into his lap, suddenly interested in the seam of his pajama pants instead of his pleading daughter. He clamped his eyes shut and unraveled my grip on his collar. "I don't want to call the cops. It'll bring too much attention to us—to the back taxes we owe, to the jewelry your mom kept from the bankruptcy auditors. I can't have them swarming the front lawn. Or don't you remember what happened?"

He raised his chin defiantly, scooting his chair back so that he was out of my reach. But I didn't care. I crawled on the concrete floor, closing the distance between us. I was not too proud to grovel. I needed an adult's help, someone to keep me safe. My dad could be that person if he wanted to.

But he wouldn't rise to the occasion.

"Of course, I remember what happened!" I banged my fist on his armrest.

"It'll all blow over. Just—just stay away from the mine. Keep close to home. You'll see. It'll blow over."

"No, it won't." I fell back onto my heels, utterly bewildered by my dad's response to the events of tonight. "You know, I never realized how selfish you really are. You really only care about yourself, don't you?"

My father's lip trembled, and he turned to look away from me. I heaved myself off the floor, my hands trembling at my sides.

"You're such a fucking coward. All you do is sit out here and put together those damn puzzles. While your family is *suffering*. While your wife has one foot out of the door. What is all this shit?" I walked over to the broken armoire, where my dad had set up another stupid puzzle. I grabbed a handful of pieces and tossed them to the ground. "I mean, this is a fucking joke!"

"I am your father! And this is my house." He jumped out of his chair, his lip still trembling. "Do not speak to me that way."

"This isn't your house. You lost that, remember? And you're about to lose this one, too." It was a low blow, but he deserved it. He had failed me time and again, and now this. I was so disgusted with him. "And you haven't been a father to me in a very long time."

I slammed the back door shut so hard the clock on the wall shuddered. Tanner was standing in the kitchen with his phone in his hand, his jaw slack in shock.

"How much of that did you hear?"

He bobbed his head to the side. "Enough to know to butt out."

I nodded and walked to the fridge. I needed cold water after all the screaming—screaming at Squid's Hollow and at home.

"B's with Squid. Said they holed up in the house with his grandma's gun. B saw a strange car pull into the Hollow and doubled back. So you were right—she did come back." He took a deep breath. "They both saw Ron and the other guy chasing after us. Which means..."

"Which means they want that." I pointed to the battered lockbox on the kitchen counter. "I can't understand why. I gave them just about everything in here. It's littered across the forest floor."

"Can I have some of that?" He nodded toward the water. "I'll get out of your hair soon. Maybe I can crash at Squid's."

I thought of that tiny house, now crammed full with Squid and B. I thought of the road going to the Hollow and how we narrowly escaped. The thought of one of us going back there was unthinkable.

"No. Stay here."

"Are you sure?" He raised an eyebrow and looked worriedly toward the garage where my dad was undoubtedly licking his wounds.

"Don't worry about him. He doesn't make the rules here." I plopped onto the couch next to Tanner with a heavy sigh, feeling the weight of my frustration take over me. "My dad won't come out of there. He hardly ever does."

TWENTY-THREE

Forty-five days until we lose the house

"A *dead body*?" Lucile squealed into the camera, her eyes bulging. I was on FaceTime with her while Tanner drove us to school. Tanner's truck rumbled down the road, hiccuping through potholes.

"I was going to tell you about it, but I just crashed." My mouth stretched into a wide yawn.

"Sis, it was on the evening news." Lucile brought the phone so close to her face that I could see her pores. "All the way in Atlanta!"

"How is Mom?" I asked. I could see the corner of my mom's shoulder in the background. There was a seat belt strapped over it. I frowned. "You're not driving and on FaceTime, are you?"

"I'm fine sweetheart." My mom's head popped into the frame. She said in a louder voice. "We're in an Uber. Going to the salon."

"Stop yelling," my sister snapped at Mom. "It's literally just like a regular phone call. You can use your inside voice."

"Hey, can you do me a favor?" I asked.

"*Another* favor?" Lucile closed her eyes and massaged her forehead with the tips of her fingers. When she opened her eyes again, her eyes were hooded, skeptical. "What do you need now?"

"Can you pull some books from the Spelman-Morehouse library for me? Anything on Toulouse." I squirmed in my seat as Tanner looked at me out of the corner of his eye. There was a part of me that felt pretty defeated about last night. Finding the lock-box with only a few coins was disheartening—and it was even more disheartening that I'd thrown them at Ron. But I couldn't help but think that the bigger mystery lay with Toulouse. All of those bullet holes and the cannonball I'd found didn't quite match the version of history I'd read about. Toulouse may have gone up in flames, but what caused the fire? There was nothing in our library about it, and that was the most comprehensive collection in northern Georgia. Maybe Spelman and Morehouse had more to offer. I waited for Lucile to respond, and when she didn't, I whispered, "Please."

"God, not you too. You know Grandma Bernie was obsessed with that town?"

"Don't you want to know *why?*" I raised my voice, shifting in my seat so that I could lean closer to my phone. "If we're going to lose our house because of Grandma's obsession with Toulouse, then we have a right to know why."

Lucile's face softened as she mulled this over. With a sigh she said, "Fine. I have some downtime, so I'll see what I can—"

The phone shook. The camera angled toward the ceiling, and then fell to the floor. There was clearly a struggle for the phone. Finally, my mom's face came into view. Clearly, she had won.

"Enough about that old town. You know, Mrs. Kinnier called me this morning. And Mrs. Tillerson. And I haven't heard from them for months. And all they wanted to talk about was you. And how you were getting a special commendation from the mayor, and..."

"Uh-huh." I rolled my eyes, giving a sidelong glance at Tanner. I mouthed the words *I'm sorry*, and he gave me a small smile.

"Don't worry about it," he said with a soft smile. He had bags under his eyes. He hadn't slept well on the couch. His long legs dangled over the armrest.

My mom was still chatting hurriedly.

"...so we'll be seated just off the stage. You know how much those seats usually cost." She pursed her lips, her nostrils fluttering. She looked absolutely triumphant, like she'd just won the lottery. This was her chance to be back in Langston society. "Oh, is this it? We're at the nail salon. Tell Dev I say hi."

"Mom, you hate him. You've always said he was a bad influence."

"Nonsense!" She rubbed her chest, shaking her head. "I've always been fond of him. Anyway, smooches."

The call abruptly ended. I put my phone facedown in my lap and laughed awkwardly at Tanner.

"She probably thinks I'm in the car with Dev since I was with him last night." My voice trailed off. I suddenly felt awkward about my mom invoking my past in the presence of Tanner. "Anyway, my mom can be a lot."

"She might be the only person who's actually thrilled about a dead body."

"I know, right?" I said as we pulled into the Langston Academy parking lot. He eased into one of the spots near the back of the lot.

We were *just* in time for the morning bell, and most of the prime spots were already taken. I opened my door and looked at him over my shoulder. "Thanks for the ride."

"It's nothing." He skipped around the front of his car so that he could walk beside me to the double doors at the front. "Thanks for letting me crash on your couch."

"It was nice." I blushed and looked at the pavement. We'd crashed on the couch after only a few minutes of mindless TV. I had woken up with my head resting on a throw pillow on one end of the sofa, Tanner on the other, a mess of our legs tangled in between under the throw blanket. It was the first time I'd only *slept* with a guy.

And it felt oddly more intimate than anything I'd ever done.

I wondered if he felt the same way. When I pried my gaze away from the sidewalk and looked at him, his cheeks were red and he too was looking at the ground.

"Look, I know you didn't ask for my advice, but my two cents..." His eyes fluttered over to mine, and he cleared his throat. "Make things right with your dad?"

I brought my hand to my face and covered my eyes, stifling a groan.

"That's complicated. But I'll think about it."

The hallway was buzzing with activity. Everyone always lingered in the hall until the last minute, but this was on another level. Seniors weren't in their strict uniforms, especially a few days before the end of school.

Dylan and Fatima were down the hallway near Fatima's locker.

Dylan raised an eyebrow at Tanner and me walking together and whispered into Fatima's ear. She whipped her head around so quickly that her hair slapped against Dylan's face. I couldn't help but choke out a laugh. And I didn't care if Dylan heard it.

"Looks like we've been spotted. Run now and save yourself." My smile faltered as those words truly hit me.

Run.

It's what he'd told me last night as he lay on the forest floor. It all came flooding back, and I froze in the middle of the hallway.

"We're okay. Just breathe." He placed a hand softly on my shoulder and squeezed. "You gonna be all right? Because we could go. Take a personal day."

"No, I'm fine." I mustered a small smile then tucked my hair behind my ear.

"My class is that way." He ticked his head down the next hallway, which led to the science wing. "Text if you need me."

He walked down the hallway, stopping to look over his shoulder before disappearing into his classroom. Fatima bounded down the hall, her shoes squeaking against the tile, as Dylan followed slowly behind her. She stood in stark contrast to Fatima's mood—her eyes hooded, her mouth a thin line. Ignoring her, Fatima bounced on her toes, waving her phone in front of my face.

"Front page of the *Langston Star*!" She squealed, sliding into the seat next to me.

"Really?" My eyebrows shot up. I knew we were in the news, not *the* news.

Fatima shoved her phone under my nose. And scrolled down to the featured headline:

TEEN DIVE YIELDS DEADLY SURPRISE

A laugh bubbled up my throat. What a dramatic title. But considering almost dying on my ascent, being chased through the woods, and dodging bullets, it wasn't far from the truth.

There was an awkward photo of the five of us standing alongside the mayor, her grin beaming as she wrapped her arm around B, who looked seriously annoyed at being touched. I was flanked on my right side by Tanner and on the left was Dev. I looked like I was holding my shoulders inward, like I was trying to make myself smaller. There had been so much attention, so many questions, so many flashing lights.

"And a seat at the Founder's Day table." Fatima squealed. "Totes unbelievable."

"I know, right?" Dylan huffed, blowing her bangs away from her face. "The mayor's been in office for like a year, and already she's changing the rules."

"I thought you liked Dev's mom," I said.

"She's just mad because that seat is usually reserved for the valedictorians and prom court." Fatima waved her hand dismissively and stepped in front of Dylan. "It's like you've already won."

"Not yet," Dylan said under her breath. "And you're definitely not going to win walking around with bedhead less than a week before prom."

I turned the camera on and put it in selfie mode so that I could see myself. My eyes were crusted in the corners, and my hair was haphazard, much bushier than I normally wore it—probably because I hadn't conditioned my hair after the dive. I'd just rinsed it and crashed.

"Did you hook up with Tanner *and* Dev?" Dylan put her hands on her hips, scanning me up and down, her eyes judging every inch of me. "Wow, you are trying to fit it all in before you graduate."

"Slut shame much?" Fatima glared at her. Then she turned back at me, wiggling her nose. "But seriously, what's the story there? You guys pulled up *together* this morning. So, that means you spent the night at his place."

"Actually it was *my* place."

"Oh." Her eyebrows shot up. "It's just…I've never been to your new house. Neither of us have."

"It's just a house." I shrugged, trying to be as cool as I could. There was a reason I didn't bring friends home to my grandma's old house. I was embarrassed—afraid they'd never speak to me again if they saw how far my family had traveled from our big house on Violet Drive. I shook my head, trying to put it all to bed. "And nothing happened."

I gulped, feeling a blush creep across my cheeks. I didn't want to tell them how I didn't even make it to my bed last night, how I collapsed on the couch with Tanner by my side. How I woke up with my legs tangled with his underneath the throw blanket. There was only time for one of us to shower and get out of the door. We'd almost been late. Was all of that really written across my face?

"Nothing happened. Sure." Dylan scoffed.

"I'm really not in the mood for this." I shoved past her on my way to my locker.

"What?" Dylan held her hands up at Fatima. "She's clearly slumming it with Captain Speedo. She's just afraid to admit it, just like she's afraid to show us the sketchy trap house she lives in."

"Take that back." I turned quickly on my heels and stalked toward her.

"Or what?" She raised her eyebrows, a challenge.

"You know what, Dylan?" Fatima raised her voice so loudly that it sliced through the chatter of the hall. "Shut up."

"What did you say to me?" Dylan blinked, her eyes wide with shock. She wasn't used to pushback from anyone, especially Fatima.

"I said *shut up*. Honestly, you've turned into such a bully. You're clearly threatened by Casey. You want to put her down as much as possible. But look at yourself."

"Fatti's got a backbone all of a sudden."

"I don't care if you call me that. Not anymore. Come graduation, you'll actually have to grow up like the rest of us." She threw her hands up. When she brought them back down, she slapped her thighs. "Do you really think people at Brown are going to find this shit endearing?"

"Whatever." Dylan flipped her hair and walked away from us. Calling over her shoulder she said, "You two deserve each other. And you can forget about the limo to prom."

A few students clapped when Dylan disappeared behind the

girls' bathroom door. But Fatima's eyes were wide, and her breathing came short and quick. She was clearly in shock from telling Dylan off in front of everyone in the hallway.

"Are you okay?" I asked, steering her to a quiet corner under the stairs.

"Oh my God." Her breath hiccupped. "Oh my *God*. I can't believe I just said that to her."

"She had it coming."

"No, you don't understand. She has a rising moon in Gemini and it's only a matter of time before—"

"Fatima." I gripped both of her arms and ducked my head, bringing my eyes to her level. "You are entitled to your feelings. Love yourself in this moment, okay? I know I do."

"I should probably go after her." She started toward the girls' bathroom, but I grabbed her sleeve, stopping her.

"I have a better idea." I lunged to my locker and slammed the door shut, leaving my books locked inside it.

"Where are we going?" Her eyes darted to the clock on the wall as I tugged her down the hallway.

"Ever heard of a personal day? I hear they're all the rage."

The wind whipped through my hair as Fatima sped her Range Rover through town. I held my hand out of the passenger side window and wove it through the breeze, feeling relief wash over me. It felt exhilarating to break free from all the pressures of school, of broken friendships, of my life in ruins. Fatima nudged my elbow on the center console.

"I don't want to go home yet. Do you?" she asked, eyeing me through the corner of her sunglasses.

"No." I shook my head with a sigh. I didn't want to go home—and I wasn't just saying that because I didn't want her to see my place. All that waited for me there was an empty house, and the garage held the empty husk of my dad. I wanted to remain in this in-between space a little longer.

"I know just the place."

The car veered to the right, and we continued along the main drag of the center of town. Most of the weekend tourists had left, so the streets were bare, the storefronts mostly devoid of customers. We pulled into the parking lot outside of Town Creamery, one of Fatima's favorite spots, then strolled across the street and to the to-go window.

"Can I get the chocolatiest things you have in the largest cone you have?" she asked the guy behind the counter. He nodded, then looked to me for my order.

"I'll have what she's having, but in a cup."

"Blasphemy." Fatima tsked under her breath. "The waffle cones make the whole thing complete."

"I like to get straight to the point." I laughed at her upturned eyebrows as I grabbed my cup from the counter. I ticked my head to one of the tables out front. "You wanna sit outside?"

"Aren't you afraid someone will see us?" She squinted down the street then tilted her head to the side. "On second thought, it is kind of a ghost town right now."

A trail of double chocolate fudge ice cream oozed down the side of Fatima's wrist as she took another bite from her waffle cone. I slumped over the bistro table, feeling the weight of my weekend exploits, watching my cup of ice cream melt in the sun. Fatima groaned in satisfaction as she took another bite.

"Whoever invented chocolate was a fucking genius. It makes everything better." She smacked her lips, her eyes rolling upward. Then she focused on me, her eyes tightening as she watched me take a tentative bite. "Are you still thinking about Dylan?"

"What?" I almost choked on my spoonful of chocolate. "Hell no."

While I still felt lingering guilt for the way things went down in the hallway earlier, Dylan was the furthest thing from my mind. My thoughts were elsewhere—lost in the dead eyes of the missing diver, in the breathless chase through the woods, in the screech of the black car colliding with the guardrail. Every time I closed my eyes, I relived it all. And I couldn't exactly tell anyone any of it. I blinked away from Fatima's probing gaze and returned to my cup.

"Sure will make for an awkward prom."

"Fatima." I groaned, tossing my spoon onto the table. "Surely that plan is dead now."

"I've already put the deposits down on the limo and the private room at the club." She bounced up and down in her chair, a guilty smile tugging at her lips. She clearly still wanted to go to prom. "Plus,

I've been looking at my chart, and I think prom's still a thing. I don't know, I have a good feeling about it."

"Spending an entire night around Dylan does not give me good feels."

"But you'll be with me." She leaned forward, batting her eyelashes. "And your hot date. Which, by the way, I still need to find for myself."

"What about Avery? You've been hanging out with them a lot. Don't roll your eyes, I saw you two in the stacks."

"That's done-so. They've been kinda flaky lately, and you know I hate that." Fatima leaned back in her chair, pursing her lips. "And everyone else is taken. I mean, no biggie just super embarrassing to not have a date."

"I mean..." My voice trailed off as I considered whether or not to suggest someone. "You could take Dev. He's been itching to go to prom more than any of us. It's kinda weird, but I think he misses his high school days."

"I don't know." Her lip jutted out to the side. "Wouldn't that be weird?"

"No. All we share now is ancient history." A low laugh escaped my lips. It was truer than she knew—Dev and I were down the Toulouse rabbit hole with the rest of the downstreamers. I frowned, thinking about the last time I'd heard from him. It was after the press conference. "Although, he hasn't been answering his phone lately. Not since yesterday."

"Then maybe a good party will pick him up. Come on, it's written in the stars. You'll come, won't you?"

"I guess." I flung my arms in the air. Then I shook my head at the trickle of ice cream oozing from her wrist onto the table. "You're dripping everywhere."

"I know. I totally need more napkins." She slid her chair away from the table and practically skipped to the creamery's counter.

I wished I shared her mood—but I was too distracted by the sight of Ron a few blocks down. His spat of red hair was unmistakable, and I could just make out a blackened eye against his pale skin, even this far away. He walked slowly with the assistance of a cane. A fresh injury—perhaps sustained just last night?

And then my blood went cold when he lifted his chin and fixed his eyes on me. He froze there on the sidewalk in front of the municipal building, staring me down like the night before. I hooked my feet around the legs of my chair. I wasn't going to run this time.

"Who's that?" Fatima said over my shoulder. "He's looking right at you."

"That's Tanner's stepdad," I said, not able to tear my eyes away from him. I was frozen in fear and defiance.

"He knows you? Wait, Tanner introduced you to his stepdad. Um, that's huge. Why didn't you tell me that?"

"It's not like that. I met him when I was...when I was at his pawnshop selling some things." My gaze drifted to her pearl hair pin fastened to the side of her hair.

Her hand grazed the pearls, and she let out a soft sigh. "So, *that's* why you haven't worn it." She gripped her cheeks with both hands, her eyes wide. "Part of me thought it was because you were kind of done with our group."

I bobbed my head from side to side. She wasn't half wrong—I was done with Dylan.

"Well, I'm not done with you." I smiled up at her.

Mayor Hornsby bounded out of the municipal building, her heels wobbling as she made her way down the marble stairs. She flung her arms up when she reached Ron, then cocked her hips to the side. Her back was facing me, so I couldn't see the expression on her face, couldn't read the words on her lips, but by the way Ron shrugged and hung his head low, I got the impression it was not a casual chat.

The mayor and Ron were embroiled in some sort of argument. I *knew* something was up between them.

Before I could think about anything else, I dove for my backpack lying at my feet and slid my phone out of the front pocket. I held it up and snapped a few pictures.

"What are you taking a picture of?" She snapped her head from my camera to the sidewalk in front of the municipal building. Her jaw fell open when she realized who it was. She plopped down in her seat, nearly dropping her waffle cone, and hunched over to make herself look smaller. She ruffled her hair, covering most of her face with her strands. "Hornsby is friends with my mom. What if she sees us?"

"She looks like she's got her hands full." I ticked my head to the sidewalk where Mayor Hornsby was poking Ron in the shoulder with her finger. His body shuddered through the force of the jab.

Fatima tapped her foot against mine, turning my attention back to her upturned eyebrows, the look of panic across her face. She was the student body secretary, and she couldn't be caught cutting school.

"Okay. Let's bounce," I said, slinging my bag over my shoulder.

Fatima jumped out of her seat and looked longingly at her ice cream in her hands. She chomped down, stuffing her mouth with as much chocolate as she could, then tossed it in the trash can.

"What a waste," she said, her lip jutting out.

I linked my arm in hers and we crossed the street. Fatima's strides were quicker than mine, and she nearly dragged me behind her in her rush to put a safe distance between her and the mayor.

When I looked to the sidewalk in front of the municipal building, I could just barely make out Ron's retreating figure, limping along the walkway. The mayor walked up the stairs two at a time, then paused to look over her shoulder in our direction. Even through her sunglasses, I could feel her eyes on me. She'd seen me.

And I'd seen her.

I jogged after Fatima, more than eager to get away from the mayor's watchful gaze.

TWENTY-FOUR

Forty-four days until we lose the house

One personal day rolled into another. Missing two days in a row would normally make me nervous, but as it was the last week of school, I threw caution to the wind.

I deserved this.

I didn't take a joyride like B did when she skipped school or tinker with projects like Squid did. All I wanted to do was sleep. My brain felt like it had reached critical mass—burnt out from running overtime on my broken family, sparse finances, and a foolish treasure hunt. The stress of it all consumed me, and the only thing I could do was tune it all out. By sleeping for hours on end.

Depression naps—that's what the internet called it.

By Tuesday evening, I was feeling semirestored, though I still had lingering fatigue I couldn't shake. I didn't know how I could possibly still be tired, but I was. Still, I managed to drag myself out of bed and pour myself a bowl of cereal.

The cereal grew soggy in the milk as I scrolled through my text messages from Tanner and Squid and Fatima—even one from B. But there was one person who was glaringly absent from the bunch.

Dev.

I still hadn't heard from him since Sunday when we'd stood on the dock and posed for pictures—political props for his mom. Something was up—he never disappeared for this long. I decided to check up on him to see if he was all right.

And to try to figure out what his mother was up to.

His house was large with gray shingle siding, old Dutch windows, a turret with bay windows. I knew the house well. I'd spent many evenings here with friends laughing through game nights in the basement where the pool table was. And then there were the nights with just us, making out in his room.

The last time I was here was last year, the night of prom when we snuck alcohol out of his parents' liquor cabinet and spent the night in the boathouse. It was only a year ago, but my goodness, it felt like a lifetime ago. So much had changed.

I parked on the street. At this point, I knew how to not be seen when sneaking around my old neighborhood. I darted across the front lawn, cognizant of where the motion-activated lights were placed, then rounded the corner of the house.

Crouching behind one of the garbage cans, I took a moment to catch my breath, surveying the grounds for any movement. A stray cat darted across the driveway, making my breath hitch. But it quickly scurried beneath a car parked in the driveway, which was draped in a tarp.

That was odd. I'd been to Dev's house countless times, and I'd never seen one of his family's cars concealed. They had nice cars, ones they'd like to show off.

My eyes darted to Dev's second-story bay window, where the

lights were on, then back to the sketchy car cover. Before I spoke to Dev, I needed to see what was under the cloth.

I ran across the driveway, taking the same route as the cat so that I wouldn't set off any of the motion detectors. The car cover crinkled as I lifted the corner up slowly. Beneath it was shiny black paint with deep gauges streaking across it. Ducking my head beneath it, I found what I'd been looking for—a Mercedes hood ornament. I traced the symbol with my fingers, my breath tumbling out in a rush.

Ron had driven this car when he was chasing us from the Hollow. He was absolutely working with the mayor.

Which meant Mayor Hornsby was also looking for the treasure.

I snapped a few pictures of the car and sent it to Squid, B, and Tanner. Then I ran around the side of the house to Dev's windows. At my feet were bits of gravel. I picked up a small rock, prepared to throw it at his window, but then I thought better of it. If it broke the window, I'd wake the whole house up—and I didn't run through the woods to escape Ron only to be caught at the mayor's doorstep.

Something was up with the mayor. I had a bad feeling about her. I always had. But this time...she had changed. She was up to something.

I tossed the rock into the grass and picked up a large piece of mulch instead.

"Psst!" I tossed the bark up at his window. "Dev."

I grabbed another handful of mulch and chucked pieces of it at the window. They hit the pane with dull thuds. I was about to reach for another when Dev appeared at the window. I let out a deep breath, a sigh of relief. I hadn't realized how tight with worry my chest was until I exhaled.

"Case?" He lifted the window up farther and stuck his head out. He whisper-yelled, "What are you doing here?"

"Great, you're alive." I clasped my hands together, slightly annoyed that he didn't seem welcoming. "You weren't answering your phone, so I thought the worst."

"Shhh. They can hear you."

I slapped my hands to my sides. What did he expect me to do?

"Well? Let me in."

"I don't know, Case." He scrunched up his mouth, his eyelid twitching nervously. "I'm grounded. My mom—she doesn't want me hanging out with you and your squad anymore."

"My *squad*?" I stifled a laugh. "And do you always do what your mommy tells you to do?"

"I see B is rubbing off on you." He raised his eyebrow at my sharp response. Maybe he was right—B's acerbic wit was formidable. It spurred people to action. After a moment, Dev threw his head back with a muffled grunt. "Okay, fine. Here."

He threw down a flimsy fire escape ladder.

"What am I supposed to do with this?" My whisper came out as a hiss.

"Climb it. Lots of people have," he said with a smug smirk. Clearly, I was not the first girl to sneak into his room this way.

I gripped the sides of the ladder then heaved myself upward. The ladder swung into the side of the house, and I hit a ground floor window with a *whack*.

Ladders were definitely not my thing.

"For chrissake!" He held his palms out, begging for me to stop. "I'll come to you."

The light in his window shut off, and I was left in the darkness. I was still for long enough for the crickets to resume their buzzing. In the quiet, I could hear the water lapping the docks, and in the darkness my eyes adjusted to the moonlight.

"Over here." Dev popped his head out of the sliding door of the next room over.

"So are you on lockdown?"

"Grounded until Mom says otherwise." His nostrils flared as he ran his hands through his hair. "She even took my phone away, which is obviously torture."

To take his phone away was almost a lethal blow. He was always on that thing.

"Oh, we're the bad influence?" My eyebrows quirked up. "Are you sure it isn't the other way around?"

"I mean, I was already in deep shit. And then we found the body at a time when we really shouldn't have been diving." He sank to the edge of the table in the dimly lit room. "It's just not a good time for my mom with the whole senate thing."

"Maybe it's not a good time for her because she's up to no good." I chewed on the edge of my lips, my nostrils flaring. I stepped forward, coming within inches of Dev's face.

"Your mom knows Ron. You saw the way they were talking on Sunday. How can you explain that? She *knew* we were looking for the Toulouse Treasure. But none of us told her that."

"You've really gone full townie, haven't you?"

"What is that supposed to mean?" I frowned.

"I mean first you start running around with *them*." He waved his arms around me as if conjuring up Tanner and the rest of the crew. "And then this treasure hunt. And now you think my mom is hiding stuff."

"Does she work from home?" I asked, changing the subject. I didn't have time to debate with him about something I already knew was true. His mom was competing against us for the treasure, and she was ruthless. Two could play at that game.

"Doesn't everyone these days?"

"No, they don't. A lot of people still go into a workplace. They work blue collar jobs, work with their hands," I said in a huff, with a little more passion than I'd intended or meant. I used to not care about these things. But now I knew that there were only a privileged few who got to work from the comfort of their own homes.

"I mean she has an office at municipal, of course, but—wait, where are you going?" he hissed after me, but I was already across the room.

I opened the door to the hallway, listening closely before bounding down the hall on my tiptoes. I slunk down the hallway, keeping close to the wall, hoping that the floorboards wouldn't creak underneath my feet.

"Wait, Case," he hissed behind me. "Where are you going? You can't be serious!"

I opened the door to her office, finding cream-colored furniture set against polished wood panels. Her home office was just below Dev's room, with floor-to-ceiling bay windows and a sprawling, million-dollar view of the lake. This was one heck of a piece of real estate—the county seat. B was right—Mayor Hornsby was the queen of the charmies.

A long glass desk sat near the wall of windows on the side. It had a full bouquet of flowers on top of it, which was beautiful but strange. It didn't really leave much room for actual work.

This wasn't a working office. This was a showroom, something to uphold the optics of the mayor. There was a key rack dangling underneath the light switch. I snatched the only pair hanging from the wall, studying the rose seal etched into the handle.

"Come on." I tugged on Dev's sleeve.

"Where are we going?" He tripped over his flip-flops as he struggled to keep up.

"To your mom's real office."

Crouched behind a row of hedges, we waited in the shadows as we scoped out Langston's municipal building. Despite the fact that it was after hours, all of the lights were on in the main entrance—probably because there was a security camera pointed at the double doors. It would be hard to remain unseen if the lights were on.

I hadn't thought this through.

And if that wasn't hard enough, the building sat directly across from the Langston police precinct.

Yep—I definitely wasn't a criminal mastermind.

The silhouette of a hooded figure appeared in the alleyway between city hall and the urgent care clinic next door. It grew larger as the footsteps grew more pronounced. It made a beeline for our little huddle in the bushes.

"Case, you there?" Tanner whispered through the greenery.

"Over here."

"You didn't say anything about him coming." Dev's eyes widened with panic. "This is a terrible idea."

He wasn't wrong. But sometimes the riskiest things had the biggest rewards.

"Hey," Tanner said, crouching down to our level. "You look good. I didn't think you'd look so well."

"Um . . . thanks?"

"Sorry, that came out wrong. It's just that you haven't been to school in a couple days, and I guess I figured you'd been sick when I said that. But you look great."

"Uh, hello?" Dev waved his hand between us. "We're in the middle of committing a crime here! So, could you guys focus? How are we going to take out the camera at the front?"

"We could push it up. Angle it toward the ceiling." I squinted toward the front steps, trying to figure out how tall the archway was. It had to be eight feet. I looked back to the boys. "Who's the tallest?"

"I think that's me." Tanner shrugged apologetically at Dev, the ghost of a grin on his lips. Then he snapped off one of the branches from the hedges. Before I had time to ask what he was doing, he said, "For extra reach. I'm not *that* tall. I'll wave when the coast is clear."

He was looking across the street at the police station to make sure the coast was clear, then bolted across the walkway, giving the camera a wide enough berth so that it wouldn't catch him on tape. He tiptoed behind the camera, making sure to stay in its blind spot, the branch raised in his hand.

He jumped and whacked the camera with the branch. It fell to the pavement, splattering into pieces.

"Shit." I bit my lower lip, praying that the police wouldn't come rushing over. Now was our chance to make a break for it. I grabbed the collar of Dev's shirt. "Come on!"

I scampered up the steps two at a time and slid the key into the door. The dead bolt clanked open.

Dev stood guard outside of his mom's office.

I was in the mayor's office, with pale cream, textured wallpaper, and a mahogany desk in the center of it. It reminded me of her home office, but more refined and functional—the woman had consistent taste. The fabrics on the chairs felt expensive.

I heard the door behind me open wider, so I darted behind the desk before someone saw me. Dev poked his head through the crack. "I think someone saw us. We gotta find another way out."

"Check the windows to see if they open," I whispered to Tanner while I rifled through the mayor's desk drawers.

I stared into the open drawer, my eyes widening as I fully processed what I was looking at. It was a crumpled bill. Like the one we'd found in the lock box.

"It's a Toulouse dollar. I threw this at Ron when he was chasing us."

"Wait." Dev blinked rapidly. "Chasing you?"

"I'll explain later." I held my hand up. I didn't want to relive the trauma of being chased through the woods. Not here. I shook my head. "How would your mom have something I gave to Ron? And look, she has more."

It was all there. All the crumpled bills were in the desk drawer. They looked like they'd been straightened, ironed out, preserved. She had babied these bills. This was important to her. Tanner sidled up next to me and bumped Dev out of the way, his eyebrows knitting together as he raided the drawer.

"The coins," he said, scraping the bottom of the drawer.

"And what's this?" I frowned, pulling out a tea-stained scroll. "It's a map."

It was a map of the most unexpected place. It wasn't a map of the old town of Toulouse. Or of the bank vault. Or even the old family homes we'd thought about raiding. It was a map of the old mine and of the excavated chambers within. It was more extensive than I'd imagined. And there was a mark along the side of the map in blue pen.

Water line.

Scrawled in a different pen color was another line farther down the bottom of the page. In hastily written cursive it said *New Water Line.* I scanned the map, slowly realizing that parts of the mine were drained of water just as the shoreline of Langston Lake was sinking in the ongoing drought conditions.

And below the map of the mine were stacks of papers, stapled and staggered. They were all cases with my grandmother's name on them. *Berenice Sutton v. Town of Langston.*

"What is this?" I mumbled under my breath, shuffling through the pile of papers. I pointed to one of the next stapled bunch, then closed my eyes, shaking my head as I finally realized what these were. These were my grandmother's lawsuits, all stacked neatly on the mayor's desk. Hornsby had been sitting on them the whole time. "I don't get it."

Tanner slid one of the packets across the desk and leaned forward, squinting in the dim light.

"Salvage rights?" Tanner read. "Your grandmother was suing the city for salvage rights."

"You better start talking." I shook a handful of pages at Dev, my nostrils flaring. "Did you know any of this?"

"What? No, *I swear.* You know my mom doesn't tell me anything. All I know is that she's been working really long hours, okay? I just thought she was taking this job a little too seriously. I mean ... she quit her job at the firm to work *less.* Now, we see her even less than we did when she was partner."

I fought back a well of tears. This was Grandma Bernie's legacy. She'd spent all of her money on these lawsuits. Everyone laughed at her. Even I did. But maybe we were all wrong. Maybe the mayor found something in it that rang true.

"Guys, the security guard is in the hall." Dev stuck his head out just enough for one eye to see past the door. He ducked back inside, worry painted across his face. "He's coming this way."

"Shit," Tanner grumbled, running his fingers through his hair, making it stand on end. "I say we take everything."

"The whole stack?" I asked. "But won't she notice?"

"Shots have *literally* been fired. This is fair game. Come on help me."

"Shh. He's coming closer." Dev held his finger up to his lips, signaling us to be quiet. Tanner gripped the windowsill, prepared to push it up, but Dev vehemently shook his head. "Nope—no time to run. Turn that flashlight off and hide."

Dev scurried across the room on his tiptoes, closing himself in the corner closet. Tanner and I ran for the thick drapes hanging over the far window. We opened the curtains, waking up a flurry of dust. My nose twitched, and I thought I might sneeze, so I quickly buried my face into Tanner's chest, hoping his shirt would shield me from the dust bunnies. He was warm and smelled faintly of chlorine, like he'd gone for an evening swim before meeting up with us.

The door creaked open, and the flashlight panned the room. I could see the light at my feet. I pressed my face farther into Tanner's shirt, and I felt his chest rise as he took a slow breath. Then it froze, like he was holding his breath.

We waited for what seemed like ages, until finally the light in the mayor's office waned and the sound of footsteps retreating grew fainter.

The door to the mayor's closet crept open, and Dev poked his head out.

"All right. I think the coast is clear."

TWENTY-FIVE

Forty days until we lose the house

The lockbox stared up at me from my desk. The old rusted thing taunted me, gave me hope by looking so important, only to turn out to be such a nuisance. This treasure was actually trash, and I still didn't understand how it connected to the old mine.

I should have left it at the bottom of the lake where I'd found it.

I'd already tried unscrewing the hinges, but they were fused on. I had a knife I wasn't afraid to use, and if all else failed, I'd use a blowtorch if only to see the lockbox burn. This thing had gotten me and all of my friends into a heap of trouble for nothing.

Mostly, I was mad at myself for giving up the meager contents of the box. It enraged me to think that the few things of value I'd gained from this stupid treasure hunt now lined the forest floor. I could have gotten a few hundred, maybe even thousands out of the coins and paper money. I could have bought a prom dress. I could buy books for school.

I was so completely disappointed with myself.

I swiped the box off my bed and slammed it onto my desk, making the contents rattle. B had taken a sledgehammer to it. That, plus a hundred years underwater—the box looked like it had seen better days. I picked it up, looking the busted lock squarely in its mangled hole. Then I turned my head and pressed my ear against it. I shook it, and the lock rattled again.

What key was Ron looking for, and why did he think we had it?

I opened the box and sighed. There was only one coin left—easy come, easy go. And only fragments of bills and the rest of the rusted lock that broke off inside.

I heard movement in the kitchen—more than the usual shuffling and darting through the house that had taken place since my mom and sister had left. I bounded out of my room, eager to see my mom.

Dad was at the kitchen table. Wearing actual khakis instead of pajama pants. He was rifling through a tool bag.

"Oh. I thought you were maybe Mom."

"Nope, just me. Sorry to disappoint." He ran his fingers through his hair and sighed. "But she said she'll be home in time for the centennial. Lucile says she might come with Bryant, too. So, you'll have that to look forward to at least."

"Dad . . . I'm sorry for what I said the other day."

"I think you meant all of that."

"Some of it. But I shouldn't have said it like that. It wasn't helpful."

"Ughhh. We both know you're right. I've failed you and your sister. And lord knows I've failed your mother. And myself. I need to start *doing* again." He lifted the wrench in his hand. "Why not start with the broken cabinet?"

I looked from him to the hallway where the box lay taunting me. That box had nothing to offer me. But maybe, my dad's company would be a balm to soothe me.

The garage was pretty much in the same condition as it was when I left—an overturned puzzle, pieces strewn across the concrete. The broken armoire cast in the corner. The lumpy old chair my father spent most of his waking hours in.

"I shouldn't have—" My voice trailed off as I knelt down. Yes, my feelings were valid, but the way I expressed them—goodness, I was so ashamed. I used my hand as a broom and swept the pieces together in a pile. Then I sank to the moving blanket, just as my dad did. And I set to putting the puzzle back together.

"Maybe I needed a swift kick in the pants," my dad grumbled under his breath. He looked up at me, his lip shaky. "I went to the bank the other day. To see what our options were."

"Oh?"

"My business may have filed for bankruptcy, but my personal credit is still relatively intact. And well, I qualified for a loan."

"Really?" My chest tightened as I held my breath. "You can save the house?"

"No, it's not nearly enough for that. But it is enough for the first semester of Barnard. Between this loan and your savings from working at the club and the money you'll get from selling your car, you'll have enough to put your mind at ease until you hear back from scholarships and work study programs."

"Dad. I—I can't take that. What about you and Mom? This house?"

"We'll figure it out, okay? Look, the bank actually had a hiring sign in the window, so maybe my finance days aren't over."

We laughed, a strained and awkward laugh to fill the discomfort hanging over us. My dad, who'd run a billion dollars of assets at his financial firm, was going to be one of the most qualified bank tellers. But at least he would be doing *something*. It reminded me of working at the Langston Country Club, a job I thought was beneath me. But at least I was doing something. And I didn't feel alone in being proactive. Not anymore.

"This one's a tough one," I said, looking at the cover of the box with the puzzle's picture on it. It was a seascape with a flotilla of boats in the background. And an expansive sky with lots of clouds. A very tricky puzzle, because when all the pieces were loose, they all looked the same—slight variations of blues and greens and whites.

And then I looked at the finished puzzles that he'd glued and preserved resting along the wall. A field of horses. A dock reaching out to a dark lake under starry skies. A cityscape of New York. He was piecing together images of the past—moments that were important to him. He was holding on to images of a life that didn't exist anymore.

"It's five thousand pieces. I don't know what I was thinking."

"You were thinking that you could do something big with your time. You can rebuild." I put the puzzle piece down and tilted my head to the side. I wasn't just talking about the puzzle. I was talking about his business that he built, the tower of success he'd stood on, and I was certain he could do it again.

And not just for the money. If I'd learned anything over the past few months, especially the past few weeks, money came and went. But it was important not to store all your self-worth in it. Otherwise, you'd be brought low every time.

"You're right though; this one is kinda impossible." I looked between several pieces that all looked the same.

"Sometimes the key is grouping the colors together and turning each piece to see if they go together. I think a lot about life when I do this. How things have a way of working out if you have the patience to see it through."

I smiled softly. And then the hair on the back of my neck stood up and my breath hitched.

The key.

"Thanks, Dad!" I yelled over my shoulder as I ran through the house, down the hallway and back into my room.

My hungry eyes looked at the lockbox. Instead of rattling it, I flipped the box upside down and dumped the contents onto the floor. And then I flipped it right side up and studied the keyhole. The lock was broken, but only a few of the fragments fit together to reform it.

There were several duller bits of metal left over. These slightly darker, rusty pieces were something else altogether.

Could this be the key?

Crouched over the pieces, I slid the metal chunks around the wood floor, turning pieces like I would a puzzle. And then one piece fit together. And after a while another did. It took me an hour to connect the mangled pieces back together. I slid the last small piece into place then sat back on my heels, my eyes growing wider.

It was an old iron key.

I crawled to my phone across the floor and texted the gang.

Guys, you've gotta see this.

TWENTY-SIX

Thirty-nine days until we lose the house

Squid wiggled a slender tube in front of my face. I squinted to read the letters on the side—*industrial strength superglue*.

"Are you sure this will hold metal?" I asked skeptically. I raised an eyebrow as I looked from the rusty key to Squid's grin. I didn't want to ruin the key beyond repair. For all we knew, it was the only copy. And it's not like we could make a duplicate. We didn't have a lock to take to a locksmith.

"Trust me. This stuff works like a charm. I've used it on all kinds of stuff—goggles, the siding on my grandma's house, B's motorcycle."

"What?" B's eye's narrowed. "You used glue on my bike?"

"No wonder it keeps breaking down." Tanner tucked his lips under his teeth, hiding his smile. He turned to me. "How did you figure this out?"

He looked at me with a mixture of wonder and admiration and my cheeks heated. He held my gaze for a moment too long and then coughed, turning his attention back to the key. He reached a finger out to touch it, but Squid slapped his hand away.

"Just give me some room to work my magic, okay?"

"Try the loop first, and see if it'll hold." We only had one shot at it. And I wanted to experiment on the part that didn't go into a lock.

"I got this." He slid on his safety glasses as he sat on the desk then laced his fingers together and pushed them outward, cracking his knuckles. He unscrewed the cap, and the smell instantly hit my nostrils—fumes and vapors, like a stronger version of my dad's puzzle glue. Squid turned to me and shrugged sheepishly.

"You're gonna want to open some windows." He bobbed his head from side to side, pursing his lips. "Unless we wanna hotbox the room. This shit'll get you super high."

"Ugh, you're such a glue-sniffer like your brother." B rolled her eyes and huffed as she walked to my bedroom window. She climbed onto my bed without even bothering to take off her shoes and pushed the pane up. She sank back on the mattress, looking at Squid with interest. "How is your brother holding up after the other night?"

"I only saw him once, and he looked okay." Squid shrugged, the tube of glue hovering over the key pieces. "He's been spending most of his time up on the mountain. Thinks he's some kind of lookout and that's his bird's nest."

"Well, for once, I agree," I said, leaning over the desk to watch him apply the first glob of glue onto the metal. "He saved our lives the other night."

Even with the window open, the fumes filled the room. I walked across the hallway and turned on the bathroom fan.

"What do you think this key unlocks?" Tanner leaned closer, brushing my arm. And then my breath hitched as I thought about the other night, when we'd slept on the couch together. My stomach churned, and my cheeks heated. I wanted to do that again.

And again.

"I don't know, but it's important. Ron wouldn't be chasing after it if it wasn't." B scooted to the edge of the bed. She pursed her lips, her eyes growing distant as she lost herself in thought. "So let me get this straight. You raided Hornsby's office and found the money you threw at Ron. So we've got her. They're clearly working together. Your hunch was right."

"Don't sound so surprised." I couldn't help but smirk at her look of wonder. "And there was a car in the Hornsby driveway, covered in a tarp. I know it was the banged-up Mercedes that Ron crashed into the guardrail."

"So, the mayor, the queen of the charmies, is responsible for siccing her hounds on us, chasing us through the woods, and is involved in a secret treasure hunt *herself*." B folded her arms, sauntering across my bedroom, her head tilted to the side.

"I know. It's *a lot*." I sighed, my head throbbing. "I just wish we knew what this key opened. The map shows the mine, but there are like a hundred chambers down there. She'll find us before we know what we're looking for."

"Then let's cut her off before she gets there first." She threw her hands in the air. "Let's hand the evidence to the cops right now. She'll get arrested. We'll be fucking heroes. We get more time to search the mine."

"You're kidding, right?" I gripped my forehead with my fingers.

"And how do you think we're going to tell the cops where we got our evidence?"

"Well…" B wrung her hands. Then her head snapped up. "We can say that we found it."

"Um, guys?" Squid raised his hand. But Tanner was already walking toward us, his hand on his hip.

"Case is right, B." Tanner shook his head. "We committed like five crimes breaking into the mayor's office. So everything we have from there is evidence *against* us. Just think it through."

"Guys!" Squid yelled.

"What?" Tanner and B said in unison, whipping their heads around to face him.

"We have another problem." Squid slid his chair away from the desk, revealing what he'd been working on. The key was still in pieces. "This key ain't opening anything."

"What did you do?" Tanner darted across the room and leaned over his shoulder. I followed suit and so did B until we were all crowding around Squid and the key.

"So remember when I said this was foolproof?" He held his hands up, as if he was turning himself in to the authorities.

"Lemme guess." Tanner narrowed his eyes at him.

"Uh, yup." Squid slapped his thighs. "This glue isn't sticking. The key is rusty and porous and it's not gonna hold."

"We could take it to the locksmith next to the pawnshop."

"Use your brain, B." Tanner groaned and turned away from her. He paced the length of my bedroom. "That dude's friends with Ron.

I'm pretty sure he'd talk about an ancient key some kids brought in to copy."

"Okay, fine. But I don't hear any better ideas! Unless you know of a way to make an exact replica of the key, this is a dead end." B raised her hands in exasperation. "The hunt is over *again*. And we can all go back to our lives."

"An exact replica?" Tanner's eyebrows shot up. "Could a three-D printer make it?"

"It would have to be state-of-the-art." Squid looked to the ceiling, wagging his head as he considered Tanner's suggestion. "One that can use a metal alloy."

"State-of-the-art like the one at Langston Academy?" I tilted my head to the side, locking my eyes with his. "You're a genius. But..."

"But what? You printed out all those goblets and chains. We'll just print out a key, and then we'll be good as gold."

"Those goblets took *hours* to print. Apiece." My heart sank. This was not a realistic plan. And after our criminal activity in city hall a couple nights ago, I didn't want to get caught doing anything else illegal.

"We could do it during prom." Tanner cocked his head to the side. "You know, if you're still up for going with me."

His gaze was intent, and I lost myself in his green eyes for a moment. B and Squid melted away, and it was just us. I nodded. Of course I wanted to go with him.

"Wait, what?" B's nostrils flared. "You guys are going to prom together?"

I nodded, vaguely registering her. "But I don't have access to the software." I may have been the president of the student body, but the keys to the copy room rested with the class secretary. That was Fatima.

How would I be able to get the keys from Fatima without telling her?

"Or I guess we could let Fatima in on it." My shoulder stiffened as I caught B's nostrils flaring. Her cheeks reddened.

"This just sounds like another charmie takeover," she fumed, taking a menacing step toward me. "First Dev. Now Fatima."

"You heard her, B." Tanner stepped between the two of us. "Fatima has the keys to the printer and the software. We *need* her. We can ask her when we go to dinner before prom, right Case?"

"I see." B laughed, but it didn't sound happy. It sounded more like a grumble. "It all makes sense now. No wonder you're taking her side on *everything*. It's 'cuz you guys are hooking up!"

"B, stop." Tanner veered his head to the side, his eyes unblinking. He was clearly ticked off, and honestly, so was I.

"Whatever is going on—or not—is none of your business." I stepped closer to her, my voice rising a few octaves. "Is this still about calling the cops? I thought we all agreed that that was a stupid idea."

"Jesus, how are you going to take her side over mine?" She pointed an angry finger at me. "This charmie downstreamer wannabe?"

"I thought you said I was one of you." My eyes tightened and I felt moisture pooling in the corners.

"I said a lot of things. But don't get it twisted. Before a few weeks ago, you didn't even know we existed. And after this little treasure hunt is over, you'll go back to ignoring us. And that day can't come soon enough. Move."

She barreled toward the door, banging my shoulder on her way out. The front door slammed. Then she revved her motorcycle loudly, the boom reverberating off the siding of my house. She sped away, leaving a trail of car alarms in her wake.

TWENTY-SEVEN

Thirty-three days until we lose the house

I nudged Tanner's side with my elbow and smiled as we approached the white Gatsbyesque facade. He gave a lopsided grin in return, then snaked his arm around my shoulder and led me over the threshold. His hand was warm and a bit clammy, and it suddenly dawned on me that he was nervous.

"Don't worry. She'll help us," I said with as much conviction as I could muster. Although if I were being honest, I wasn't entirely sure Fatima would help us hack the school's 3D printer. As the student body secretary, she would be breaking her oath of office by helping us commandeer school property for our own devices.

Squid was right. We *were* pirates.

"I'm not nervous," said Tanner. "What makes you say that?"

"Your hands are sweating. And you're doing that thing with your eyebrow. It twitches when you're amped up. It happens before races sometimes."

"You came to the swim meets?"

"A few. You never noticed?"

"I'm actually really surprised. I thought your crew was all about football."

"I hate football."

"I don't look in the stands at swim meets. There's too much pressure. If I meet my mom's eyes or my coach's, I can feel the pressure. And it really does a number on my headspace. So I focus on rolling my shoulders and warming up. It's kinda like a trance."

"I wish I could do that."

"Don't you?" His arm stiffened as he turned to me. "Sometimes I look at you, and you look like you're on another planet."

"I have a lot on my mind." I shrugged, feeling the weight of the world on my shoulders.

"I know." Tanner nodded resolutely. "I hear you."

And I looked up into his eyes, and saw how earnest he was. He heard me. He understood me. He saw me like most people never did. And my heart hiccupped at the thought of finding that in someone. And then my chest caved inward at the thought of this all being over soon.

Summer would end, with or without the treasure.

We walked side by side, our forearms knocking against each other as we neared the roundabout. Colonel Langston still sat atop his horse, his eyes following us as we strolled. The decorations for the centennial had already started to go up, and there was a red, white, and blue sash draped over his shoulder, and his pedestal was trimmed in patriotic bunting.

"Give me a break." I snorted under my breath. The casual observer would think that Colonel Langston singlehandedly saved the Union, that he was a great hero. But he was a Confederate soldier, fighting to uphold slavery. And then there was his connection to

Toulouse. I wasn't sure about his involvement in the town before it became abandoned—not yet. But from what I kept learning about him, I had a hunch that it wasn't going to be praiseworthy.

The myth of Langston the great benefactor was a lie.

"I always thought this statue was kinda creepy." Tanner linked his arm with mine, steering me away from it and toward the white marble stairs of the club.

Dylan and Fatima's limo was parked out front, so I knew they were already inside, probably partying it up in the private room. But I was in no rush to get there, not with my hand in the crook of Tanner's elbow.

"Ahh, the original deed to Langston," I said, gazing through one of the display cases that lined the hall. This piece of paper had granted all the land of Toulouse to Colonel Langston for mere pennies. It had enabled him to build the dam. It was arguably the foundation of all of our lives.

So why did I think it was a lie?

"It's strange though." I leaned over the case, trying to unlock this document's secrets. "How he was given a deed to the whole entire city. A city that was abandoned. Something doesn't add up."

"Well, if anyone's going to solve it, it's you." He cocked his head toward the private dining room.

"Ready to go into your trance?"

"Not a chance. Not while I'm with you."

The host guided us down the hallway with backlit portraits of old white people, the founders of Langston and the heads of all the top families. My family was never featured up there, even though we went back generations in this town. I always thought it was odd—but then again, we were Black. The host led us through the mahogany lined bar, past the dining room with the thirty-foot ceilings and circular tables lit by the dim glow of candlelight. The back wall was lined with French doors that looked out onto the lake. The moonlight twinkled on the still water. And there were a few people walking down the pier/boardwalk.

We entered the intimate private dining room, where there was raucous laughter. Dev was trying to twerk in the corner with Dylan and Pierce. Fatima stood with her arms folded, shaking her head as she looked at Dev, her last-minute date, with tight eyes—a touch of regret. She grabbed a water bottle filled with dark liquid, and guzzled down a few gulps. When she set the bottle down, she rubbed her chest, soothing the burn. Whatever was in that bottle, it clearly wasn't water. Their behavior seemed incongruous to the staid atmosphere of the old club. Or perhaps it was fitting—the rich kids with nothing to do but drink and make a mess. This was our life.

Well . . . it wasn't mine. Not anymore.

"Y'all missed a hell of a limo ride," Dev said from the other side of the room. He boomed "Shots, shots, shots!" Fatima's date jumped out of his seat and pumped his fist in the air. "Shots, shots, shots!"

"I love your dress." Fatima turned away from him, likely happy to have a distraction. "Omg, you look *so* good."

"I feel like I've seen it somewhere before." Dylan tilted her head to the side, her eyes alight with venom.

That backstabbing bitch.

"On the runways of Paris," Fatima suggested.

"Rent the Runway, more like," Dylan mumbled under her breath, but I could hear her. And I'm sure others could.

"She's charming," Tanner said as he pulled out my seat.

"Once a charmie always a charmie. Isn't that what B says?"

"With a few exceptions." Tanner smiled, an intimate knowing smile, one that stopped my heart.

He'd said I was one of them. And I was starting to believe him.

We sat at the end of the table. The waiters placed the menus in front of us. I nearly choked when I saw the prices. It had been a while since I'd been to the club—we weren't members anymore, and I couldn't bear to use Dylan or Fatima's guest pass. I didn't like being seen here anymore. I fidgeted in my seat. Tanner placed his hand over mine, and leaned closer to my ear.

"Who's nervous now?"

"I don't have much money," I said apologetically. My eyes flitted to the floor. I was too embarrassed to meet his gaze.

"Tonight, you can order anything." He lifted his chin proudly.

"No, I can't let you do that." I shook my head. I knew he worked overtime at the pawnshop and at his other odd jobs just to afford a new suit. I already felt bad enough. He had already been trapped into taking me to prom, because Fatima cornered us in the stacks.

"Between you and me, B is working tonight, so it's on the house." He squeezed my hand tighter. "She'll make sure of it."

"Are we sure she won't spit into it?"

"Just don't order that." His finger trailed across the page and landed on the surf and turf option—a filet and lobster combo for a whopping eighty-seven dollars. It had to be the most expensive thing on the menu.

Our shoulders shuddered as we both giggled.

"What are you two lovebirds laughing about?" Dylan asked from the other end of the table, her chin lifted. She looked like she was holding court.

"Just an inside joke." I bit the inside of my cheek. "You wouldn't get it."

"Already have inside jokes. Cute." Dylan rolled her eyes, clearly still annoyed at me, but I didn't care.

Dylan was not my friend. I didn't want to get mixed up in her energy, and clearly she didn't want to mix with mine. And I was cool with that.

The past few weeks had shown me what real friends could be like. I felt a pang in my chest at the thought that I had unresolved issues with B. We still hadn't spoken since the argument at my house, and I wanted to make sure we were cool. I set my palms against the table and scooted out of my chair.

"I'll be right back," I said, sliding my chair back to the table. Tanner shifted in his chair, looking up at me as if to ask me if I needed him to come, but I shook my head. This was between me and B.

I opened the double doors of the dining room and wove my way through the crowded restaurant to the back.

The chef de cuisine was behind the line, wiping her brow with the back of her hand as she plated a foie gras over roasted vegetables. B stood behind the cash register, a messy bun bobbing atop her head as she typed in an order on the computer—from memory of course. Her gaze flitted to me and then quickly back to the screen.

"What?" she mumbled under her breath. "If this is about the wait, we have a lot of people here, so you're gonna have to—"

"You know this isn't about the food," I said, cutting her off. "Can we talk about the other day?"

She didn't say anything—the only noticeable acknowledgment to what I said was the tightening of her jaw. I opened my mouth, prepared to apologize for overstepping, for even suggesting I bring in Fatima. But B beat me to it. She set her notepad on the counter with a huff.

"Look, can we not do this?" she asked through gritted teeth. "You'll call me an asshole, and maybe I deserve it, and then I'll beat myself up about it and feel like shit. So can we not?"

"You're not an asshole."

"Please. Like you haven't thought that. I know I'm no angel."

"You are *challenging.* I'll give you that." A nervous laugh escaped my lips at that generous characterization. "But you're also my friend. At least I thought you were."

B shrugged. "I've lived my life on the other side of people like you. I honestly don't get you sometimes."

"I've kept it one hundred with you. What else do you want?"

"I don't know." She crossed her arms and cocked her hips to the side. "You probably don't remember this, but your girl Dylan, ran her fingers through my hair—and I mean, fully grazed my scalp—right in front of you. And you said nothing."

"Are you sure I was there?" I frowned, hoping that she had me mistaken with someone else.

"Oh yeah, you were there. But not really." She held her chin up. "I just always thought you were in the sunken place."

"Ouch." The sunken place was where suppressed Blackness went to die. I thought about the times Dylan had run her fingers through my hair without my permission, all the times I'd heard a white classmate casually drop the n-word when they thought I was out of earshot.

The other Black one—that's how customers sometimes differentiated me and B. And I didn't correct them when I should have. Instead, I always swallowed my pride to appear unfazed.

B was right, I had been in the sunken place, tamping down the Blackness buried within me and below the lake's surface.

"Part of me still thinks that you'll turn your back on me and the crew. That you'll take the treasure and run. Because that's what charmies do."

"I'm not a charmie. And I don't need to keep proving that to you." This time I held my chin up automatically, from the confidence within. "I'm about to break into my school's lounge for our downstream crew. I just wish I knew we were still on the same side."

"We are." She tucked her lips in between her teeth and looked down at the keyboard instead of looking me in the eye.

"Then stop fighting with me. Seriously, I get enough of that with Dylan."

"She's a piece of work." B rolled her eyes.

"So are you. But in a good way."

TWENTY-EIGHT

Tanner led me by the small of my back as we walked down the hallway, lined with gold tinsel streamers. The glitter banners that I'd constructed with Fatima billowed softly from the hallway rafters. Langston Academy had been transformed into a glitzy wonderland.

We halted at the doorway where a small photo line was forming. The camera flashed as couples took their obligatory prom shot. When it was our turn, Tanner and I stepped up to the photo backdrop of Langston in its early days—a photo taken straight out of the pages of Langston's Gilded Age history books.

"Is this okay?" he asked as he snaked an arm around my waist.

"It's perfect."

We walked to the cafeteria, our elbows knocking against each other. I had the compulsion to reach out and grab his hand, but for some reason I didn't go for it.

The cafeteria had undergone a metamorphosis. It was even better than our party planning renderings could have imagined. The ceiling was draped in a soft tan tulle, making the tall ceiling appear lower. The tulle came to a point in the center of the room, like a grand and lush tent. And in the center was an elaborate chandelier with glass fixings and faux candlelight. Round tables surrounded a wood-paneled dance floor. And atop each table was a dimly lit candelabra surrounded by gold chalices and goblets, printed by the 3D printer.

All of those after-school party planning sessions had paid off.

"Last one to the dance floor has to get the drinks." Dev bolted to the dance floor, leaving Fatima with a frown.

"Who has the flask?" Dylan wafted her hand in the air, waiting expectantly for Pierce to pass her the booze.

"We'll catch up with you later." I linked my arm in Tanner's and gave the group a small wave.

"Dipping out so soon?" Dylan raised a judgmental eyebrow.

"We'll be back. We just wanna hit the photo booth real quick."

"Ahh, right. The photo booth in the stacks." She rolled her eyes. "No one ever reads in the stacks."

Fatima tapped the edge of her nose with her finger, then followed Dev to the dance floor. He looked over his shoulder, giving Tanner and me a knowing look, then flashed a wide smile.

Tanner and I scurried back to the hallway and sidestepped the prom photo stand as we made our way around the corner to the main staircase.

The printer was no longer in the hallway. It had been moved to the computer lab across the hall. We pressed our noses against the glass, our breath fogging up the windowpane as we stared at the 3D printer. Triumph surged through my veins, giving me a shot of adrenaline. This would work. I gripped the door handle, prepared to breeze into the room, but it didn't turn.

"Come on!" I jiggled the door handle again. When it refused to open, I kicked the bottom of the door with my shoe. "It's locked."

"We need *another* key?" Tanner brought both of his hands to his face and rubbed his temples. "This is just endless."

"Not really. I know how to get it."

I grabbed Tanner by the sleeve of his suit jacket and tugged him back toward the dining hall. His black leather shoes squeaked against the floor as he scrambled to keep up with me.

Fatima was seated at one of the tables with Pierce sitting across from her. Her eyes were hooded, half open as she listened to him drone on about the investment business his dad owned. Hearing him attempt to explain things way over his head was equal parts amusing and terrifying. He'd bored me thoroughly at dinner.

"Hey, guys." I slid into the seat beside her.

"Join us." Pierce nodded excitedly. "I was just telling Fatima that this is, like, a great time to buy. Like, the rate of return on—"

"Actually." I coughed, rubbing my sternum with my hand. "One of the chips from the snack table kinda scratched my throat. Could you guys get us some drinks?"

"Uh...yeah sure." His eyebrows knitted together.

"Thanks."

"Ugh! I owe you one. Dev left to go to the bathroom and left me alone with him." Fatima collapsed onto the table, her arms splayed out against the tablecloth. "Why can't he just shut his mouth and look pretty?"

"He *is* a talker." I jutted my lip to the side and gave her a conciliatory pat on the back.

"He talks more nonsense than Dylan. And that's saying something."

"Where is she, BTW?"

"Who knows. Probably stuffing the ballot box." She rose from the tablecloth, looking lazily around the room. "The girl is obsessed with being prom queen."

"Well, I have something that might liven the night up." I looked at Tanner, who was standing across the room at the drink table with Pierce. I twirled my finger, signaling for him to keep him occupied. *Stall him.*

"Oh?" Fatima perked up, and she sat up straighter.

"We need to get in the student council room and print something on the 3D printer." I squinted my eyes shut and scrunched up my face. Saying it out loud sounded way sketchier than I'd intended. I opened an eye to peek at Fatima's face.

"This has something to do with what you and Tanner have been up to?" She followed my gaze to where Tanner was standing with Dylan's date. He grinned and gave a sheepish thumbs-up. I smiled and hid my face on the side of my shoulder, hoping he didn't see my blush. Fatima nudged my foot with hers underneath the table. "You really like him, don't you?"

"Yeah." I caught my lower lips between my teeth. "It's so

unexpected. I tried to resist it. There's no point in catching feelings for someone right before graduation. It's so unfair."

"You can't help what the stars have in store for you." She squeezed my hand, even though I was rolling my eyes. Fatima had her charts and horoscopes, her planetary alignments and fate. But I didn't have faith in the universe. I'd spent so much time fighting against the forces that shaped my life—pushing my father to be better, lamenting over my grandmother's legacy, trying to shove my way back to the top—that I hadn't left room to trust in the stars. That was all fluff and nonsense, yet in this moment, Fatima seemed more grounded than I was. She gripped my hand tighter, her voice softening as she said, "You deserve happiness. You know that, right?"

I nodded slowly at first, then faster as that realization hit me to the core. I'd been singularly focused on finding that treasure to save my family, so that I could singlehandedly pull us out of the bank-ruptcy trenches. I'd lost sight of my needs along the way.

"Here." She slid her purse strap from the back of her chair and dug inside it, eventually pulling out her keys. Plucking the right one out of the bunch, she held it out for me to take. "Don't tell me what you're doing. I want plausible deniability. Wanna make sure I'm at Cal for my first day of classes."

My hand closed around the key, my chest caving in at the thought of my best friend being on the complete opposite side of the country as me. A couple weeks after graduation, she'd be in California.

"Fatima, you're the best." I choked on a fresh wave of tears.

"I know." She fluttered her eyelashes, her eyes dewy. "Go raid the lounge. Then make sure you leave room for some actual fun tonight."

"It's done," I whispered into Tanner's ear, making him jump in his folding chair. He was seated at one of the round tables to the side of the dance floor.

"Already?" He turned in his seat, and leaned closer toward me. "I thought it was going to take hours."

"No." I bent my head and giggled into my fist. "It's modeled and being printed now."

He cocked his head and pursed his lips.

"Why do you do that?" He reached out and touched the side of my wrist with his finger. "Why do you hide your facial expressions. You do it a lot."

'I didn't realize I did." I blinked, startled by the intensity of his expression. I wanted to turn away, but I didn't want to give him yet another example.

"You don't have to hide yourself with me."

"Would you like to dance?" I could feel my cheeks heating, but I squared my shoulders and kept my eye contact with him, feeling bold and confident.

"Lead the way." He held out his hand, and I took it gladly.

Feeling the warmth of his hand made my insides feel like they were melting, I had never felt like this with anyone before. When we got to the dance floor, he swayed back and forth to the rhythm of the music. Each song morphed into another, and I lost myself in the beat of our bodies, in the thrum of the bass, until a microphone squeaked to life.

"May I have your attention please?" The dean of Langston Academy raised his hands, lowering them slowly to encourage quieter chatter. "I'd like to announce the winner of prom court this year."

He opened the envelope in his hands and slid his glasses down the bridge of his nose.

"Your choice for prom king is Pierce Burns, and for prom queen it's—" He squinted at the page, raising his eyebrows. "It's Fatima Haldipour."

My jaw dropped as the hall erupted in cheers and applause. I twirled around to find Fatima in the crowd, who was clasping her cheeks with both hands, the shock evident on her confused face. She took a hesitant step toward the stage, her shoulders shuddering as other students patted her on the back and hollered out her name.

Pierce sidled up next to her, leaving a stunned Dylan standing alone, her cheeks flushed.

"Go, Fatima!" I yelled above the crowd.

All those funny flyers she'd made for Dylan, all that campaigning she'd done on behalf of an undeserving friend, had paid off anyway. It must have increased her exposure to the student body, and when it came time to vote, she'd left the most-lasting impression on everyone.

She deserved this.

The winner's waltz began to play, and the crowd of students backed away, forming a circle around Pierce and Fatima. Pierce held his hand out, but Fatima shook her head, choosing instead to twirl to the music on her own. She would dance to the beat of her own drum, with or without a crown.

When the dance ended, all the students closed in on her, congratulating her on her win, taking selfies with her to commemorate the occasion. Tanner wrapped his arm around my shoulder, his face flushed with excitement.

"You wanna take a break?" I pointed to our table at the edge of the room. It seemed far enough away from the heat of the dancing crowd.

"Take a walk with me." He flicked his head to the double doors that led to the terrace. His voice was thick, deeper than it usually was.

And my stomach did another somersault as we went outside.

"Thank you for coming to prom with me." He leaned against the stone railing, looking out onto the placid waters of the lake.

"I should be thanking you." I covered my face with my hands remembering Fatima finding us in the stacks and how she'd thrust us together. I was still so embarrassed.

"Don't do that. Not now." He touched my wrist again, requesting that I not hide my true emotions. It was dark, but his green eyes caught the light of the lampposts, and in them, I could see their intensity. "The past couple weeks have been pretty fun—hanging out with you. I know we still haven't found the treasure, but we've gotten so far. And, well, we couldn't have done any of this without you."

I looked to the lake, my eyes tightening as they closed in on the Drop Point. "That's high praise coming from the state's number-one freestyle swimmer."

He squinted skeptically at me. "There go my stats again. Why do you know them?"

"I looked you up, of course. Because, ya know…" My voice trailed off as I tried to think of something funny—like *I had to know who I was swimming with the other day.* But his penetrating eyes could see right through that—because that wasn't the truth. He wasn't holding anything back tonight, so neither would I. "Because I… like you."

I gripped the back of his neck, my fingers rubbing the small hairs at the nape. He leaned forward and paused, as if he was unsure of what to do next. I pulled him closer.

Our lips touched, softly at first, as if we were figuring out each other. He breathed softly against my lips as he repositioned. And my hands gripped his neck tighter. His hands slipped into my hair, pulling the tendrils loose from the nest of bobby pins. And then the kiss deepened into something hungrier, more urgent.

I turned my face to the side, catching my breath, and his lips moved to my neck and my ear, nibbling it softly.

"I had no idea you liked me like that." His breath was hot against my face, sending goose bumps up my spine.

"I do." I whispered with a chuckle. "I just wish I'd said something sooner."

I didn't know what this key would hold, if it would yield the treasure we so desperately sought. I didn't know if I needed the treasure anymore when I had Tanner in my arms right now. We had only now, only this summer, until we parted ways for college and for lives that would undoubtedly be separate.

But I couldn't think about that now.

I pulled him closer for another deep kiss.

TWENTY-NINE

The next morning, I leaned against the side of the galley near the club's kitchen, reading the calendar to see where Ms. Harold had assigned me. I was supposed to be in the private dining room, rolling cutlery napkins and steaming glasses. I followed the soft clank of glasses and silverware and found Tanner wiping down the stemless wineglasses. I knocked on the doorframe, making his head snap in my direction.

"Dish duty again?" I asked.

"Those pesky fingerprints. They never quit." Tanner shook his head, his mouth drawing into a wry grin. He waved his gloved hand at me. "Hi."

"Hi, yourself." I covered my mouth with my hand, hiding my smile. But then I remembered what he'd said last night—that I hide my expressions, my emotions. I lowered my hand, letting him see my wide smile. I wanted him to know how glad I was to see him. Grabbing a stack of napkins off the dining room table, I set up my station next to his.

He reached over me to grab another glass, even though he had plenty beside him. His gloved fingers grazed my arm, and for a second, I was lost in the memory of our kiss last night. My face heated so much I thought I was going to implode.

"You're doing that on purpose." I coughed, clearing my throat and trying to sound unaffected.

"Maybe I am." He set his glass down and tilted his head to the side, his dimple growing deeper as he looked at me.

I couldn't help but lean forward. I was drawn to Tanner. I had been for a while. But now I didn't have to hide it. I was inches away from his face when I heard a loud smack on the doorframe. Tanner and I jolted apart, our breathing heavy.

"So, last night was a success?" Squid asked, his hands clasped expectantly.

"Oh, yeah." Tanner nodded emphatically then gave me a side-long glance. His fingers grazed against mine. "We took the night by storm."

"Why do I get the sense that we're talking about two different things?"

"Because you are, Squid." B draped her arm over his shoulders and pointed two fingers at Tanner and me. She whispered loudly so that we all could hear: "Different lock and key situation over there."

I rolled my eyes, praying for the ground to open up and swallow me whole. Tanner and I hadn't banged last night, but I didn't exactly want to get into those details with the rest of the gang. That was between us.

My phone buzzed in my back pocket, a welcome distraction from the awkward conversation. It was a text from my mom.

"Oh," I said. Tanner raised his eyebrow. "My mom. She's actually coming home this week. And she says she has a surprise."

"That's great news, right?" He nudged me with his elbow. "I know you've been worried about it."

"*Very* good news." I nodded, feeling my chest deflate. It was as if I'd been holding my breath for weeks, wondering whether my mom would actually return home or if she'd choose to stay in Atlanta forever.

"How's your head?" B reached up on her tiptoes and tousled Tanner's hair. "I saw you guys pounding shots in here last night."

"I really didn't get that drunk. I mean...yeah, I was tipsy. But I knew exactly what I was doing."

"Well, you're miles ahead of Dev. He's not looking excellent."

"He's here?" I cocked my head to the side, surprised to hear that Dev was out of bed before noon.

"He's in my section and looks like shit." B poked her head out of the doorway to the dining room and checked him out. A small chuckle escaped her lips before she turned to me. "He was asking for you."

I thought I caught a flicker of a frown on Tanner's face, but I wasn't sure. I stepped away from my folding station and smoothed my apron, then swiped one of the iced water carafes off the galley counter and made my way over to B's section.

Sure enough, Dev sat hunched over his table near the window, his sunglasses still covering his eyes, even though he was inside. He gave me a limp wave when I approached his table.

"You look like you could use this." I poured more water into his glass. "I can't believe you're even alive right now."

"Me neither. Fatima went hard last night." He ran his fingers through his hair, sighing heavily. Then he paused, his mouth widening. He slid his sunglasses to the top of his head, revealing a pair of wide, bloodshot eyes. "Shit, I just realized how that sounded. Nothing like *that* happened."

"It would be fine if it did. Seriously." I tried to stifle my laugh, but I couldn't help myself.

"I actually had someone else in mind," he said, tilting his head toward the veranda where B was handing out entrées.

"Stop." I gawked at him, my eyes darting to B and then back. "You serious?"

"I think she might go for it if I play my cards right." He watched her for a moment longer, but when her gaze flitted over to our side of the restaurant, he blinked away. He smiled guiltily at me, his eyes begging me not to give him shit about it. Then he leaned forward and whispered, "So you got the key?"

"Yeah, thanks for your help. It's actually in my pocket. If you wanna see?"

"Don't pull it out. Not here. My mom . . . she has eyes *everywhere*." He looked over his shoulder as if someone at the next table was eavesdropping on our conversation. "And it's not paranoia. She knows something's up. Ever since her office was broken into, she's been fuming."

"Does she know it was us?" I lowered my voice to little more than a whisper.

"No. But I think she suspects. She's been asking me questions, everywhere I go, every call I get. So...just be careful."

"Got it." I nodded and picked up the water carafe. "You'll let me know if she starts to make another move on the treasure?"

"You know it."

Thirty-one days until we lose the house.

My mom stood in the kitchen, slightly breathless from carrying all of her luggage into the house. Her cheeks were flushed and slightly raw looking, like she'd spent a lot of time out in the sun. There was barely any sign of her haggard appearance of late.

"Hello, darling." She opened her arms, beckoning me into them.

"Hi, Mom." I closed the gap between us and squeezed her tightly, breathing in the familiar smell of her. I pulled back and laughed at the mess of bags surrounding us. "You have more stuff than when you left."

"Just a few things here and there. Lucile's roommate is purging everything from her closet in preparation for her summer at *Marie Claire*. And well, there were a few tasteful things in there." She bobbed her head from side to side, her lips pursed with an edge of indignance. "I couldn't let them go to waste, and I still have my figure. I may have lost everything else, but I still have *that*."

"You look good." She did look youthful and less hollowed out than she had a couple weeks ago, albeit a bit sunburned.

"You think so?" She grazed her cheeks with the tips of her

fingers. "We went to this spa and Lucile told me to get anything within reason, and so of course I opted for the new mini mélange chemical peel. Lucile says it gives you *Jell-O* skin, which apparently is all the rage now."

"That explains it." I mumbled under my breath. My mom wasn't sunburned. Her raw face was self-inflicted. She'd had a chemical peel.

"Speaking of your sister, she also wanted me to give you this." My mom dug around in her purse and pulled out a thumb drive, which she shoved into my unsuspecting hand. "It's apparently got some old cases on it—though I wish you two wouldn't dig into your grandmother's past. She was clearly not in her right mind, and dwelling in the past isn't going to help us now."

Those haggard shadows crept up beneath her eyes as she sighed heavily.

"I know," I said, stuffing it in my pocket. I didn't really need these cases. I'd stolen the mayor's copies and had already combed through them.

"And she wanted you to get a chance to thumb through this." She held a weathered book out to me and then snatched it away as it grazed my fingertips. "And she said—well, I'm not going to give the exact wording, because honestly your sister's vocabulary is in the gutter these days. But she said it's very important that you not lose this, because it's quite old and out of print and on loan from the library."

I grabbed the book out of her grasp, my eyes widening as I read the title.

THE TIMES OF TOULOUSE

"No way! I've been looking for this book everywhere." I traced the embossed lettering on the cover, my eyes growing dewy. I gripped my mom's sleeve. "Thank you. Seriously."

"You're welcome, Case." She shook her head slowly, clearly surprised that this old, tattered book had such an effect on me. She tapped her manicured finger against the cover. "She'll want it back when she comes for Founder's Day next week."

"Wait—she's coming?" My eyebrows shot up.

"Yes, and she's bringing her boyfriend—such a sweet boy. She lent me her car, so she'll be driving it back. It'll be marvelous, all of us together." She clasped her hands, her nostrils flaring. "Speaking of Founder's Day, we thought you might be interested in this."

She pulled out a bag from her pile of belongings and reached in, pulling out a glittering jewel of a dress. Red with thin straps and a sweetheart neckline.

"For me?"

"This one's all yours. What do you think?"

"It's perfect." I held it up to my body, turning so that I could see my reflection in the window.

"I thought so, too." She smiled over my shoulder as she appraised my reflection in the kitchen window. Then a frown formed on her face. "I'm sorry I didn't get to see you in your prom dress."

"It's okay." I shrugged. "I wore the same one I wore last year."

"Still . . . I wish I could have been here. It's just . . . I needed a pause if that makes sense."

"It does." I flung the dress over my shoulder and turned to face her. "I'm just glad you came back."

"Always." She grazed the backs of her fingers against my cheek. She scrunched up her nose, the light returning to her eyes. "Try it on and tell me what you think."

"Oh," Dad said, poking his head out of the garage. He opened the door farther, revealing his polished appearance—he was wearing khakis and his beard was trimmed. He looked more put-together than he had in a long time. He'd clearly made an effort for my mom.

"Hello," my mom said in a breathy whisper, her raw, peeled cheeks deepening their pink color.

"I thought I heard your voice." He took a tentative step forward and then stopped. "It hasn't been the same without you."

They stood there, exchanging tender looks. And I suddenly felt like I was intruding.

"I'll let y'all catch up."

I tucked *The Times of Toulouse* book under my arm and grabbed my dress and backed away from my parents, smiling as I rounded the corner to the hallway. They had a lot of catching up to do. I gripped the book tighter, feeling hope on the horizon.

THIRTY

Twenty-six days until we lose the house

The school was empty by the time I picked up my cap and gown from the administration office after my last exam Friday afternoon. My head was crammed full with facts from *The Times of Toulouse*, swimming with pictures of the town before it was destroyed, and after the buildings were bombed. Personal accounts of the carnage lined the pages. It confirmed my suspicions about Toulouse. Toulouse did not die of natural causes. It was burned down by cannons and gunfire, by a mob led by Colonel Langston, who had everything to gain by their demise. The people of Toulouse did not want to relinquish their land in favor of the dam, so Langston found a way to drive the residents out. And then the colonel covered it up with eighty feet of water. It was hard to not let my thoughts drift to the gunfire, hard to focus on my exams. But I managed to eke by.

School was officially over, our lockers cleared for next year's students. With my bundle of graduation clothes tucked under my arm, I strolled down the empty hallway, stopping at Mr. Brown's classroom. The door was ajar, but I knocked anyway before pushing it open farther.

"Ms. Whitecroft!" He looked up from his desk, his smile widening. "The conquering hero. How does it feel to be done?"

"A little weird, I guess." I shrugged. This was all I'd known for the past several years. Breaking the routine of coming to the academy would be an adjustment. And my absence would be even more profound for my parents. We still did not have enough money to pay my grandmother's back taxes, and I couldn't really help them, besides searching for the treasure. And that was a long shot.

I did not feel like a conquering hero. I felt kinda beat down.

"Can I ask you a quick question?" I asked, leaning against the doorframe. "I've been reading up on salvage rights and saw that it mostly applies to international waters."

"Yes, navigable waterways is also a component." He shook his head with a chuckle. "You know, you're the second person to mention salvage rights to me this week."

"Really?" I pushed off of the wall, standing at attention.

"This doesn't have anything to do with Mayor Hornsby's thing?" He shifted in his seat to face me in the doorway.

"Mmhmm." I nodded, hoping I sounded convincing enough. "I—we're helping her with . . . the thing."

"It's a pretty elaborate idea to have a scavenger hunt on Founder's Day, but . . ." With a small chuckle, he scratched his bald head. "But I don't know how many people will want to run around the old mine in their tuxedos and ball gowns."

"You know the mayor." I laughed awkwardly. "She's full of surprises."

"She is indeed. Always keeping me on my toes." He opened a drawer and took out a notebook with his scribbles on it. "Tell her that the law of salvage is pretty antiquated and it applies to the lake only, so I'm not sure how much water that would hold when we're talking about the mine. But she is right about one thing."

"Yes?" I said in a breathy whisper. I desperately wanted to know what conclusions she'd made about the lake and my grandmother's cases. "What did she say?"

"The theory of abandoned property is a better angle for the scavenger hunt." He ripped the page out and held it for me to grab. "You can give this to her if you want, but please do remind her that I'm no lawyer. I'm just a history nerd."

"So," I said, reading the page as quickly as I could. "The property in the lake is salvageable, but the stuff in the mine is not in a navigable waterway, so it's abandoned property?"

"That's right." He smirked. "But it's just a game, right? I don't think the other participants will care either way how she words the premise of the game."

"I know. This is probably more detail than anyone wants to know." I folded the page and slid it carefully in my back pocket. "But I'll make sure she finds out."

I held out my hand to shake.

"Thank you for everything you've taught me. Truly, I learn so much every single time I talk to you, especially today. See you tomorrow at the Centennial Founder's Day."

Toulouse had lost something long ago—its brick and mortar, its identity, its wealth. Grandma Bernie had lost her legacy in those ruins. And it was time to get it back. The mayor's map was clear: the key would unlock something in the mine. And that something was the treasure.

Right?

We gathered at the Hollow, toting our contributions to the supply list Squid had drawn up. It was a hodgepodge of gear. A couple of hydro-flasks and a duffel bag from the Dive, donated by Dev. Some climbing rope and hooks from Tanner. And flashlights from my garage. I surveyed the supplies, wondering if we were truly prepared to go into the mine. B brushed my shoulder as she set a long slender box onto the table next to the rest of our mishmash of supplies. I studied the label and it read—*Ultimate Party Pack, 100 Glow Sticks.*

"Did you go to a rave or something?" I raised my eyebrow at B.

"You know it." She smirked. "It's only about half full, but I figured it would come in handy."

"And last but not least." Squid grinned as he set his safety glasses and a pair of swim googles into the duffel bag. "For eye protection. Could get dusty down there."

He then placed a bundle of brownish sticks into the mix. Tanner reached out and stilled his hand. He shook his head, slowly at first and then faster.

"Dynamite? You've really lost your mind this time." He grabbed the sticks by the fuses, as if he was afraid to come into contact with them. Then he walked to the corner and dropped them into the trash can.

"What if we need to blow something up?" Squid asked over his shoulder as he ran to the trash can to retrieve his explosives.

"I think Squid should stand guard outside." I eyed Squid warily, seeing the fire of adventure in his eyes, the twitch of his trigger-happy fingers. He could not be trusted to do no harm in the mine.

"Oh, come on. I even provided the safety goggles."

"All in favor of not letting pyro-Squid blow up the mine." Tanner raised his hand, casting his vote. My arm shot up in swift agreement.

B chewed on the inside of her cheek and shook her head apologetically.

"Sorry, dude." She patted him on the shoulder before raising her hand.

"Okay, the ayes have it."

"Fine. We'll need these." He handed over two walkie-talkies.

THIRTY-ONE

The paved road ended shortly after Squid's Hollow—a sign that we were leaving the outskirts of Langston and into the no-man's land of the unincorporated township. The gravel crunched underneath the tires as we ascended up the steep hill.

There were tents scattered around the top of the hill. And the trail leading to the old mine was littered with beer bottles and discarded trash. This was beyond the reach of utility services, beyond the grasp of rules, in the gray area of law enforcement and land ownership. This was the forgotten edge of town where the burnouts and ruffians ruled.

After Tanner put his truck in park, I opened the passenger side door and felt their eyes on me, watching me as I walked toward the mine entrance, feeling their scrutiny on my back. I wondered if I was welcome up here. I gravitated closer to Squid. He was the closest link to this crowd that any of us had, because his brother hung out up here.

"You can't park there," said a long-haired guy with bangs swooping over his eyes.

"Where should I move it?" Tanner asked.

"About two miles back down there." He pointed down the gravel road—the one we'd just traveled up.

"Very funny. Where's Seb?" Squid asked.

"Who's asking?" The guy nodded at me and Tanner and B. He pointed at the duffel bag that was full to bursting at Tanner's feet and laughed. "Look at this corny motherfucker."

"Hey, new guy. Tell Seb his brother's here. And that it's important." Tanner's voice boomed, reverberating off the entrance to the mine. He took a step forward, his nostrils flaring. "Seriously dude. We don't have a lot of time."

"Yo, Scuiducci?" The guy with bangs leaned against one of the metal beams supporting the entrance. "We got a situation up here."

"What?" Seb ducked his head as he scampered out of the mineshaft. "What the hell are you doing here, Squid? I told you not to check up on me."

"I'm not checking up on you, dude." Squid cowered away from his brother's imposing stance. I linked my arm in his, hoping to lend him some extra strength. He straightened his back, puffing out his bony chest. "We need to get in there."

He pointed behind his brother's back. Seb turned slowly, following Squid's finger to the entrance to the old mine. His chest rumbled as he barked out a laugh.

"No way, bro." He waved his hands, his chuckle subsiding. "Thad, tell 'em what you told the other charmies trying to get in here."

"This is a restricted zone." Thad crisscrossed his arms into an X, looking serious. But then a smile tugged at his lips and he dissolved into a fit of laughter. He shoved Seb's shoulder. "You 'member that part in *The Terminator* when that bro was all like—"

"Wait," I said, cutting him off. "Someone else tried to get in here?"

"This guy comes up here a couple months ago. Says he's gonna go *swimming* in there. Had all this snorkeling equipment and everything. And we're like, you're crazy, dude. And then he leaves, right. But check it. He comes back a few weeks later with like…this letter. What was it called?" Thad frowns and turns to Seb for support.

"A cease and desist." Seb slaps Thad's arm. "Signed by the mayor and everything."

"But that shit don't work up here." Thad held his arms up in another X. "So we kicked him off the mountain again. Dude hasn't been back since."

"And he ain't coming back." Seb folded his arms, smiling smug—clearly pleased with himself.

"That's because he's dead," Tanner piped up. He walked up, scrolling through his phone. He held up a picture of the missing diver's driver's license. "Is this the dude?"

Seb stepped forward, squinting at the screen. His smug smile waned as realization swept over him. His jaw slackened.

"We didn't do *anything* to him," Seb stammered, looking to Thad and then back to Tanner. "We just scared him off with a few bang snaps that we threw at his feet."

What was with the Sciiducci family and explosives?

"Do you have any more of them?" Squid stepped forward, his eyes wide with excitement. "Maybe some bigger Pop-Its? Those really let it rip."

"Wait." Seb scratched his head. "You actually *want* us to fire off explosives? You *never* want us to do that."

"Today is your lucky day." I shook my head. I couldn't believe that I was encouraging him. But we really needed his help. "Because I have a feeling that guy's friends are coming back."

"And they have guns." Tanner raised his eyebrows. "Like the gun they fired last week."

"You scared them away with those bottle rockets." Squid gripped his brother's arm. "And we need you to do it again."

"Sick." Thad nodded, his grin wide as he looked to his friend. But Seb wasn't smiling. He peered at Squid with concern. "Who'd you piss off?"

"Oh, just the mayor and her goons. Found a dead guy, broke into her office, stole her stuff." Squid gave an exaggerated shrug, his shoulders rising to graze his earlobes. "You're not the only delinquent in the family."

Seb's lips twitched, flitting between disbelief and pure joy. Finally, he broke out into an earnest smile. He gripped his brother's shoulder and shook him, rattling his wiry frame.

"I knew we were related." He laughed for a moment and then looked to the rest of us. "I don't know what y'all want down there. It's nothing but shafts and water. But even most of that has dried up."

"We're counting on it," I said.

"But if more people are coming after you, we need more hands on deck." Seb released his hold on Squid and held his hands out. "So who's it gonna be?"

"You keep watch, okay?" I nudged Squid with my elbow. "This is your moment to fire off that dynamite. Oh come on, I saw you put it back into the duffel bag when you thought no one was looking."

"What?" Tanner flung his head back. "You didn't!"

"You heard my brother. We need emergency firepower." He hung his head low, hiding his guilty smile. "You three go in. Don't worry. We've got it covered up here."

"Come on, let's go." Tanner gestured to B, then grabbed my hand as we stepped toward the mine. B took a tentative step forward with us, then she staggered several steps back.

"Wait. Uhhh." She shook her head as she looked into the dark mineshaft. "I'll stay out here, too."

"You're not coming?" I asked.

"*No.* No, I'm not going in *there.*" She slowly backed away from the hole, her footsteps echoing off the rocks around the entrance as she picked up the pace. She pressed her back against the outside wall of the mine. Tilting her head toward the sky, she took a deep breath of the fresh air outside.

"What's up with her?" Seb scoffed.

"She's claustrophobic," Squid said, elbowing him in his side.

"It's tight. Dark. Small spaces." She blinked rapidly, her breathing quickening. "I can't. I just . . . *can't.*"

"Then this is definitely not your cave, girlie." Seb patted her on the shoulder, rumbling her uneasy stance.

B scowled at him so forcefully that he looked away. She did not like being called *girlie*. It was likely worse than calling her *Barbie*.

"Okay, just breathe." I closed the gap between us and wrapped my arms around her. I hugged her for a while, waiting until her breathing slowed and her heart rate normalized. "We'll be okay. Seriously."

"I'll signal for you if anything goes south," she said, her breathing still ragged from her frayed nerves.

"What's the signal?" Tanner asked.

"Call of the wild, dude." Seb threw his head back in a howl, followed by Thad.

Then Tanner and I gripped each other's hands and stepped into the mouth of the mine.

THIRTY-TWO

The entrance to the mine was narrow, smaller than the size of a standard doorframe. I couldn't imagine being a miner, working here day in and day out, crouching down into the darkness. It smelled damp and stale, like wet earth and mildew.

The lighting instantly dimmed. It was no longer the middle of the day. It felt like it was twilight, moments away from complete darkness. I took out my flashlight from the duffel bag and clicked it on.

I ran my fingers along the rough stone walls, tracing the veins of browns and tans that streaked across the rock. A gust of wind whooshed out of the mine with enough force to blow my hair back.

"It's been doing that." Squid's brother shrugged before ducking into the mine.

He knelt down as he walked, trying not to bump his head on the low clearance of the ceiling.

He slowed when he reached the end of the passageway, and I shined my flashlight at his feet, where there was a man-size hole. A wooden ladder poked out just above the rim. I leaned over, trying to see to the bottom of the chamber, but I couldn't see anything. The ladder seemed to plunge into darkness.

"I went down there once." He shook his head, and his eyes grew distant. "It's darker than dark down there. And completely flooded. You can't touch the bottom."

"You sure about this?" Tanner asked. And I could tell by the way he looked that he was having second thoughts. Before I had a chance to respond, a low whimper sounded from behind him. B poked her head into the mouth of the cave, giving us a thumbs-up.

"I'll go first," Tanner said with a gulp.

"No. I'll go. Keep B calm." I stepped in front of him and knelt at the ladder. Carefully I took the first step onto the top rung. "I hope this doesn't break."

"Wait." Tanner grabbed my sleeve just before I stepped down to the next rung. "Tie this rope around your waist and loop your flashlight string into your belt loop. Yeah, thread it through like that. I won't let go of the other end, I promise."

I stepped down the ladder, feeling the rope brushing against my back. It was a reminder that Tanner wasn't going to let me fall.

My sneaker tore through the third rung, and I slid down the ladder. I tightened my grip around the sides of the ladder, feeling stray shards of ancient wood puncture my skin. I screamed in pain and released my right hand, seeing the large splinter poking out of my palm.

"I can't hold on!" I yelled. My left hand was the only thing holding me up. And my hand was sliding down. My feet wiggled, trying to find the next step. I stepped on it, and the wood immediately collapsed under my weight.

"It's rotted. The wood!" I yelled up. The wood, which had been underwater for the better part of a hundred years, could not bear any weight.

"I've got you."

I abandoned the ladder and grabbed the rope, tightening my thighs around it to find more support. I slid down it as I went deeper and deeper into the bottom chamber. The blood made it slick and slippery, and I lost control of my speed. It was rope burns and screams until I touched down on the floor, crashing to the stone with a splatter.

"Casey!" Tanner's shaky, urgent cry echoed all around me. "Casey, are you okay?"

"I'm alive!"

Or at least I thought I was. I dragged myself onto my elbows, blinking my eyes, rubbing the back of my head. I tried to turn on my flashlight, but it wasn't working.

Panic crept up my spine, prickling the little hairs on the back of my neck. I could feel goose bumps dot my skin. I was at the bottom of a mine shaft with no light. There could be any number of things lurking in the shadows. Creatures who could see in little to no light.

I whipped around, my breathing ragged as I tried to orient myself. I blinked furiously, trying to speed up my eyes' adjustment to the darkness. All I could see were tiny glimmers, twinkling glows as the walls picked up the light from Tanner's flashlight.

The stone ground was wet, with intermittent pools of water.

And my footsteps echoed, louder than they had up top. This had to have been a bigger room than before—than even the map indicated.

"Hurry," I called up to Tanner, as I untied the rope so he could use it to climb down. And my voice reverberated off the cavernous walls.

I gasped, suddenly remembering that I had some of B's glow sticks in one of my pockets. I fished in my back pocket and yanked one out, bending it until I heard the familiar crack. The artificial glow strengthened as the chemicals reacted. And then I brandished it in front of my face, as if it was a weapon I could use to ward off the monsters that lurked in the shadows. I spun around and around until I was certain that the only living creature was me—and Tanner dangling from the rope above me.

As my eyes refocused I could finally see the walls and what was causing the dim shimmers.

"Whoa." I twirled around, looking at the veins of silver streaking throughout the rock. "You've gotta see this."

This silver mine was not past its prime. It was obviously still very lucrative. I was told that Toulouse was a defunct mining operation, that ore dried up and the town shrank with it, that it was essentially abandoned when Langston stumbled upon it. But these shimmering walls told a different story—a buried history. It spoke to the wealth of Toulouse, the promise of its people, and just how much its citizens had lost.

Everything—*every single damn thing* about the history of our town was a lie.

And that realization buckled my knees. I sank to the ground, my jaw slackening as I craned my neck to look at the splendor. I tucked my hand under my arm, and my palm bled into my shirt.

"I'm almost there," Tanner said as he climbed down the rope. He didn't look at anything else but the rope, occasionally looking down to check on me. He hopped down to the ground with a splash.

"Are you okay?" He gripped both of my shoulders, stilling me. He lowered his head to survey the damage, tracing his fingers along the scratches on my elbows and forearms. He held my hand, swiping his finger over my bloody palm. "This might hurt."

"It can't be worse than how it feels now."

He held his flashlight underneath his chin and clamped down with his hand. His firm grip on my hand tightened as he pinched the wood shard and tugged slowly, I winced as the tinier barbs of wood caught on my skin. My eyes filled with tears, but I refused to scream. I brought my fist to my mouth and hissed through the pain.

Finally the tugging ceased, and I blinked my eyes open, catching on tears, sending the dim light into prisms.

"Are you okay? I don't have any first aid. How could we forget first aid but remember glow sticks and dynamite? We have to go back up."

"I'm fine," I lied. I tucked my hand behind my back. "Plus, how are we going to get back up?"

That same panic spiked through my veins.

"Squid could tie the rope to the back of the truck and then pull us up."

"The rope isn't long enough. It was barely long enough to get down here." He looked up to the broken ladder, to the hole where Seb was. "Seb, can you get a ladder or some more rope? And first aid."

"Sure thing." He sounded relieved, like he would be willing to do anything other than be down here with us.

I slung the backpack off my shoulder, wincing slightly as I nicked the wound on my hand. Tanner's eyes widened. He opened his mouth as if to admonish me, but I glared at him.

"I said I'm fine." I unfurled the map and pointed to the path.

"But you're not." He gripped the hem of his shirt with both of his hands and pulled them apart until it ripped. He tore off a long strip and grabbed my hand. Gently, he wrapped it around the wound and fastened it with a knot on top of my wrist. "Better?"

"Yeah, thanks." I nodded, then ticked my head in the right direction. "Let's head that way."

We treaded down the narrow path that slowly sloped downward into the water. Our shoes sloshed through the water. I tried to tiptoe around the puddles, but they got wider and deeper. Eventually I stopped trying to avoid them and just splashed through them. My sneakers were soaked through. And then my socks became heavily laden with water. Wet socks were so gross.

Ankle-deep in musty groundwater, we came to a gate in the mine. The black rose of Toulouse was emblazoned on the rusted wrought iron.

I shook the gate, hoping that it would break open—it looked fragile enough to shatter. But no dice; it was sturdier than it looked.

Tanner tapped my shoulder with something cold, and my head snapped in his direction. In his hand was the 3D printed key—the copy of the key that we'd found underwater in Toulouse.

"It's worth a try," he said, shrugging warily.

"Moment of truth." My breath was shaky as my wet, bloody fingers gripped the key. I slid it through the lock. And a wave of anticipation surged through me. This is what we'd been working toward for weeks. I hoped it hadn't all been for naught.

The key slid into the lock, and I released my breath, my chest tightening as I struggled to breathe. I turned the key and it got jammed. I jimmied it, careful not to force it too hard. The alloy the 3D printer used was not a very hard metal, and I didn't want to snap the key in half.

Turning it slowly, I tried again but the key wouldn't budge. "I don't get it! Why aren't you opening?" I yelled at the gate, willing it to reveal its secrets to me. I racked my brain, thinking about the lockbox and the map of the mine we found in Mayor Hornsby's office. All signs pointed to this mine, to this gate.

So why wasn't it opening?

I was afraid to look at Tanner's face—this was all my fault. I'd led us all the way down here with a key that clearly didn't mean anything.

"Maybe we should turn back." I shrugged and turned slowly, the beginnings of an apology on my lips. But before I could finish, he gripped my shoulder, tugging me away from the gate.

"I think I can do it." His eyes tightened as he surveyed the metal.

He removed his hand from my shoulder, then grabbed one of the gates and shook.

"Do *what*?"

"Break the gate down." He tucked his lips between his teeth and shook harder this time, then grinned speculatively. "This could work. It's all rusted at the edges and not sturdy at all. Stand back."

He swished his hand to the right, motioning for me to get as far to the side as I could. But there wasn't much room—the pathway was narrow, barely wide enough for two people to stand side by side. I tried to make myself flush with the jagged rock wall as Tanner walked backward as far as he could go without dipping back into the deep water, his gaze intense as he looked at the gate.

"Here goes nothing," he grumbled under his breath; then his legs hitched into motion as he ran as fast as he could.

His body collided with the gate, its frame screeching and groaning under the pressure of his impact. He, too, let out a muffled cry as he tumbled forward, tripping over a jumble of jagged metal and rusted nubs.

"Holy shit!" I choked out. "You did it. You *actually* did it."

I clasped my hands on either side of my face, gazing at the passageway beyond, at all of the possibilities that awaited.

"Don't sound so surprised." He chuckled under his breath as he escaped the mangled mess. His leg nicked a piece of sharp metal, and he hissed under his breath, "Ow!"

"Are you okay?" I scampered forward, rushing through the maze of metal so that I could help.

"Careful." Tanner removed his hand from his calf, the cut oozing blood in the absence of his firm pressure. He held up his bloody fingers. "Move slowly, okay?"

"How bad is it?" I asked, stepping through to the other side. Crouching to his level, I assessed the damage on his left leg—a shallow gash several inches long that slashed across his skin.

"I'll be fine." He shook his head, swatting my worried fingers away from him. He heaved himself upward, wincing as he put weight on his legs, and I could tell he was in pain, try as he might to mask it.

Tanner shined his flashlight down the hallway before us. It was half flooded, deeper water than we'd encountered thus far. I could barely see where the pathway continued above the waterline farther down. There was no way around it but through the water.

"I'm calling it." Tanner threw his hands up. "It's too dangerous."

"The map says that it's not underwater anymore."

"It's just money, Casey. You do not have to sacrifice your limbs and life for money we don't even know exists."

"It's about more than that. Did you see that chamber? It's chock-full of silver. We've been lied to. Toulouse wasn't just some Podunk town with failed mines. It wasn't abandoned. There was war in the streets. And I need to know why."

I edged farther down the pathway, but felt a tug on my sleeve. Tanner was trying to stop me, was trying to save me from doing something I might regret. But I was in too deep now. I ripped my arm away and continued down the pathway, feeling the water soak through my jeans, higher and higher as I continued.

The water lapped around my waist when we heard a crackle on the walkie.

"We've got trouble." Squid barked through the microphone. It was staticky, like he was struggling to reach us, and I could hardly understand what he was saying. But he continued, "I repeat, we have trouble. Ron and his friends are trying to get in the mine."

"Stall them."

And then there was the pound and boom, like the shots we often heard coming from the old mine. Tanner and I turned to face each other, a look of worry on his face. It was the signal we'd hoped would never come.

"There's trouble up top." He looked over his shoulder at me, his eyes wide, jaw slackened.

I ticked my head deeper into the mine, toward the maze of chambers that undoubtedly awaited us.

"Then we have to keep going."

THIRTY-THREE

After wading through waist deep water for several yards, the path began to slope upward, ending at a set of steep steps. We ran up them two at a time, making sure to keep tabs on each other. I held my hand out behind me, and Tanner took it as we entered a dusty chamber.

This cavity did not feel wet. It smelled like dry earth as if the waves of time had not touched this tiny chamber. We crouched down and squeezed in.

"It's an air pocket." Tanner looked amazed. "Sometimes caves have them. If water rushes in too quickly, it floods the biggest compartments and sometimes leaves pockets."

"Look over there!" I gasped.

There was a large chest on the far end of the room. It was over-turned, haphazardly stashed. We ran to it. I took the key out of my pocket.

Tanner shined his flashlight onto the lock and I turned the key. It turned easily this time, followed by an internal click—as if the lock was perfectly preserved. Tanner was likely right—this chest may not have seen water.

I heaved the lid off of the chest and a mirror of silvery light beamed back at me. Tanner set his flashlight on the ground so that the light pointed upward. He coughed out a shocked laugh and squeezed my shoulder.

"The treasure," I said, and my voice quivered as I cried out, "We fucking found it!"

I dug my fingers into the coins, the perfectly minted coins that gleamed and tinkled as I moved them. They hadn't felt human hands in over a hundred years.

I burrowed my fingers deeper into the chest, trying to make my way to the bottom, and the tips of my fingers grazed something.

"There's something else." I pawed at the paper. It was thicker than paper—almost like cloth, the way a dollar bill felt.

I slid out the pages and read through the words.

"It's a deed." I dug into the chest and pulled out another stack. "They're all deeds. Secured by the Bank of Toulouse."

"The missing deeds." Tanner sifted through them, careful not to bend the weathered pages.

"So, the one in the Langston Club is a fake."

"This is what the mayor was after." He set them back into the box. "I'd bet my life on it."

"But why? I'm not even sure they're valid anymore."

"What does she always say? *Optics matter.* And she has big plans for herself. For this town. For her upcoming senate run. It would not be good if her family was the cause of a massacre and one of the greatest land thefts in the history of our country."

"Hardly the greatest. Land theft is as American as . . . America."

"Well, what are you waiting for?" Tanner scooted toward the chest, hungrily scanning the silver. "Let's grab as much as we can."

We stuffed our backpacks with handfuls of silver until they were full to bursting. I rolled up the deeds, which were printed on that linen paper our teacher told us about, and I shoved them into the side of the bag before shoveling more coins into the bag. My breath hitched at the sight of one of the deeds.

"It's Anderson. It's my grandmother's maiden name. This was her family deed. She was right. She wasn't senile. Her land *was* stolen. And she and her family had to struggle to rebuild everything."

"How do we get out?" Tanner looked behind him, at the passageway we'd used to enter the chamber.

"We can't go back the way we came." I shook my head. We'd heard the explosion up top, heard Squid's warning over the walkie. Ron and his cohorts had already breached the mine. They were coming for us. I snatched the map of the mine from Tanner's hand, searching for another way out. I pointed to a small vein jutting out from the main path, my wild eyes meeting Tanner's worried gaze. "It's worth a shot. The map's gotten us this far."

"You've gotten us this far." He bobbed his head from side to side, laughing. "I'll pretty much follow you anywhere."

If the map was correct, there was an opening to the lake on the other side of this wall. The only thing was, we weren't certain if it was filled with water or a continuation of the air pocket.

I heaved my leaden backpack over my shoulder and headed to the back end of the chamber. My gaze lingered on the treasure chest. It was still quite full, and I wondered when we'd be back to claim the rest. With a heavy sigh, I turned my attention to the alternate exit. Crouching down, I left the treasure behind me and focused on finding our way out of the mine.

Instantly, the smell of wetness hit my nostrils. I peered over at Tanner, whose nostrils were flickering. He could smell it, too. There was water down here. And a lot of it.

The path slowly sloped into water, our shoes sloshing through the puddles until a sharp drop-off had us wading in chest-deep water.

"We're almost there." I gasped. The water lapped around my neck, licking at my chin.

My backpack was completely saturated with water. Combined with the coins, it weighed me down, dragging me below the water line. I took a step farther and the water rose above my lips, sloshing into my nostrils.

I hopped onto the tips of my toes and gasped for air. Tanner grabbed the strap of my backpack. He looked worriedly down at me. He was much taller than me, so his face had not reached the water yet.

"Give it here." He tugged at the strap more forcefully.

"No, I'm fine."

"Quit the crap, Casey. You are *not* fine. I'll carry the backpack. I'm a stronger swimmer, and I have more upper body strength."

I handed him my backpack, shoving it into his arms.

"Okay." I took a deep breath, trying to expand my lungs as much as possible. "You ready?"

"Take these." He handed me the goggles that Squid had packed. They were flimsy, but they'd be useful.

"What about you?" I waited for him to produce another pair of goggles, but he slung the bag over his shoulder. There was only one—deep down I'd always known that.

"I'm used to getting water in my eyes. I can do it." He clenched his jaw shut, nodding resolutely. "Deep breath. Okay? Deep, long breath. It's about twenty yards to the end of the tunnel, and maybe another fifteen feet to the surface. Conserve your energy by taking long strokes, glide in between strokes. Swim straight for the surface and don't worry about me. I'll be right behind you."

"Ready?" I rolled my shoulders, loosening them up for the swim strokes ahead.

"Now!"

We took a breath together then sank into the dark waters below.

THIRTY-FOUR

The water filled my ears, drowning out sound. It was dark, eerily quiet. We only had one flashlight, and it was tied around Tanner's waist. It bobbed with every swim stroke, sending the light ebbing and flowing in my direction.

I kicked my feet, holding my hands out to guide me as they touched the sides of the walls. I tried to do what Tanner told me, to push hard and glide forward to conserve my energy, but it was difficult. I was already overexerting myself, and I was only halfway down the hall.

Instinctively, I floated to the ceiling to see if there were any air pockets. But there were none. I looked back at Tanner, who pointed forward. I pushed off the ceiling and swam down the tunnel.

A dull glow at the end of the tunnel appeared. It was the open water. We were almost to the opening.

I wanted so badly to take a breath. My chest was spasming. I tightened my lips shut so that I would not be tempted to take a breath—because my mind was playing tricks on me, and there was no air down here.

With a thrust, I burst from the mineshaft and reached the open water of the lake. I flapped my arms upward, reaching for the surface. Forty feet below me, the most remote ruins of Toulouse lay in pieces, swallowed up by the same water that claimed its mines along the hillside. I followed the slopes upward to the shoreline, feeling my lungs cave in from lack of oxygen.

My vision was blurring. My chest caved in. I was light-headed from the lack of oxygen. If I could just make it to the surface and take a gulp of air, I would be fine.

With one last surge of energy, I burst through the surface. Gasping for air, my arms flailed about as I turned in the water, trying to orient myself, searching for Tanner to emerge behind me. I dipped my head beneath the surface, searching for him.

In the distance, fifteen feet below, I could just make out Tanner's flashlight tied around his waist. His feet kicked furiously behind him, but his upward momentum was limited, given the heavy load of silver he was carrying. He had both of our bags draped over each shoulder. Even as strong of a swimmer as he was, there was no way one breath of oxygen two minutes ago would sustain him to the surface at this rate.

He would never make it.

I gulped down a big breath and then dove after him, my feet kicking as fast as I could. Tanner's strokes had slowed. His determined expression slackened, and he looked like he was losing steam.

I collided with him and gripped underneath his armpits and tugged, but he was too heavy. I had to make a choice. Get rid of some of the excess weight.

I slid one of the backpacks off his shoulder and watched it plummet down into the lake, disappearing into the darkness. Tanner was instantly lighter, and I grabbed the other strap, and his hand stilled me. Then his arm loosened and went limp at his side, floating sickeningly at his side.

I kicked him to the surface.

Just a little farther. Just a few more feet. Please, please make it.

I emerged to the surface with a primal cry with my arms hooked around Tanner's.

I towed him to the nearest shoreline, and dragged him against it until he was away from the water.

"Tanner?" I shook him. He didn't move. "Oh no. Oh God, please tell me I'm not too late."

I plunged my face against his, touching lip to lip and breathed into his mouth a few times, pinching his nose closed. Then I crossed my hands over his heart and pounded hard, trying to get his heart pumping. Trying to get him to start breathing.

"Please." I whimpered as I continued doing CPR.

Water bubbled out of his mouth, and my face perked up. I pinched his nose and breathed through his mouth again and pounded his chest. More water gurgled up, followed by a cough.

He rolled over and coughed up more water. I clasped my hands over my mouth and started to sob. Fat tears rolled down my cheeks.

"I thought you were dead." I sniffled.

"You came back for me."

"Of course I did. You're important...to me."

"I'm sorry I couldn't carry both bags."

"It's not important. Certainly not as important as your life. We'll know the true story. And who knows, maybe we can search for the bag on a dive. Bring the deeds to the surface."

He smiled weakly. "The deeds are in this bag."

"Seriously?"

I gripped the back of his neck and pulled him closer to me. And then our lips collided. And of course it was different than CPR. His lips were warmer, and more urgent as they pressed against mine.

A loud whistle shot through the sky, followed by a crackle. And a fan of fireworks exploded above our heads. After being shot at and hearing dynamite explode and almost drowning in the lake, we didn't even flinch, didn't even stop kissing as the fireworks blasted above us. Well, we only stopped for a moment to take the show in before turning our attention back to each other.

I leaned my forehead against his, steadying my breath, closing my eyes and drinking in his warmth.

"Should we take up our spots at Founder's Day?"

"Let's shake this town up."

Slick with mud and blood, we stepped onto the boardwalk. We were in stark contrast to the people around us. They were in pastel maxi dresses and seersucker, wearing smiles and raising champagne glasses. We were smeared in filth, our clothes tatty, our faces grim. I felt like I'd just been through battle—in many ways, I had been. But this was not the first time this town had known battle. The people at Founder's Day didn't know that.

Not yet, anyway.

On the edge of the boardwalk, on the sprawling lawn of the country club, stood a large white tent with a smaller canopy set up behind it for the service staff. I trudged up the grassy knoll, my legs wobbly beneath me, with Tanner at my side.

"Do you know who's working today?" I turned to Tanner. "We need to borrow a cell phone to call B and Squid."

"Well, they're both supposed to be working." He smiled, a bit of color returning to his cheeks. "I think Marco's cooking. We can ask him."

"Shit, Harold alert." I darted behind the canvas flap, and Tanner scrambled after me, just as Ms. Harold barged in the service tent with two bags of ice. A firm grasp tugged my shoulder back, nearly knocking me off balance.

"Holy shit. I *knew* that was you." Lucile's mouth hung open as she picked a clump of grass out of my hair.

"Shh." I held my pointer finger up to my mouth.

"Why are you all wet and covered in mud again?"

"Seriously, keep your voice down. Ms. Harold will hear you."

"Sis," she hissed, leaning forward and sloshing water from her glass and onto the ground. "This look is loud. You're going to stick out like a sore thumb anyway."

She stepped back, her arbor green maxi dress swishing against the grass. She looked absolutely stunning compared to my wet, bloodstained shirt and Tanner's ripped T-shirt and pale pallor. She eyed him up and down, her expression growing more worried by the second. Behind her stood an equally handsome guy in a maroon dinner jacket and black slacks. He snaked his arm around my sister's waist.

"You were not lying about your family." He clamped his lips shut, trying to hide his smile. "I'm Bryant. And you must be Casey."

"Bryant!" My eyes widened as I looked from him to my sister. "I should have known from the Morehouse maroon."

"It goes with everything." He smirked, straightening his lapel jacket. He craned his neck around me and nodded at Tanner. "Who are you?"

"Tanner." He held out a hand caked in mud.

"You mind if I don't?" He backed away from Tanner, his hands held up. "I just washed my hands."

"It's cool, I get it," Tanner said, slumping against one of the serving tables.

"I've heard so many good things about you." He looked nervously to his side, where Tanner was drinking out of Lucile's water goblet. "Was actually hoping to talk to you about your grandmother's cases you found. Lucile let me take a peek, and I have to say, they're fascinating. But it can wait until after you . . . go home and change?"

"You read the cases?"

He nodded. And all of a sudden, I lunged forward and gripped his hand.

"What can you tell me about land theft and buried treasure and abandoned treasure? Ever come across salvage rights?"

"Whoa, dude." Bryant gently but firmly removed his wrist from my grasp. He shot my sister a nervous look. "Is she for real?"

"Unfortunately, I think she is. But at this point I guess you're used to getting grilled by my insane family." She grabbed me by the crook of my elbow and drew me closer to her.

"Can I borrow your phone?"

"Where is *your* phone?" She released her hold on me, slapping her hands at her hips. "Look, Casey, tell me what's going on."

"I lost it in the lake, and I need to call my friends, okay? Just give it here, and then I'll tell you everything. And, Bryant?" I raised my eyebrows. "I need your legal opinion on the whole thing, okay?"

THIRTY-FIVE

The main stage stretched before the party. A long table atop the stage was adorned with a white tablecloth and candelabras and a lectern for the impending mayoral speech. My parents were seated at their table just below the dais, an honor bestowed to them for having a daughter as the town hero. I wasn't sure if they would consider me a hero after my appearance tonight.

My mom looked like she was in her element in one of her favorite maxi dresses, with her hair pulled back into a high loose bun. She clinked glasses with her tablemate and took a sip of her drink, but she turned her head to the side as she stroked her sternum—a telltale sign that she was nervous. She turned her face to the other direction, clearly scanning the crowd. She was searching for something.

She turned in her chair, craning her neck to search the crowd. Her eyes flitted past me and then back again, and when our eyes locked, she exhaled, as though I was the thing she was searching for and she was relieved.

But then as she scanned me from head to toe, that relieved smile slowly waned, and when her eyes moved to Tanner beside me—covered in sand and dirt from when I dragged him onto the shore—a crease began to form in between her eyebrows. She was fully frowning by the time she threw her napkin on the table and scooted out of her chair.

"What *happened?*" It came out more as a heavy sigh. She held her forehead up with her hand, breathing heavily. "Go home and change into that dress I laid out. Please?"

"Mom, I love you, but I'm not leaving here." I leaned in and gave her a kiss on the cheek—a real kiss, and not one of those fake air kisses she was fond of. Then I sidestepped around her and made my way up the steps, gripping the railing for added support. My legs were weary, my body was tired. I could have collapsed into an exhausted heap in one of the chairs.

But I couldn't back down now. I had something to say.

Water pooled at my feet, wetting the podium. I tapped the microphone to make sure it was on, then cleared my throat.

"Sorry I'm so underdressed." I dropped my hands to my sides, slapping my soiled jeans. I was slightly embarrassed before I stepped up to the podium, but now that all eyes were on me, I wasn't anymore. "My name is Casey Whitecroft. Last year my dad's business lost big in the stock market. And instead of telling his firm the truth, instead of telling his family the truth, he mortgaged our house to pay for his losses and to try to turn his company around. But it didn't work, and we lost everything. Everything except my grandmother's house, a world away on the other side of the lake.

"I've thought about this a lot. And I'm sure he's thought about this a lot, too. If he'd been honest about his troubles, maybe we'd be in a different place now. Maybe the trust between my family members wouldn't feel so broken. So, we made a commitment to ourselves to always be honest with each other going forward. And there's hope for us, I think.

"That's why I think there's hope for this town.

"This whole Founder's Day is really not what it seems. And I think if we really stopped to think about it, we'd know it was a lie. Old Langston did not *discover* this town. There was already one here—Toulouse. Toulouse was a majority Black town that not only survived the Jim Crow South, it thrived. They did not sell this land to Colonel Langston. This land was stolen. And I have proof.

"The deed that hangs in the country club—for the select few movers and shakers who have access to that building—that deed is a forgery. It's a big fat lie.

"I know it's a forgery, because we found the real deeds. I also know for a fact that Toulouse printed their deeds on a mixture of linen and cotton stock—just like what our country uses for our money.

"Colonel Langston, along with the help of Eustice Hornsby and a group of white men, opened fire on the city of Toulouse. Just because they refused to sell him their homes. They didn't want to—"

"Oh, my *God!*" the mayor screamed from the other side of the boardwalk. Her hair was wild, and she was out of breath as she wove through the crowd. She slicked her hair out of her eyes then snapped her fingers at the security guards on the edge of the stage. "I want her off that stage. Now!"

The guards moved onto the platform, but I gripped the lectern.

"Let me finish talking." A security guard wrapped her arm

around mine and tried to pull me away from the microphone. I gripped the podium tighter, refusing to leave without finishing what I came here to do.

"No. You've had quite enough time talking."

I wriggled free from the guard and pulled out the roll of old deeds from my back pocket.

"These are the real deeds to the land we stand on. The Black and Indigenous owners of this land never relinquished their property. Their city was ransacked." I pointed the roll of papers at the mayor. "You knew about this. You could have been a part of a whole wave of reconciliation. You could have talked about the *real* history of Langston. Not the made-up *fellowship of friends and neighbors* you always talk about."

"She's just a disgruntled teenager." The mayor gripped the railing on the edge of the stage. "She doesn't know what she's talking about."

"All of you," Sheriff Gutierrez cut in, taking the stage steps and stepping to the center of the stage. She pointed to Tanner, Squid, B, Dev, me, and the mayor. "Let's take this down to the station. *Now.*"

THIRTY-SIX

A cacophony of voices erupted in Sheriff Gutierrez's office, a war of words as each person fought to be heard. The sheriff held her arms up from behind her desk, raising her voice above all of ours to regain control of her office, but we still didn't stop. Finally, she slapped the desk with her palms.

"I said, one person at a time." Gutierrez hunched over her desk, speaking deliberately slowly.

She looked to the left of her desk where I was seated next to Tanner. He still had a sickly pallor—remnants from his brush with death in the lake. His pale arms snaked around the backpack filled with silver and the deeds to Toulouse. Squid and B stood behind us in their catering uniforms. Dev stood awkwardly in between us and his mom, who sat to the right of the sheriff's desk, flanked by Ron and her assistant, Brenna, who fidgeted behind her. The mayor's voice roared with an authoritative edge.

"The point is, these kids are *reckless*!" She shot us a reproachful glare. "Months and months of planning the centennial are down the drain because of their foolish stunts. I mean, look at the state of them!"

"Oh, sorry we can't all be in evening gowns." B slapped her sides, shooting the mayor a grimace that could rival her own.

"You *should* be sorry." She whipped around to face the sheriff again. "Not only did they hijack tonight, but they broke into my office last week."

"That's only because you stole our money!" I yelled back.

"Because you interfered with an official investigation!" she scoffed. "Oh, and I guess we're also supposed to overlook the fact that you also trespassed at the mine, city property. With explosives, no less!"

"Well, *you* sent henchmen to rough us up." Squid puffed up his chest, standing tall.

"And chase us down the mountain," Tanner said in a shaky voice.

"I didn't do those things." The mayor folded her arms, the heat from her eyes diffusing. Her face was impassive as she looked away from us. "You can't prove a thing."

"What about the car?" B gripped Dev's sleeve, pulling him closer to our side. With upturned eyebrows, she pleaded with him to back up our version of events.

"The car is a mess." Dev hung his head low, avoiding eye contact with his mom. "It's almost totaled."

"Because he crashed into the guardrail while he was ramming the back of my truck." Tanner flared his nostrils. For the first time all evening, the color had come back to his cheeks. They burned red as his eyes bored into Ron's.

"Sheriff Gutierrez." The mayor tucked her hair behind her ears.

"That's obviously a domestic dispute. It has absolutely nothing to do with the matter at hand."

"It has everything to do with this." My shaky fingers unzipped the backpack in Tanner's lap. I reached in, feeling the coins shift between my fingers then pulled out a handful of silver. I dumped it onto Gutierrez's desk and the coins scattered atop the surface. One of them rolled into her hand resting on the table.

"I'll be damned." Her breath caught as she held the coin up to the light.

"That's what she's been after this whole time." I ticked my head toward the coins on the sheriff's desk. "And she was *ruthless*."

"Enough! These kids are *criminals*. They broke into my office—in city hall, for chrissakes! And they conspired to defraud the town and Langston's heirs of the treasure." She scooted to the edge of her seat, her hungry eyes fixed on the silver.

"But it's not Langston's, and you know it." Tanner dug into his bag and pulled out the rolled-up deeds. They were a little bent out of shape from being jostled around in our struggle to escape the mine. But they were still intact.

Tanner stood up, his stance a little wobbly before he braced himself on the desk. Carefully, he unfurled the coarse paper. "These are the deeds from Toulouse. Never granted to Langston. Never sold to anyone. Toulouse was stolen."

"Those are *mine*," the mayor growled, then lunged across the table.

"No, they're not!" I leapt from my chair and dove for the deeds, but the mayor's hand shot out, grabbing my arm before I could snatch them off the desk and stow them safely back in the bag. Her viselike grip cut off my blood circulating to my hand. It went numb under her hold.

"Get your hands off my daughter." My mom barged into the office. She straightened her dress, which was twisted and ruffled, like she'd had to fight her way in. Her frown deepened as she zeroed in on the mayor's hands on me. She crossed the room in a few strides and grabbed Hornsby's wrist, shooting daggers from her eyes. "Let go. *Now.*"

The mayor released her hold on me and shrank back against the wall, putting distance between herself and my mother's venomous scowl.

"Your family is nothing but trouble, especially your daughter. I will have the full weight of the prosecutor's office levied against her." She lifted her chin, holding out her hand. "Give those deeds to me."

My hand twitched against the deeds, but my mom shook her head.

"Don't you dare." She stayed my hand. "This is what my mother was looking for."

She traced her fingers over the clothlike paper. She mumbled as she read the text, her eyes dewing as she flipped through the stack.

"What does Grandma have to do with this?" I asked, tapping her on the shoulder.

"I've been doing some digging into my mother's lawsuits, racking my brains trying to figure out what she was thinking. And now it makes sense." She set the deeds back onto the desk and grazed my cheek with the back of her hand. "Your grandmother was suing the city for salvage rights."

"So, *that's* where all of her money went."

"Every last dime. But she couldn't prove ownership. Even though she was born in Toulouse. Even though she knew what was buried down there, and no one would listen. Hell, I thought she was crazy. But she persisted." Mom blinked away a few unshed tears, then looked up into the mayor's brown eyes, her expression hardening. "And *you*. You kept her running around in circles. Getting her cases dismissed on technicalities. Dragging it out until she'd drained her savings. And now I know why. How could you? I thought we were friends."

"Your mother was peddling conspiracy theories about our town and our forefathers—my forefathers."

"No, she wasn't." My mother sighed. "Not by the look of these documents."

"You can't just expect us to just rewrite history." She gestured to Gutierrez. "This is about more than treasure. It's about preserving our heritage."

"That's exactly what we're trying to do," I said, standing to join my mom at the front of the desk. "And Langston is a blemish on our history."

"Oh, really." Hornsby scoffed. "What's next? Tearing down his statue?"

"Actually, for starters," B said, cocking her head to the side. "That's not a bad idea."

"We could blow him up." Squid bounced on the balls of his feet. "Send him off with a bang."

"Read the room, Squid." B gave him a playful punch to his shoulder.

"Langston owned the land, passed it down through generations." Mayor Hornsby pursed her lips defiantly. "Possession is nine tenths of the law."

"All right. I suggest we hand these over to the county clerk's office. May I?" Sheriff Gutierrez gestured to the papers on her desk. When we nodded, she slid them toward her, a look of awe splashed across her face. "These are really something. Quite a find."

Tanner reached out and squeezed my hand.

"I will instruct the clerk to handle these documents with care and properly preserve them. They can provide copies to both counsels, and then you can adjudicate the issue if you desire."

"But—" Tanner started, but the sheriff cut him off.

"It's up to the courts to decide. But I will say, from what I hear. You have a good case."

"And the treasure?" My voice cracked as I looked at the silver scattered across the desk.

"Well, this is abandoned property. Looks like salvage rights haven't been established yet. Mayor Hornsby is right." The sheriff's stern look melted into a smile. Her eyes twinkled as she pushed the coins in my direction. "Possession is nine tenths of the law. So, it's yours until declared otherwise."

EPILOGUE

I leaned against the car, a chuckle escaping my lips. *Scuiducci Luxury Motors* was emblazoned in large green letters atop an all-glass building. It was the mechanic shop of Squid's dreams—and then some. Beside the mechanic's bays there was a showroom with sports cars on display. I eyed the townhouse next to it, wondering if that was the new home he'd built for his family. I'd done the same for my parents, given them a hefty portion of the treasure to buy back Whitecroft and set things right. But they chose to pay off Grandma Bernie's back taxes and stay in her old house—with a few major renovations, of course. They were adding a second floor and a large infinity pool that overlooked the lake.

But it was still Grandma's house—our family seat.

An Aston Martin zoomed into the parking lot. The tinkling horn blared as the car slowed to a halt next to mine. The window rolled down, and there was Squid. He leaned over the passenger seat and waved.

"Casey Whitecroft has finally come home."

"Hey, Squid." I slid my sunglasses off my face and beamed at him. I raised a playful eyebrow. "Or should I call you Mr. Scuiducci?"

"Only in front of the patrons." He patted the seat next to him. "Get in. We don't want to be late."

I grabbed my purse from my car and hopped into the passenger seat of his. And then he screeched out of the parking lot and down the street toward the center of town.

The turnpike curved down the mountain, through the trees and away from Squid's Hollow. It was a familiar ride, one that held memories of our chase to find the treasure. That seemed so long ago.

Maybe it was. A lot could happen in a year.

The tree line broke at the final curve, revealing a town in transformation. The downstream side had started to trade in its ramshackle shopping centers and vacant storefronts for new and revitalized buildings. Cranes spotted the skyline indicating that work still continued.

"Wow, this side of the lake is really built up," I said under my breath. We slowed at a light, blocks away from marquee signage that read THE ROSEWATER @LAKEVIEW in big blue letters. I leaned closer to the passenger side window, marveling at the scale of the development. I'd seen pictures of it, but they didn't do it justice. "I barely recognize the place."

"Just wait. You ain't seen nothing yet." Squid slapped the steering wheel. "We'll show you around after dinner."

"No way." I nudged him with my elbow. "Pull over."

"All right, but we don't have much time." His eyes darted to the dashboard clock. Then he huffed as he eased onto the side of the road. Clicking the button for his hazard lights, he shifted in his leather seat to face me. "What do you think?"

"It's incredible. I mean, I saw pictures in the early stages. But it's grown so much."

"I know, right? It's amazing what some buried treasure will buy you these days." He smirked and pointed to a cluster of shops on the new boardwalk by the cove. "That's the new Holmes Pawn Shop— where Ron definitely is out of the picture. And B's restaurant is right there on the water—just opened last month. Chef Alessandra is gunning for a Michelin star. And you know what? She just might get it."

"She finally got her restaurant." I shook my head in wonder, looking at the two-story building with the terra-cotta roof. I thought B would take the helm of her ship, but she'd opted to poach Chef from the Langston Country Club. Now the Toulouse Tavern was the best restaurant gig in town. The entire downstream side was booming in the midst of rapid revitalization, and B's restaurant was at the center of it. I tilted my head to the side, thinking of my headstrong friend. "Is it weird that she's not the top chef? How is that dynamic going? I bet they're butting heads."

"Sometimes." Squid bobbed his head from side to side, a sheepish smile crossing lips. "But most of the time, B's there to learn from the best. She's really come into her own. You'll see."

"And those—" I gestured to the gaps between the buildings, the undeveloped land where the grass was at least knee high. "Those are the empty lots my mom has been telling me about?"

"Yeah, she's really made it her mission to ensure every last Toulouse descendant gets their slice of this town."

"I know." I chuckled. Lately, the ongoing lawsuits involving the

Toulouse land theft was all we ever talked about. "It's good to see her have purpose. And maybe fighting for Toulouse gives her a closer relationship with Grandma Bernie, which she didn't have when she was alive. At least that's what my dad told me. He's starting to sound like his therapist."

"Your parents have been a huge help with all this." Squid craned his neck so that he could see behind my seat. "There are some lots over there and more scattered on this side of the lake. Some of the Toulouse descendants have come back and started building. But others have been harder to trace. And some of the families don't exist anymore, so the courts have had a tough time doling out the property. But they'll figure it out. Hopefully."

"We should make some sort of memorial for them." My head dipped as I thought of the firefight in Toulouse, about Colonel Langston's rampage of the town so that he could steal their land. Countless people were killed or displaced in that massacre. My grandmother spent her adult life trying to get that land back. The harm was immense. "I'll chip in for it."

"Another monument?" Squid raised a skeptical eyebrow. "Doesn't this town have one too many of those?"

"Ahhh, the old colonel." I winced, thinking about the shadow his statue cast in the town square. After all we'd uncovered about him, it was an eyesore that needed to be rectified. I drew my lips into a hard line. "His days are numbered."

"Let's tear that sucker down." Squid rubbed his hands together.

He pulled back onto the road and sped through a yellow light. The touchscreen on the dashboard chimed with an incoming text message—it was from Tanner. I shifted nervously in my seat. Squid raised his eyebrow.

"Have you seen him yet?"

"Who?" I asked, even though deep down I knew who he was talking about.

I could feel Squid roll his eyes as we turned onto the bridge and crossed the water. But he didn't push me further, which I was grateful for. The truth was, I hadn't seen Tanner in a while, and although I was curious and excited about the prospect of seeing him again, I was nervous.

It had been a year since that crazy summer when we almost drowned in the mines. He'd gone off to school in Connecticut, and I'd headed to New York. I wondered if he was a different person now. Or if I was so different that he wouldn't recognize me.

We pulled into the center of town, where a crowd gathered in front of the Langston statue in front of the country club. It wasn't as pristine and well taken care of as I remembered. It looked like it hadn't been power washed for quite some time. And there were ropes tied around him, binding him. As if they were binding him from doing any more harm.

"Looks like B saved us some seats," Squid said, pointing to the front of the crowd.

"Oh my gosh." My mouth fell open at the sight of B. Her curly coils were picked out into a thick and luscious Afro that fell past her shoulders. She wore large designer sunglasses, much fancier than the ones I was wearing. They rested atop a nose where a red septum ring hung.

The girl was really leaning into her power. And it looked good on her.

An arm draped around her shoulders and tugged her closer. It was Dev, also with longer hair. It was slicked behind his ears. He gave B a kiss on her forehead, and I had to struggle not to burst into laughter at the absurdity of it all. I collapsed into the seat next to both of them, hoping my eyes didn't look as wild as they felt. My eyes felt like they were popping out of their sockets.

"Um, hi?" I said, my mouth hanging open.

"Hey, yourself." B lifted her chin defiantly and scooted away from Dev. He hugged her shoulders closer and chuckled.

"She still *loves* PDA, don't you, sweetie?"

"Sweetie?" I said under my breath. And now I thought I'd seen everything.

"Tanner, over here!" B yelled. She waved her wrist—which had a small tattoo of the black rose of Toulouse on its underside—beckoning him toward our group.

He was wearing a gray V-neck and dark skinny jeans. I had spent the past year in New York with some of the world's finest men on display for me every time I stepped onto the sidewalk. But nothing beat the tall and slender, subtly muscular, confident stroll of Tanner. After all this time, he still made my breath catch.

"You came." He leaned in to give me a hug, and when I wrapped my arms around him, I had a flashback to our last kiss. I cleared my throat and leaned away from him, an awkward smile tugging at my lips.

A crane rolled onto the lawn, the beep of the backup gears blaring until it came to a halt next to the statue.

The guys jumped out of the truck and lowered the crane with a control panel in the tailgate of the truck. The crane lowered, and they attached the hook to the ropes tied around dear old Langston. With a wave of his hand, the crane lifted, shuddering under the weight of the monument. Then with a more forceful tug, the stone mount dislodged itself from the grass taking bits of dirt and grass with it as the crane lifted the statue higher.

The guy on the ground secured the bottom of it to the truck to stop it from swaying. And then the truck left the town square, leaving a hole in the ground where Langston once stood.

"I thought I'd feel more." I scrunched up my face, pushing my sunglasses back up the bridge of my nose. "But it was so anticlimactic."

"You should feel proud of yourself." Tanner nudged me with his elbow. And there it was—that little flutter in my stomach. It had been a while since I'd felt that. He shifted in his seat, giving me the full force of his green-eyed gaze. "How long are you in town?"

"Why?"

"Because I'd like to take you on a date. Somewhere that doesn't involve jumping down mineshafts or finding dead bodies."

"I know just the place." I smiled and flicked my head toward B's restaurant on the downstream side—the Toulouse Tavern, named after the Black settlers of this great town.

THE END

ACKNOWLEDGMENTS

This book could not have been possible without the help of my mom, who spent hours and hours on the phone with me discussing the story elements, asking probing questions that only made it better. Your meticulous reading and attention to details made this book complete.

Thank you, Dad, for reading this book cover to cover, like you do with all my books. Your insight is invaluable.

To my rock star beta readers Gabe Dover and Sasa Schwartz: thank you for your notes in the margins and your late night texts with suggestions. I appreciate your friendship and support.

To my powerhouse critique group: Sophie Meridien, Linda Cheng, Maya Prasad, Flor Salcedo, and Sunshine Bacon. I am so honored to work with you all. Your work inspires me, and I am so incredibly grateful for you expertise and general awesomeness. You all make me a better writer.

Carrie Pestritto, you are the best agent a girl could ask for. Thank you (and your interns!) for pulling me out of the slush pile in 2018. From story brainstorming to strategy chats, you have helped develop my career in too many ways to count. Thanks for being the GOAT.

To Kieran Viola for acquiring *Good as Gold* and to Kelsey Sullivan for editing: thank you for making me a Disney princess. Laylie Frazier, your artwork gives me goose bumps. I'm absolutely obsessed with this cover artwork, and Tyler Nevins for the amazing design.

Last but not least, Jonny Metts. Thank you for finding the sun with me, for adopting another puppy, and for reading all my fresh pages.